Trayis

VLG – Book Eleven

Vampires, Lycans, Gargoyles

By Laurann Dohner

Trayis by Laurann Dohner

Growing up mostly human in a Lycan pack has been hard for Shay. Shunned and distrusted by most, she wouldn't have survived without the support of her foster family and alpha. She's had a longtime secret crush on Trayis, her alpha's VampLycan half-brother. Shay thinks he's hot and finds the courage to approach Trayis during one of his infrequent visits. She's hoping for just one night of ecstasy before she spends her life alone, unwanted.

Trayis is stunned when he realizes the sweet, timid Shay is interested in bedding him. He's also furious when some pack women attempt to humiliate her in front of him. He's more than happy to pick her over one of them. She might not be his type but it's just sex. He's up for that. What he doesn't plan on is how she makes him feel.

So much for a simple vacation and a one-night stand.

VLG Series List

Drantos

Kraven

Lorn

Veso

Lavos

Wen

Aveoth

Creed

Glacier

Redson

Trayis

Trayis by Laurann Dohner

Copyright © May 2019

Editor: Kelli Collins

Cover Art: Dar Albert

ISBN: 978-1-950597-03-1

Trayis - VLG – Book Eleven

By Laurann Dohner

Chapter One

Shay stared with longing at the mated couples who had arrived at the party from her spot near the trees. They all looked so happy. The single people were hooking up as well. It seemed she was the only person by herself.

Someone bumped her arm and she gasped, turning her head.

Marcia smiled. "Hiding again? You're allowed to go down there to join in, Shay."

"We both know how that will go over."

Her childhood friend sighed. "Fuck them."

Shay snorted. "As if anyone would touch me long enough."

"Well, actually—"

"Don't. Werewolves hate condoms."

Marcia stepped around her, turned, and then frowned down at her from her taller height. "There's always humans, then."

"Because the two times I dated them worked out *sooo* well."

Marcia gave her arm a gentle squeeze. "Maybe you just chose poor specimens when you gave dating humans a try? I've heard some of them aren't bad."

"One showed up on our third date with another woman's scent all over him, and the second jerk decided not to take no for an answer. He would have hurt me if I wasn't such a good fighter. Pass." She shrugged. "Life isn't fair. If anyone knows that, it's me."

"I still think you should go down there to celebrate the birth of our alpha's third son. You're part of this pack."

"Technically...but not according to some. This is a celebration. I don't want to cause a scene if anyone decides to be a jerk. The focus should be on our alpha pair's newest addition to their family."

"Bullshit! This is a celebration for the *entire* pack and that includes you! I know you're lonely, and it's not okay to go without touch, Shay. Our kind needs it."

"I don't go into heat."

"It's not just about that. You're half Werewolf. Sex and being held is a big deal for us. We need it like air and food. Even humans crave touch. *Everyone* does."

"I'll never be that desperate. The men just want blow jobs or anal sex. *That's* what the pack guys offer me, Marcia. I can't accidently get pregnant that way. And not once has the offer changed."

"I could talk to Rod."

She wrinkled her nose. "Ewww. Keep your brother out of this. First off, I don't want a pity fuck. That's what it would be. Secondly, he'd be horrified if you even brought it up, since he sees me the same way I see him. We're family."

"Okay." Marcia got out of her way and stood next to her.

Shay watched as more of the pack joined the gathering. Minutes passed before Marica spoke again.

"You're just going to stand here then and watch everyone? You're really *not* joining in?"

"Yes. Go. Have fun. I'm not going to let you hang out up here with me all day."

A tall, muscular man strode out of the tree line across the clearing below, and Shay recognized him immediately. That blond streaked hair was unique compared to her pack. Most of them had dark brown or black hair.

Her heart rate picked up and warmth spread through her chest. "Trayis came."

Marcia leaned in closer, pressing their arms together. "Damn, he's as hot as he is terrifying. Is it just me or has he bulked up on muscle since the last time he visited?"

"He's not terrifying. Trayis is actually very sweet."

Marcia snorted. "To you, maybe. The rest of us have all gone running with him at one point or another. I take it you've never seen him shifted?"

"No. Why? Is something wrong with his Wolf? Is he a bit aggressive or something?"

"Or something."

Shay couldn't look away as Trayis approached their pack alpha and gave his half-brother a big hug. He grinned widely as he spoke to Arlis's mate, revealing his looks only improved when he was happy. Ginny handed over the infant in her arms to him. The sight of Trayis holding his tiny nephew had Shay's stomach clenching a bit.

It had been five years since he'd last visited from Alaska. The alpha pair's twin boys had been born that time.

Speaking of, the identical twins rushed to their uncle, grabbing hold of his legs.

"Explain," Shay urged, tearing her attention from the touching scene of a family reunion. "What's wrong with Trayis when he's shifted?"

"He's a VampLycan, Shay, not a full Were. Let's just say when shifted, he looks like a creature out of one of those human horror movies about us. Not that he's mindlessly violent or anything, but nobody wants to so much as brush up against him. Hell, even go *near* him during a run. Only Arlis risks playing with him; he obviously knows his older brother won't kill him. Ginny too. Trayis is her brother-in-mate, though. Our alpha pair are the only ones who feel comfortable around his beasty side."

"Huh. I've never heard any rumors about him." It made her feel sad for him. She knew what it was like to be avoided for being different.

"That's because Trayis is highly respected in the pack. Do you really think they'd dare talk trash about how he looks on four legs? Nobody wants to offend him." Marcia leaned away and ran her fingers through her dark hair. "How do I look? Kale just got off duty and has arrived."

Shay studied her friend. "Beautiful. Fierce. You should just tell him how you feel."

Marcia frowned. "Maybe I'm too dominant for him."

"It's his loss if he needs some submissive woman to cater to his every need."

"Oh, I'd cater alright, if his need was to get me naked. I'd even get on my hands and knees to let him take me from behind."

Shay laughed. "You've been drawn to him since he hit puberty, the second he started growing all those muscles and shot up in height." She glanced at the clearing, hunting for Kale. He'd approached a group of young women Shay hated. They had always been mean to her. "Shit. Bitch Trio alert."

A snarl tore from Marcia. "Why does he always flirt with them?"

"Because they'll sleep with any guy who smiles at them?"

Another snarl came from her best friend.

"Go rescue him from himself. Show him what's he's been blind to." Shay grinned. "Just walk up to him, grab him by the shirt, and kiss him. He might like the direct approach."

"That's easy for *you* to say."

"You're better than those idiots he's flirting with, Marcia. Be yourself and take what you want. What do you have to lose? I heard he's thinking about settling down."

"Who told you that?" Marcia was in her face a heartbeat later, her eyes partially going Wolf. Blackness surrounded her irises. "Who's he been seeing that I don't know about? He never gets serious with anyone!"

"I ran into Darlene this morning in Arlis's office, when I had to have him sign some correspondence I'd printed out. Ted is retiring from an enforcer spot, and Kale wants it. She said if he takes a mate, it would give him an advantage over the others who might want the honor. Darlene admitted he'd discussed it with her only because they're cousins. She wants him to win the spot, of course. It makes sense. A mated enforcer is more focused on his job, not busy trying to impress potential sex partners to get laid."

"Fuck," Marcia sighed.

"You don't want him to end up with a mean girl, do you? Show him you're interested and go get your mate."

"Who says he's my mate?"

Shay rolled her eyes. "Give me a break. I'm your best friend, and you freaked out over what I just said. It's obvious. He's *yours*. It would make you miserable if he claimed someone else."

"I'd leave the pack," she admitted quietly.

Shay felt sick to her stomach hearing those words. Marcia was her best friend. Shay herself was stuck and couldn't transfer somewhere else. Only Arlis would offer someone like her protection and a place with a pack. And likely only because she'd been born there. "You're better suited to Kale than one of those bitches. He's always screwed around with submissives. Show him how good it can be with a dominant. Kale isn't the type to back down from a fight. He probably craves it. Challenge him to get him into your bed. Hell, tie him to it until he's ready to bite."

Marcia stepped in front of her again, smirking slightly and peering deeply into her eyes.

"What?" Shay crossed her arms.

"Great advice from someone who's too chickenshit to mingle at pack parties. You've never gone after a man, either. If you did, you wouldn't be sleeping alone every night."

"I'm different from you."

Marcia lifted her eyebrows. "I'll make you a deal."

Shay detested seeing that mischievous glint in her bestie's eyes. "What?" She knew she'd regret asking.

"I'll go after Kale with everything I have…if *you* pick one man to go after with the same gusto."

"But I'm not a dominant."

"You're a *woman*. We've got the same thing between our legs that men want so desperately to get at. At least they know *you* won't tear strips out of their skin if they aren't great at fucking."

"Crude. Kale also won't fear knocking you up. *You* can control your ovaries. I can't."

Marcia reached back, pulled something from her jeans pocket and held it out.

Shay stared at the items in her open palm, stunned.

"Four condoms. Take them. I *was* going to ask Rod to fuck you tonight. You don't want him? Find someone you're attracted to."

Shay's hand shook as she took the foil-wrapped condoms. Mostly out of fear that someone would walk up on her and Marcia and catch sight of the things. She slid them into her bra cup, happy she'd worn a baggy shirt to hide the slight bulge they created.

"Deal?" Marcia narrowed her eyes. "I'll find the courage if you do."

Shay thought about what would happen if Marcia left the pack. Not only would she be without the person she spent the most time with, but the mean girls might target her even more. She'd be miserable. "Fine."

A grin split Marcia's face and she turned. "Pick."

Shay stared down at the clearing. Tim was a submissive who worked with children. She felt zero attraction to him, though. Her gaze lingered on Trayis...and stayed there. Memories of her childhood filled her mind. He'd always been nice to her on his rare visits. It was probably because they were both half-breeds. Of course, she wasn't a kid anymore.

He also wasn't part of the pack. He'd stay for a few days, and then be gone for years. Worst case, no matter how badly it went, at least she wouldn't have to face him every day.

"Trayis." His name left her lips.

Marcia gasped. "Are you crazy? *Anyone* but him. How about Ruffus?"

She wanted to gag. "You mean STD waiting to happen if he wasn't a Were? Gross. He'd hump a tree if it had a hole. Plus, he's one of the jerks who harass me the most. Like he's doing me a big favor to even offer to let me blow him. I'd rather sell my ass to a stranger on eBay."

Marcia barked out a laugh. "Okay. Bad choice. What about Zander? He doesn't act like a man whore or treat you badly."

"I think he likes men."

"That's kind of hot."

"True, but I'm clearly not his type." Her gaze stayed on Trayis. "I'm only attracted to one."

"I never knew you were nuts. Fine. I'll go after Kale. You hit up Trayis." Marcia held out her hand. "Just don't say I didn't warn you if it goes bad." She jerked her hand back before Shay could shake on it. "You know…Trayis could hurt you." Concern laced her voice. "He's part Vampire. What if he drinks blood? You're just a little shit."

"He won't hurt me. He's a protector. And stop calling me that. I hate it."

"You *are* a little shit. You're all of five foot nothing."

"Five-three, thank you very much. Not everyone is lucky enough to grow to be almost six feet, Marcia. I envy you the ability to reach all your kitchen cupboards without using a chair."

Marcia held out her hand again. "Fine. Trayis better not suck your blood though. Half-brother to our alpha or not, tell him you have a bodyguard who will come after him if he harms you. You're family."

Shay clasped her hand. "Deal. Let's do this."

But panic swiftly hit as they released each other. Had she honestly just agreed to go hit on Trayis? *Crap!*

Desperate times call for equal measures. It was a saying her foster mom, Sylvia, had told her thousands of times.

"I go for Kale and you go for Trayis. Let's do this. Pretend we have cast-iron balls."

Uncertainty sounded in her best friend's voice. Shay stepped close and leaned against her side to show support. "Kale's meant to be your mate. You can do this. He's perfect for you, even though he's been a moron not to see it. You intimidate men, but that's not a bad thing. Go intimidate the hell out of him. You can bet none of those brainless bitches he ever nailed matched him in bed for passion or aggressiveness. You know he's had to hold back. You won't let him. He'll love that—*and* you."

Marcia laughed. "Okay. What's your game plan to get Trayis into bed, oh short one?"

Shay's mind blanked. "Beg?"

Marcia snarled low.

"Joke." She wasn't so sure though. "I don't know. I'll wing it. He's always been nice to me. And besides, I wouldn't mind a pity fuck from *him*. He's gorgeous."

"And dangerous. Don't forget that part."

"He stopped a group of kids from bullying me once, when you were visiting your cousins. He's a protector."

"Of *kids*. Weren't you like ten years old at the time? Maybe we should call this off."

"You're using me as an excuse now. Kale is looking for a mate. It's going to be *you*. You'll blow his mind once you get him naked and show him how good it can be between the two of you. We both know it. Go after your Were. I'll be fine. I've got something in common with Trayis. I'll work with that."

"You're half human and Were. He's half Vampire and Were. *Nothing* alike. He can shift into something scary as fuck. You can't even get your fingernails to grow long."

"But I'm a woman. He's a man. It's not like I'm chasing after him during a run when he's in fur. *Then* we'd have problems. But in skin? Even playing field, right?"

"Right."

"We can do this." Shay had everything to lose if she couldn't get Marcia to go after Kale. It wasn't a sure bet, but she really believed they belonged together. "Let's go." She took the first step and Marcia stayed at her side.

They broke apart at the bottom of the hill.

Shay was glad that Trayis had moved away from the large group of the pack to sit at a picnic table to eat. No one shared it with him. He tended to be a bit of a loner when he visited, only spending time with his brother's alpha family. She changed directions, grabbed a plate of food off the buffet, and had to ignore some pointed shocked looks from her pack over her presence as she made her way over to him.

"May I sit with you?"

Trayis looked up and nodded, putting his half-eaten hamburger down. "Shay?"

She took a seat, flattered that he'd remembered her name. That had to be a good sign. He was so handsome it was hard to look at him. He had beautiful eyes. They were a soft brown with a lot of gold streaks. "Yes. How's your visit going?"

"Good. I had to come meet my new nephew."

"Joshua is adorable. I got to hold him this morning when I was in the office. You can already see the intelligence in his eyes. He's going to grow up to be as wonderful as our alpha pair. And the twins are super protective of their baby brother. It's adorable."

Pride flashed in his eyes. "It almost makes me regret not having children of my own."

She could relate. She'd never have children. Or a mate. Unless she left the pack to live with humans. It wasn't a happy thought. "You haven't found a mate yet?"

He shook his head and went back to eating his burger, dropping his gaze. "No. I did adopt a fully grown human. Though it's not the same as having young."

That stunned her, and it must have shown on her face.

He grinned. "It's a long story. She became mated to someone in my clan."

That made sense. Sometimes humans needed a family bond to be accepted into a pack. Trayis must have offered to be that bond for the human. It proved he really was as compassionate as she'd always believed. It made her want him even more.

It was a relief that he was still officially single, too. It meant she stood a slight chance of talking him into her bed.

She glanced around, spotted Marcia with Kale, and watched as her friend grabbed him by the front of his shirt. She hauled him toward the trees instead of kissing him, though. He didn't put up a fight but a look of pure confusion creased his features as he was led away. She grinned.

"What's amusing?"

She gave her attention back to Trayis. "A friend of mine just made her interest known to the Were she wants."

He smiled. "Ah. I guess that's the good thing about pack gatherings. Celebrations mean a lot of single people finding an excuse to have sex. The same thing happens in my clan."

"Do you like living in Alaska?" There was a lot she didn't know about the VampLycans.

"I do. The winters can be harsh, though. We get around it well. It's like a different world up there."

"You mean because it's remote? Arlis once said you live far from cities."

"That too. There are a few small towns that have popped up but nothing like here. The populations are usually just a few hundred or less. Humans mind their own business and stay out of our territories."

"That must be good. You know, to run around in fur and not need to worry about being spotted or shot at by hunters."

He nodded as he finished his burger and picked up the second one on his plate. It made her glance at her own; she could only eat one burger. She hoped that didn't put him off, but no way could she eat as much as a shifter. She picked at her chips, desperately trying to think of something seductive to say or do. She had to gain his interest to get him into bed.

He sniffed the air when the breeze teased her back, blowing her scent his way. "You're not mated. I'm surprised."

That jolted her. "Why would you say that? A lot of women in their early twenties are still single."

He studied her face, not even being discreet about it. "I just figured someone would have snatched you up once you hit maturity."

She wasn't sure how to take that and was tempted to ask. Did he think her so weak that someone would need to take her under their protection? "No mate. No boyfriend." She shrugged. "I work for your brother. I handle all the pack correspondences, which keeps me busy. Our territory borders four other packs. It's like Werewolf central around here."

That didn't help her, either, since none of the Were men from other packs would give her the time of day...but she didn't mention that. At least one of those other alphas had outright forbidden any of his pack from even dating humans. She figured mating to a half-breed wouldn't be allowed, either.

"Arlis must trust you a lot."

She smiled. "I can't tell you how wonderful he is."

"Don't let Ginny hear you speak in that tone about her mate. She'd be jealous, and maybe feel the need to remind you that he's her mate."

The very idea horrified her. "Oh no! I'm not attracted to him."

Trayis arched one eyebrow, staring at her. Then his eyes narrowed as if he didn't believe her.

She dropped her gaze, seeing his dominance—and feeling it as well. This conversation had gone wrong in a bad way. "Arlis is my hero, but that's it. It's nothing sexual. Just gratitude." She dared to look at him again. "My mother was human. Once it became known that I couldn't shift, some of the pack wanted me banished."

Anger glinted in his eyes. "Why would they do that?"

"Some don't see me as worthy of being part of this pack. Not all of them…but enough that they went to Arlis. He put me under his protection and allowed me to stay. I was terrified at the time that I'd be sent to live with humans. I wouldn't have fit in with them, either."

"That's the stupidest thing I've ever heard. You faintly carry the scent of a Lycan. Other packs would target you. You wouldn't be able to blend in or stay hidden with humans."

"That's what Arlis told them. I was born here, and therefore pack. He gave me a job when they questioned how someone like me could be a useful member of our society. He saved my life. I do think he's wonderful, but it's in a protector type of way. No one was happier than I was when he found Ginny. He's a fantastic alpha who takes care of his pack and deserves the best mate. And she's it. Their love is something to inspire everyone."

His smile returned. "I understand."

She blew out a relieved breath. "Good." It took a few seconds to work up her courage to speak again. "Um…are you seeing anyone?"

That wiped the smile off his face. "Why?" His gaze held hers.

Heat warmed her cheeks, and she swallowed hard. *Be brave. Be gutsy. You can do this.* Marcia had gone after Kale. She could do the same. "You mistook my attraction to the wrong brother."

The words came out soft, not exactly steady, but she'd said them.

Surprise widened his eyes and his lips parted, but he didn't say anything.

"Look—the mouse dares to show her face," a familiar bitchy voice stated from behind Shay.

Her spine stiffened but she refused to look over her shoulder. She'd been paying attention to Trayis, not her surroundings. Her instincts were shit for a Were, but good enough to know at least a few of her regular tormenters had arrived. *Damn. Now is not the time for them to pull their shit. What else is Kendra going to say?*

Whatever shot she'd at getting Trayis into bed, however small, would be gone by the time they were done insulting her.

"Do you know who you're eating with?" That was Lucinda. "I don't think your half-brother would approve, Trayis. She's the lowest member of our pack."

Barbie snorted. "Member? Try charity case. Our alpha has a big heart, and he took pity on her. The rest of us are smarter. She should go throw herself in the trash where she belongs."

Anger surged, and Shay slowly twisted her body, glaring at the tall bleached blonde with cold blue eyes. "Smarter? You just insulted our alpha. Perhaps your parents stuck you with the name 'Barbie' once they realized you have plastic between your ears instead of a brain." Her gaze dropped to the bitch's breasts and low-cut top. "Speaking of plastic, nobody believes you went from an A cup to a D while on vacation for a week without plastic surgery. Which seems to be a theme with you."

Barbie unleashed her claws but Lucinda gripped her wrist. "You can't do that. She's too weak and pathetic to actually, you know, have claws of her own."

21

"Yes," Kendra snickered. "Don't forget that. We're not allowed to claw the special-needs girl. Laws had to be written just for her."

The other two laughed. "Pathetic," the both said in unison.

The bench seat across the table creaked, and Shay glanced away from the trio to watch as Trayis rose to his feet. She wouldn't blame him if he walked away but instead he glared at the women. "Are you insulting my brother—again?"

His viciously growled question sent a chill down Shay's spine. She glanced at the Bitch Trio and saw them go pale. Barbie stumbled back a step, dragging Lucinda with her.

Kendra, the idiot, held her ground. She jerked her chin up and scowled.

"No. We're not."

"It sounded that way to me. You're also insulting *me* by questioning who I decide to keep company with. Shay was invited to join me. You aren't. Get lost."

Kendra seemed to have a death wish when her friends took off but she remained. "We were trying to be friendly and do you a favor."

"A favor?" He lost the growl but his voice came out icy cold.

Kendra pointed at Shay. "She *never* comes to these celebrations. Nobody wants her around. You only visit every blue moon, so she's clearly targeting you."

"For what?"

"No other male will waste time on her. She probably figured she had a shot with *you* since you're not from the pack. She's a fucking mistake that never should have been born! Her mother was a *murderer*. The only reason she's allowed in our pack is because our alpha pities her. I didn't want her to fool you into believing she was worth even a minute of your time."

"I'll considered myself warned. Now get the fuck away from us."

Kendra hesitated.

Trayis snarled.

She spun, stalking away as quickly as her high heels would allow on the grass.

Trayis sank back onto his seat. Shay lowered her chin and refused to meet his gaze. She gripped her plate. "I'll leave."

He shocked her by reaching out faster than she could track with her eyes and gripped her wrist. His touch was gentle but firm. "I didn't say you had to."

She still couldn't find the courage to look at his face. "I'm sorry they did that. It's because Marcia isn't here to scare them off."

"Who's Marcia?" His voice came out soft now, a bit husky. She didn't hear any anger anymore.

"My best friend. She's a dominant who's beaten on them in the past for targeting me." She paused. "Her parents took me in when I was orphaned as a toddler, and they raised me."

"I have questions, Shay. Would you mind answering them?"

She closed her eyes, hating this. "Ask."

He hesitated.

23

She opened her eyes and peeked up at him for a split second. His handsome face held no expression. She focused on her plate of food. Everyone else in the pack knew her history, but he didn't appear to. It was better to just spit it out than to wait for him to probe her with uncomfortable questions.

"My father always wanted to learn how to surf," she began. "He took a two-week vacation to California. He met my human mother on the beach on the first day he arrived. They hit it off, she got pregnant, and he brought her home." She paused. "I don't remember them, but Dean and Sylvia, my foster parents, were best friends with my father since childhood. It was tough for my mother to leave her family and friends, and not everyone in the pack was nice to the human girl. She was only eighteen at the time.

"Humans live more sheltered lives. It was difficult for her to become a young mom, accept the reality that she had a Werewolf mate, and live amongst people who weren't supposed to exist. When I was two...my father came home to find her barely breathing. He tried to save her but she died in his arms. He loved her, and the grief was too much. He made it three days before he stopped breathing, too. He just couldn't go on without her."

"Fuck." Trayis rubbed her wrist, which he still held. "I'm sorry."

"Some of the pack considers it murder because my mother committed suicide," she whispered. "She'd taken sleeping pills. They aren't even sure how she got them, since my father kept a close watch on her because she was having such a hard time adjusting to life here." She shrugged. "It's also not a secret that I wasn't planned. My dad loved my mom, but he'd decided to leave her in California since he knew it would be too difficult for her to learn the truth about him and give up everything she knew. He didn't want to be selfish by taking her from her life. Her scent changed, though, and he realized he'd gotten her pregnant. I was assured he was happy about that. He wanted us both. I was loved. It just ended in tragedy for us all."

"I'm so sorry, Shay. He must have loved her with everything he was, not to have survived their bond breaking. Don't allow *anyone* to tell you otherwise."

She nodded, blinking back tears. "They were right about one thing, though."

"What?"

She dared hold his gaze. "I did come to this celebration because of you."

"Why?"

"I was hoping you'd see me as just a woman, instead of the way the rest of the pack does. I wanted to take you home with me. You said it yourself...these celebrations make people want to have sex." Heat flamed in her cheeks, and she had to look away from him again. "But that was ridiculous. I'm sorry. I'll leave." She pulled on her wrist, and he let go.

She stood, her legs shaking, and stepped over the bench. The trash was nearby, so she dumped her plate, hurrying to leave before the Bitch Trio had a chance to come after her again.

Footsteps sounded on the grass behind her, and she whirled, prepared to do her best to defend against an attack.

25

Trayis smiled down at her. "My place is probably closer." He jerked his head toward the woods. "I'm staying in the trailer near here."

She was stunned speechless.

He held out his hand. "You don't want those bitches to win, do you? They were sniffing after me last night. I turned them down flat. Imagine how annoyed they'll be when I choose *you* to bed instead?"

She lifted her hand and he took it, pulling her close.

"You don't actually have to have sex with me...but they're watching."

She tore her gaze from him and scanned the area, seeing the Bitch Trio near the grills. All three appeared utterly enraged, glaring directly at her.

She smiled and stepped closer to him. "I brought condoms."

His eyebrows rose.

"I'm more human than Were. I'm sorry but...I took after my mother. Is that a deal breaker?"

"No. I've been with humans before."

She breathed out a sigh of relief. "Thank you."

"Don't say that as if you think you should be grateful. I want you, Shay. But it's been a while since I've done this. My life keeps me very busy. I could become a little impatient or aggressive once our clothes are off. I don't want to scare you."

She liked that he hadn't been with anyone recently. "I'll risk it."

Chapter Two

Shay had never thought she'd get to see the inside of the alpha's new, fancy travel trailer that he'd bought to house special visitors. It was off limits to pack. Trayis unlocked the door and gestured her to enter. She climbed up the three steps and got a view of a living area. It was compact but even nicer than she'd suspected it to be.

Sections of it expanded out of the sides, making the interior feel roomy. The modern kitchen was tucked to one side in the center area, a table across from it, and down the hallway she could see a bed.

She made room for Trayis as he followed her inside, locking the door behind them.

He flipped on some lights and pulled down the shades on the windows. It would give them privacy if anyone tried to spy. He didn't say anything until all the windows were covered. His head nearly touched the roof of the trailer. He was that tall, standing over six feet.

He held her gaze. "I do have a question still."

"Okay. Ask them." She'd give him total honesty.

"Of those laws that were written for you, does one of them declare you hands off? Is Arlis going to have a problem with me touching you?"

"No one is allowed to force me. But I willingly came here with you. You have my permission."

He cocked his head, staring at her with confusion. "No one is *ever* allowed to force another pack mate to have sex."

"In my teens, a few of the boys saw me as an easy target. I couldn't shift, and I lived with a foster family. They didn't think I'd be protected, didn't think I counted as a full pack member because of my human blood." She crossed her arms over her chest, hating to admit such weaknesses to a man she was attracted to. "Horny boys. Girl without claws. I'm considered extremely submissive in pack terms." She shrugged. "A few came after me."

He straightened his head, anger glinting in his eyes. "Were you sexually assaulted?"

"No." She lowered her hands to her sides. "Can we drop this?"

"I just don't want to set off triggers if you have any."

As she told Marcia, she knew he was a protector. It was sweet. "Do you want blunt?"

"Yes."

"Fine." She sucked in a sharp breath and blew it out. "They may have thought about forcing the issue, but fear of getting me pregnant was too high. I don't have control over my ovaries. Rod and Marcia both told me that when I'm ovulating, it's extremely faint. They couldn't pick it up most of the time. No one could be certain when I was fertile or not."

"Who is Rod?"

"My foster brother. We're family. Nothing more."

"Go on."

"Pack boys never wanted to, um…fuck me, because of the fear of knocking me up. They thought they could use some of their dominant vibes to get blow jobs, though." She knew she blushed, and Shay lowered her gaze to his chest. "They were wrong. I could fee! what they were doing, even though my human side is stronger. They couldn't just make me drop to my knees by tossing out vibes, or cause enough fear for me to blindly follow orders on instinct. *Especially* if it was to suck their dicks."

"That's fucked up."

She lifted her gaze, holding his. He looked angry now. "I know. Sylvia found out what they were attempting to do when she overheard a boy snarling, and me yelling at him. He was frustrated that his vibes didn't work, and I was angry that he'd tried that bullshit on me. So she went to Arlis."

"Sylvia is your foster mother?"

She nodded.

"No male should ever use his dominance on a female that way."

"Arlis agreed."

"So, what laws did he write specifically for you?"

"No one is allowed to challenge me. No fighting with or physically harming me. I don't have the shifter ability to defend myself. I can't grow claws. He felt they'd have an unfair advantage even in skin. Which is true. I'm stronger than a human woman would be, but I'm not nearly as strong as a full Werewolf. They'd kick my ass, and I fully admit it. No dominant-vibes bullshit to force me to someone's will." She dropped her gaze again, because his stare was too intense for her to withstand. "Not that it works anyway. And anyone willing to bed me must mate me if they get me pregnant. Hence the condoms." This was so embarrassing. "But no forcing me to mate with them. It must be my decision. That about covers it."

"Okay."

"Oh, and they can't hurt me during sex. But I know you won't. We don't have to go into that." Her blush burned hotter in her cheeks.

"Arlis actually needed to make that a law?"

She nodded. "He sat me down when I was sixteen to explain shifter sex, and how my body was different from other girls'. That's the age when most of our teens begin having sex and fooling around. My alpha cares about me, and he was worried someone would become too rough. I heal better than a human does but not as fast as a Were. He wanted me to know that he'd explained to the boys that I had more brittle bones and skin, and they'd be punished if they weren't careful."

"What is their punishment?"

"He'd beat them in front of everyone. The severity of the beating is his judgement call, depending on the injuries they may have inflicted."

He frowned.

"You know...break my arm, and he'd break theirs repeatedly for the amount of time it took me to heal, so they'd understand the pain I'd have to endure. That kind of stuff."

He smiled slightly. "Good to know."

She glanced at his mouth. "You're not part of our pack. The laws don't apply to you. It's okay if you need to bite me. I won't mistake it for a claim, Trayis."

Surprise flickered in his eyes as she studied them.

"I know you're part Vampire, and they drink blood. So that would likely be why you'd bite me, instead of the reason a Werewolf might."

30

"That doesn't scare you?"

"I'm not afraid." That was the truth. "Maybe I have bad instincts but...I'm drawn to you."

"What do you want?"

"Just you, Trayis."

"Condoms." He held out his hand.

She reached inside her bra and withdrew the linked wrappers, warm from being against her skin. He took them without comment and jerked his head toward the bedroom.

She felt nervous as she made her way to the back of the trailer. The bed was a large one for the space, taking up most of the room. It had also been made. She turned to find Trayis blocking the doorway, filling the entire frame.

"Clothes off," he rasped.

Her hands trembled a little as she began to strip. "Aren't you going to get naked, too?"

"You're shaking. Are you certain you're not afraid?" He inhaled through his nose.

"I'm not afraid but a bit nervous," she confessed.

"And you're sure you want me?"

Worry surfaced that he'd change his mind and ask her to leave. "Positive."

Shay shed all her clothes, grateful that she'd showered and shaved that morning. She reached up and pushed her blonde hair back over her shoulder.

31

His gaze lowered down her body—and she swore the golden streaks in his eyes brightened. Then she remembered his Vampire bloodlines. It wasn't a trick of her imagination. She'd never seen a Vampire in person, but she'd heard about their traits. They could control minds, and she'd also heard their eyes could take on a luminescent quality when they were hungry or sexually aroused.

"Stretch out on your back and spread your legs."

She did as he asked. Warmth heated her face as she bent her legs and then parted them wide, exposing her sex to him.

He growled low and tore his shirt over his head, tossing it on the floor. His legs moved as she guessed he was kicking off his shoes. He reached down, unfastening his jeans. She locked her attention there and masked her features in case things turned scary.

He dropped to his knees, though, before he exposed his cock, reached for her, and his big hands slid under her ass. She gasped when he jerked on her, pulling her closer. Her bent elbows propping her up slid out from beneath her, and she ended up lying flat on her back.

That hadn't been expected when he lowered his face without warning and snarled.

She tensed when she felt his lips on her inner thigh. He licked her skin, pressing a kiss there, and then lightly raked his teeth against. She felt the sharp tips of his fangs but there wasn't any pain. It was possible he needed to feed before sex.

"Do it," she urged, hoping it wouldn't hurt. She sealed her lips tightly together, silently promising not to cry out in pain if it did.

Instead, he kissed her thigh again, ran his tongue along her skin, and inched upward. Her eyes widened as he nibbled his way closer to her sex. Trayis slid his hands out from under her ass and splayed them on her inner thighs, pushing them even farther apart and pinning them against the mattress.

The first brush of his tongue across her clit had her jerking under him. It felt odd—and amazing. He focused his attention on the sensitive nub. He licked at her, sucked, and she closed her eyes. Pleasure jolted through her and a moan escaped.

Trayis growled, adding vibrations as he ruthlessly attacked her clit.

She tried to buck her hips to get away. She couldn't think, swamped by ecstasy so strong it nearly hurt. It was too much, too intense, and she arched her back, clawing at the bedding.

Shay threw her head back and yelled his name as climax tore through her.

Trayis stopped as she panted and tried to pull herself together. Embarrassment came swiftly. It shouldn't have happened so fast. But *nothing* had prepared her for that. She tried to think of some excuse for her quick trigger and wondered if she should apologize.

She opened her eyes, staring at the white ceiling above her, not daring to look at him. He probably thought she was even more pathetic than her pack did.

"Roll over and get on your hands and knees," Trayis ordered. His voice didn't sound right. It came out too deep, too husky.

She rolled, still avoiding his gaze. It would have been nice if he'd decided to take her missionary style, but she wasn't going to ask. She got on her hands and knees, spreading her legs about six inches apart and arching her back to shove her ass higher. Her foster mother had given her the sex talk about Werewolves. It was the standard submissive position for a female to take with a dominant.

The mattress dipped, and Trayis got on the bed behind her. Something landed on the mattress next to her, and she turned her head, seeing three of the condom packets. Shay assumed he was putting the fourth one on. She licked her lips, breathed deeply, and waited.

He put one hand on her hip, getting a firm grip, and his legs braced outside of hers. Slight fear surfaced but she pushed it back. Trayis wouldn't hurt her.

His finger slid between the folds of her pussy, and he rubbed her clit. It was oversensitive but it still felt good. Shay moaned.

"Damn," he growled. "Are you ready?"

"Yes."

"You're not as big as I'm used to."

She wondered if he meant her private area or her body in general. It didn't matter. He wanted her enough to willingly use a condom, and he'd just given her an orgasm by going down on her.

He stopped playing with her clit, removed his hand—and something much thicker than his finger nudged the slit of her pussy. He rubbed against her flesh, and she felt how wet he'd made her. He positioned his cock right at her opening.

Trayis pushed a little.

She closed her eyes. He felt *so* big.

34

His other hand gripped her hip to get a better hold and she locked her arms straight. He adjusted his legs a little, pinning hers in place.

"Are you sure you want me?"

"Yes."

"Your heart is racing. I can hear it."

"It would be bad if you were boring me," she teased.

"True. Here we go, doll. No turning back now. I'm going to make it good for you."

The way he sounded, the tone of his sexy voice, excited her like nothing else. He pushed against her a tiny bit more. He growled and tightened his hands on her hips. There would probably be minor bruising from his fingers but she'd heal fast from that. She tried to stay relaxed, remembering *that* part of Sylvia's talk, too.

It was supposed to feel better if she didn't tense up.

Then he pushed all the way inside her in one powerful thrust that almost made her arms collapse.

Raw pain tore through her, and she was pretty sure that cry she heard had ripped from her own throat.

Trayis froze over her, his cock buried inside her deep. He wasn't big—he was *huge*, and she thought maybe something inside her had broken.

A snarl filled the room before his hands eased their hold on her hips. He released her and came down over her back, almost crushing her beneath him. One of his arms wrapped around her chest, the other hand splaying on the mattress next to her head. She barely saw it through the tears that filled her eyes.

"Son of a bitch," he rasped near her ear. "Why didn't you tell me?"

She couldn't talk, still catching her breath from the pain.

He moved his hips, slowly beginning to withdraw from her body. She cried out because it hurt.

He froze again, still embedded inside her. "Give me your neck, *now*."

It wasn't a request. He snarled the words, sounding furious.

She managed to twist her head to expose herself to him. His mouth came down on her neck and he licked her skin. She tensed as he opened his mouth wider...then she felt his fangs prick the area he'd just licked. He bit down—and she gasped. It didn't hurt nearly as much as his cock had, breaching her.

The pain faded as he took blood, feeding off her. Her tense muscles relaxed as a kind of euphoria took over, making her mind float a bit, her thoughts jumble.

She was aware when he turned them on their sides, his body spooning hers and holding her tight. He began to thrust his hips, this time gentle and slow. She clutched at his arm circling her breasts, needing something to cling to. Pleasure gripped her, a need for more, and she moaned.

He kept that pace as his mouth suckled at her throat. Her clit throbbed. He shifted his arm down her body, pressed his hand between her thighs, and found that needy spot to rub.

She moaned louder, eyes closed, and felt a building inside her that grew and grew, until another climax exploded through her body.

Trayis snarled as he came so hard, it damn near hurt. He was pretty sure he now understood the term "busting a nut." In his case, it felt like both had ruptured.

He withdrew his fangs and licked Shay's neck where he'd bitten her. She panted in his arms as he kept her tight against him, his body curled around hers to prevent her from struggling if the urge struck.

He had to catch his own breath as he tried to calm himself over what just happened.

She'd been a virgin. He was pissed she hadn't told him. The assumption that she'd been fucked before had been a given, considering her attractive looks and the conversation they'd had. Not once had he suspected. He also wanted to kick his own ass for what he'd had to do, once he realized how much pain he'd caused.

"Shay?"

She turned her head and peered at him with those light brown doe eyes of hers. He inwardly cursed, seeing her dilated pupils. His Vampire traits had done that to her. It was a blessing and a curse. He'd stopped her from hurting, but he'd also effectively drugged her.

"Why didn't you tell me?"

She released his arm and reached up, gently stroking his jaw. "I wanted you." A yawn widened her mouth, and her eyes closed.

Her hand fell away from him as she passed out cold.

"Fuck." She was a little thing, and he'd taken blood from her. Probably too much. He gently shifted her on the bed and withdrew from her body. He looked down, seeing blood on the condom. "Damn it."

37

He focused on her heartbeat, listening to it closely. It was slow and steady, but strong.

He got off the bed and stormed into the bathroom, disposing of the condom in the trash. Blood turned his fingers red from removing it. He washed them, wet a hand towel with warm water, and returned to the bed.

"Arlis is going to want to kill me." He gently rolled Shay onto her back and spread her legs, cleaning her with care. "You should have told me, Shay. Hell, *warned* me."

He pulled back the covers on one side, lifted her, and placed her upon his sheets. They were black, and her pale skin and dark blonde hair were such a contrast against the bedding, she seemed even more fragile.

He wanted to throw back his head and roar in anger.

Instead, he forced himself to calm. Shay was fine. He'd taken blood but not too much. It didn't matter if she still bled a little from the sex. It wasn't enough to cause her harm. He tucked the covers over her and backed away, staring at her sleeping form.

His little brother would lose his shit once he found out Trayis had taken Shay's innocence. He was still stunned she'd been a virgin. What in the hell was wrong with the pack males? Shay might be mostly human, but were they all blind? Stupid? She was attractive, with a killer, compact body. More than that, she had a gentle personality and a sweetness to her.

In *his* clan, the men would have been fighting to seduce her into their beds. She'd have had her pick of any single man she wanted.

How has she remained a virgin? And why did she want me?

He wanted to ask, but she slept on.

He rose to his feet and walked into the kitchen area, yanked open the fridge, and grabbed a beer. He twisted the cap off and took a long drink, closing his eyes. A vibrating noise caught his attention, and he returned to the bedroom, bent, and snagged his jeans off the floor. He removed his cell, seeing that he had two missed recent calls. They must have come in while he'd been fucking Shay.

He tossed his jeans back on the floor and returned to the kitchen.

"Fuck. And it gets better." He decided to return Wen's call first.

"Hey, how cute is the new baby? Or is it ugly?"

"You're talking about my nephew, asshole."

Wen chuckled. "You're in a bad mood."

"You have no idea. Is something wrong there?"

"No. I hadn't heard from you all day. I was checking in, fearless leader."

"Things are complicated."

Wen's tone became more serious. "Problems with the pack? Do you need reinforcements? Is someone fucking with your brother, since his focus is on his new son? Is another pack thinking about a territory war?"

"It's nothing like that. Don't send anyone. It's not that kind of problem."

"You sound stressed. What's up?"

He hesitated.

"You're worrying me."

"It involves a woman."

39

"Oh." Wen paused. "Do you want me to get Gerri?"

"I don't need advice from your mate, and I sure as hell don't want anyone to know about this."

"Hang on." Seconds ticked by and a door closed. "I'm in your office now. No one can hear me. What's going on?"

"I fucked up." Trayis ran his fingers through his hair. "Now I have to figure out how to fix it."

"You pissed off your brother's mate? So the kid really *is* ugly, and you said something? Made a face of disgust that insulted her? I think all babies look like aliens at first, but they get cuter as they grow. Their twins are proof of that."

He sighed. "I fucked a virgin."

Wen laughed.

Trayis ground his teeth together. "Knock it off."

"Are you serious?"

"Yes."

"I'm sure it wasn't your first time popping someone's cherry. Why are you upset? Oh shit—how old is she? I know you don't go for the young ones, but some girls these days look far older than they really are."

"She's an adult. End that train of thought. She's a half-breed who lives with the pack."

"Then what's the problem?"

"She chose me."

"And?"

"Why *me*?"

"Why don't you ask her?"

"She's currently passed out in my bed." He stared down the hallway. "She was in pain. I panicked and bit her."

Wen gasped. "Did you mate her?"

"No. The blood exchange only went one way."

He sighed. "Then it's all good."

"Nothing about this is *good*."

"Trayis, I don't understand the problem. We've all basically popped someone's cherry. Hell, we were *all* virgins at one point. Then we weren't. No big deal. Women are attracted to you." He paused. "You think she's a status hunter or something, will maybe use this to try to guilt you into mating her?"

"I don't know. My brother isn't going to take this well, though, when he finds out. She works for him, and I get the impression he looks out for her because she's one of his weakest members."

"She's an adult and she climbed into bed with you. I know you, man. You didn't pressure her into anything. Women fall all over themselves, coming on to you. And you always turn them away...but not this one. I'll assume she's pretty hot?"

"She is."

"There you go. Just tell her you aren't interested in a mate. Be firm. Problem solved."

He nodded. "Yeah."

Wen remained silent for a few seconds. "But? I hear a but. I know you too well. You're freaked out over something. What is it?"

41

"I've never fucked someone like her before."

"A virgin?"

"Yes."

"Oh. I never would have guessed."

"I liked older Lycan women when I was younger, before they left. Experienced ones. Then when I first took over the clan, our single women always came to me. *They* were experienced, too."

"So you feel guilty. Maybe you were too rough or went too fast. Am I right?"

"Didn't I say as much when I told you that she was in pain and I panicked?"

"It happens. Hell, the first time I had sex, I think I came in under a minute. It wasn't ideal for the woman. My first virgin didn't go so well, either. We're big, and she was human. I used my eyes to distract her from the initial pain until she adjusted to me."

"I'm going to go now. You're not helping."

"Talk to me, Trayis. I'm your friend."

He took another sip of beer and sighed. "It was…intense, okay? The biting and fucking part. I've never come so damn hard in my life. It's messing with my head. Plus, Arlis really *is* going to be mad. She's someone he considers to be under his protection. My fucking her might piss him off. But the thing is, I *like* Shay. I don't want to hurt her if she's set on me mating her, but it wouldn't work out."

"Why not?"

"She's more human than Lycan."

"Not an issue."

"She's gentle and sweet."

"You think you'd crush her spirit or something? That you'd be too strong of a personality for her to handle?"

"Maybe. I'm also not ready to settle down."

"Tell her that. As for your brother, you said this female is an adult. Period. You didn't force her to fuck you. She made her choice. End of story."

"Right." He sighed again. "I have to go."

"I'll keep my cell close. Call me if you need to talk."

"Will do. And Wen? Don't repeat any of this."

"You have my word. Gerri understands there are things I can't tell her. Important clan business."

Trayis snorted and ended the call. He put his cell and the beer on the counter before returning to the bedroom. Shay still slept, looking entirely too innocent and vulnerable in his bed.

"What in the hell did I do...and how am I going to fix this?"

Chapter Three

Shay woke and stretched. There was a slight soreness between her legs...

One glance at the ceiling had memories returning in a flash and she sat up. She clutched at the covers, instantly realizing she was naked.

Trayis crouched against the wall in the corner of the room, sporting a pair of navy sweatpants and nothing else. His eyes were golden, revealing a lot of bright streaks in his irises. It made them appear predatory and dangerous, reminding her of a wild animal about to strike.

"How do you feel?"

His chilly tone sent a shiver up her spine. He didn't look happy in the least, but not exactly angry, either. "Fine."

"I'm trying to remain calm, Shay."

She swallowed, clutching the covers tighter. "I should have told you I hadn't had sex before but I was worried it would matter."

A low rumble came from him.

"You might have changed your mind. But I wanted you. It's really no big deal. I'll get dressed and leave."

He rose to his feet, hands fisted at his sides. She stared at his white knuckles and fear crept down her spine.

"Don't do that," he barked.

Her gaze shot to his face. *Now* he looked furious.

"Don't you dare get frightened. I'd never hurt a woman. Even one who tricked me."

That was just insulting. "I didn't trick you. Did you tell me how many women you've slept with? No. The subject didn't come up."

"You were a *virgin*."

"Not anymore. What do you want? A thank you?"

"Shay." He growled her name.

"I said I'll leave." His reaction and his words hurt. She'd heard things could become a little awkward after casual sex encounters, but never this bad. She tried to hide her emotions as she shoved off the covers and crawled down the bed to avoid him. Her clothes were on the floor at the end of it where she'd left them. She refused to look at him, feeling vulnerable and exposed as she began to dress hurriedly.

A dizzy spell hit as she bent, and she almost fell on her ass. Trayis lunged and wrapped his arm around her waist, hoisting her off her feet. He sat on the bed, planting her across his lap. She tried to stand again but his arm tightened, locking her there.

"I'm fine. I just moved too quickly." She tried to wiggle off his lap.

"Keep doing that, and we're going to have a problem. You'll make me hard again. Hold still."

She froze, staring at his face inches from hers.

"Why me, Shay? Why come to *my* bed?"

"Why not?"

A muscle in his jaw flexed as his lips pressed together tightly. He glowered at her with narrowed eyes.

"You're attractive, nice, and we have things in common." She shrugged. "Happy? I'm *fine*, Trayis. You can let me up. I'll be out of your hair within a minute and you never have to see me again." She tried to get off his lap once more.

She gasped when he twisted his upper half and her back hit the bed, then he pinned her under him. He adjusted his big body, throwing a leg over her to press hers down. He leaned in, almost nose to nose with her, as he stared deeply into her eyes.

"That's it? You find me attractive? You didn't want to guilt me into making you my mate?"

Her mouth fell open on another gasp as shock rolled through her. "*What?*"

He scowled.

She put her hands on his warm, solid chest and gave a hard push. It didn't budge him an inch. "I'm not like the Bitch Trio. I don't play mind games, and I sure as hell would *never* try to trap a guy. I brought condoms, remember? To prevent me from getting pregnant. That's *not* how a woman forces a man into mating her. Get off me!"

He rolled away, releasing her in a flash.

She sat up and found herself in the bedroom alone.

He hadn't gone far, though, since she glimpsed him down the hallway through the open door. She stared at his back as she grabbed her remaining clothes on the floor, putting them on.

He turned as she left the bedroom and blocked her way to the exit door. "Do you want to cause trouble between Arlis and me? Were you lying when you said you didn't feel anything for him? Was fucking me payback because he mated Ginny?"

Her mouth opened as myriad emotions—from anger to shock to disbelief—all slapped her at once. "You're insane!"

"Am I?"

"If you believe any of that bullshit, then yes. You are! Paranoid, too. I don't feel that way about Arlis. I never have. He's more of a father figure to me than anything else. What is *wrong* with you?"

"You were a *virgin*," he snarled.

Anger vibes rolled off him and her knees weakened, almost collapsing her. She locked her legs and her fear spiked. None of the dominant Weres had ever made her almost buckle before. It meant he had to be stronger than all the Weres she'd ever known—including her alpha. Arlis had never unleashed his vibes her way, but she'd been close before when someone else had pissed him off.

"It doesn't make sense. Why me, Shay?"

"Why *not* you?" She pushed down the fear, battling her instincts to cower. She didn't think he was doing it on purpose, but his rage still affected her. "You were always nice to me, Trayis. You saved me from getting bullied when I was ten. Do you even remember that? It was at a party and the other kids were being mean. You walked up and snarled at them. They scattered and left me alone. And when you were here for the welcome party for the twins five years ago, I watched you from the trees all day. I was just barely legal and had a huge crush, but I couldn't work up the nerve to approach you.

47

"And now you're back to celebrate the birth of our alpha's newest son, and I found myself even more attracted than ever. I wanted the first and probably *only* man I let touch me to be someone who'd leave me with a good memory. I thought that would be you. Boy, was I wrong! Now get out of my way, and stop trying to intimidate me with your temper."

The anger faded from his expression and the vibes coming off him instantly halted.

She dropped her gaze to his chest. "I want to leave now. Don't worry, Trayis. I won't tell anyone you touched me. Ever. You can just forget it happened."

He stepped aside, pressing his body against the table.

She had to brush against him in the tight space but she made it past him. The door was locked when she tried to jerk it open to escape. She flipped the lock and finally got the door open, breathing in fresh air. The sun was about to go down, the woods around them shadowing.

"Shay?"

She refused to glance back. "I'll avoid you when you visit in the future."

"I took more blood from you than I'd intended. Eat something with red meat. Maybe drink some orange juice. Will you let me walk you home?"

"I don't need an escort. Goodbye, Trayis."

She fled, slamming the door behind her.

It was easy to avoid the pack by staying off the regular trails until she reached her cabin. She punched in the code for the keyless lock she'd installed and entered.

Tears streamed down her face once she was alone. She'd made an even worse mess out of her life.

"Good going. You did the impossible," she muttered aloud.

His scent probably lingered on her. She made her way to the bathroom and stripped, tossing her cloths in the trash, never wanting to see that outfit again. It would remind her of Trayis. She didn't even wait for the water to warm before she was in the shower to wash down her body and hair. Too bad the memories wouldn't disappear down the drain, too.

He hated her...he had accused her of horrible things.

None of it made sense. Maybe he hadn't figured on her being a virgin, but *she'd* been the one to suffer the pain. Not him. He'd also bitten her and gotten blood as well as sex out of the deal.

"Why was *he* bitching?" she grumbled.

The cabin held no answers for her.

She finished her shower, put on her pajamas, and tossed a frozen pizza in the oven. It was tempting to call Marcia to pour her heart out to her bestie, but she didn't reach for the phone. Her word was solid. Trayis didn't want anyone to know what had happened between them. She would keep it a secret. Even from her best friend.

She got the pizza out of the oven, poured herself some soda, and flipped on her TV. "I'll just forget. Pretend it didn't happen. I hope things went better for Marcia." She put her plate on the coffee table and plopped down on the couch.

She winced as she landed on the cushion, a reminder that she was still a bit tender in that area. "He's a dick. A big painful one, in every sense."

* * * * *

Trayis drank his sixth beer and finally returned Arlis's call. "What's up?"

"I was going to invite you to dinner but you missed that. Ginny can warm you a plate if you want to come by. I thought you'd planned to spend as much time as possible with us while you're here."

"I'm sorry. I was on the phone with my clan. I had some things to deal with." He hated lying to his younger brother. But the truth wasn't an option. At least not until he got his head on straight about Shay. "It put me in a bad mood. It's best if I come by in the morning."

"Is everything okay in Alaska?"

"Just typical stuff. You know how it goes. I'm sure you have internal struggles with your pack."

"Always. I had to settle a dispute half an hour ago."

"What kind?"

"One of my females came to me with a problem."

He tensed, hoping it wasn't Shay.

"Maggie dumped Tom, and he wasn't taking it well. He's been lurking around her place, being a general pain in her ass. I had to warn him to keep his distance. I don't put up with that stalker bullshit."

He relaxed on the couch. "Do you think he'll listen?"

"He better or I'll lock his ass up for a week."

"He'd go nuts."

"Exactly. It put the fear in him. They weren't together long, but he said she was good in bed. As if that's a valid excuse to harass anyone. I reminded him that there are plenty of other single women for him to sleep with. He's not a bad guy. Just a bit pussy whipped and thinking with his dick."

Trayis wondered if Tom would go after Shay next. She was single...

He clenched his hands, almost breaking the beer bottle he held. The idea of some horny Lycan sniffing after her didn't sit well with him. "Speaking of internal issues, I got a glimpse of one today."

"What happened?"

"I ate lunch with Shay, and three women came up to us, talking shit about her. They said they wanted to warn me about her, but it seemed more like they wanted to hurt her feelings."

"Let me guess. A blonde showing off way too much cleavage, a redhead with a rude mouth on her, and a brunette who really needs to gain some weight?"

"One of them was named Barbie." He smiled, remembering what Shay had said to her. She had a quick mind for insults.

Arlis sighed. "I told them to leave Shay alone. That poor girl has enough to deal with. I'll talk to them."

"Why do they treat her that way?"

"Did you notice how the three of them dress? That their hair colors aren't natural? How much makeup they wear?"

"Not really."

"They're shallow. More concerned about their looks than anything else. Meanwhile, the three of them don't have a fully functioning brain between them. Shay's the only pack member they can pick on without getting their asses handed to them in a fight. I take it Marcia and Rod weren't around?"

"No. We were eating alone."

"I'm surprised those three even worked up the nerve to pick on her after the last time they pulled a stunt. Her foster siblings are very protective of Shay. About five months ago, the three of them cornered Shay and really upset her." He chuckled.

Trayis felt rage. "You think that's funny?"

"Let me finish. Her grandparents didn't want Shay after she was orphaned. Marcia and Rod's parents took her in. As the two youngest children, they bonded with Shay. All three of them are tighter than shit. Marcia and Rod decided to get even with those bitches by putting blue dye in Lucinda's Jacuzzi. It wasn't the kind that washed off easily, either. The trio likes to soak every night and get drunk, talking trash about other pack members." He chuckled again, darkly. "It left their skin colored for almost a week before it faded away. Marcia took full responsibility, but I know Rod helped. She stood in my office not one bit sorry, and told me they deserved it for being trolls. I don't allow physical fights unless it's to protect from harm. I couldn't disagree with her reasoning. I laughed and dismissed her without punishment."

Trayis had calmed but he still wasn't amused. "What do you mean, the grandparents didn't want Shay? She has family?"

"Mildred and Elvis. You've met them in the past. They used to run the pack store for decades. Their only child was Marcus, Shay's father."

"Why didn't they raise Shay after he died? Did they leave your pack before she was born?" He could understand being hesitant to hand over a pup into the care of an unknown alpha, especially since Shay was half human. Some packs were prejudiced.

Arlis sighed. "No. They were still pack members. I knew they were grieving but it was messed up. They viewed Shay as tainted, said I should put her down. They were bitter and upset when I rejected their request. Then I demoted them after they made threats. No way in hell did I trust them to supply groceries to the family that *did* take in Shay, or even trust them enough to live near her. I worried about them trying to hurt her."

Trayis jerked into an upright position and put his beer on the floor. "Put her down? *Tainted*? What the fuck?"

"They couldn't stand the sight of her, or the fact that she looked so much like her mother, Layla. Let's just say they weren't happy when Marcus mated a human, and they took their grief out on Shay when he died. They blamed *her*, as if any of that shit was her fault. It wasn't fair or right. They made actual death threats against a two-year-old after I refused to put her down myself. I'll tell you flat out that if *anyone* was to blame for their son's death, it was Mildred and Elvis. They treated their son's mate like shit and made her life miserable until Layla broke.

"Shay was an innocent child and cute as shit. Hell, I would have adopted her if I'd been mated. Instead, I transferred the grandparents to the far north sector and stuck them in a cabin to be lookouts. It's fucking miserable out there. Regardless, when Shay hit puberty and still hadn't shifted, they reached out to friends to petition me to banish her. They claimed Shay wasn't eligible to be part of the pack. That's when I'd had enough of them stirring up shit and kicked them out of the pack. It would be a death sentence for Shay to be on her own in the human world."

"Damn."

"Shay's had it rough. Probably always will. I've done my best to make certain she's not harassed."

By writing laws just for her. He couldn't say that, though, in case Arlis asked how he'd found out. "She seems nice."

"She's a sweetheart. Not that she's a pushover. She's got backbone. Always had to. She'll stand up for herself, but there's not much she can do against other women who could rip her to shreds with their claws. No one in the pack is allowed to touch her that way."

"Who are you talking about?" came Ginny's voice over the phone.

"Shay. The wannabe models were at it again today," Arlis explained to his mate. "I'm talking to my brother."

"Hi, Trayis!"

"Tell her hi back. Now go spend time with your mate and sons. I'll be by at breakfast."

"We'll see you at eight sharp."

Trayis ended the call and sighed. He stood and paced the narrow space between the couch and two chairs. Shay's words echoed in his head about why she'd chosen him. If she'd expected kindness or some great first sexual experience, he'd let her down.

"Fuck."

He showered and left the trailer naked, shifted, and then sniffed the ground. It didn't take long to pick up Shay's scent. He growled when he realized she'd stuck to the woods and avoided any of the trails that ran through the area. He lost her scent a few times but found it anywhere she'd brushed up against bushes and trees, since she'd had to make her own path through the vegetation. As he continued to track her, most of the pack cabins were left behind...until he finally came to a lone cabin sitting far from the others.

He raised his head, studying it. Lights glowed behind closed curtains.

It wasn't a big place, probably no more than six hundred square feet, if that. He softly padded onto the porch and sniffed at the swing. Shay's scent covered it. He'd found her home. He went to the door and cocked his head, picking up the sound of a television.

He hesitated, debating on shifting back to skin or returning to the trailer. She'd made it home safely. He'd worried about her passing out from blood loss.

He sank down and curled up on her porch, resting part of his body against the door. It creaked slightly, and the television muted. He could hear her breathing, though, and her steps when she came closer to the door.

Trayis got up and shifted. It would be better for her to find him naked in skin than to see his animal form. It tended to freak out his brother's Lycan pack when he ran with them.

"Go away," Shay muttered. "Today was more than enough. Don't make me call Marcia."

He cleared his throat. "I thought you said you weren't going to tell anyone what happened between us."

A lock clicked and Shay jerked open the door—then gaped.

He took in his fill of her, too. She had damp hair from a shower and wore a cute two-piece pajama set with short sleeves and pants that fell to her calves. He grinned, unable to help it.

"I take it you like cats. Does your pack know?"

She glanced down her body to stare at the print of various kittens, but her gaze froze when she realized he stood there without anything on. She gasped and jerked her chin up. "I thought you were the Bitch Trio. What do you want, Trayis? Why are you here?"

Studying her as she spoke, he noticed subtle things...like how her eyes were red and a bit puffy. How her voice sounded a little huskier than normal. It twisted him up inside. She'd been crying. He felt like a bastard. "I came to apologize."

"Minus your clothes?"

"I had to track where you lived. I do that better in fur."

She spun away but left the door open. "Come in before you're seen." She yanked a blanket off the back of her couch and held it out, keeping her gaze averted from his body.

"By who? You live pretty far away from the others."

"Sentries patrol every hour because I'm out here."

He stepped inside and closed the door behind him. The place was as tiny as he thought. The living room barely contained the couch, a slim coffee table, and a television over the fireplace mantel. The kitchen was an eight-foot-long strip containing a small counter with an oven, stovetop, and fridge that had all seen far better days. She didn't even have a dining table. The compact bathroom sat at the back under a loft section. A ladder rested next to that door, and he glanced up at the open loft. It couldn't have been more than six feet deep and seven feet across.

"You sleep up there?"

She shook the blanket. "Put this on. I refuse to talk to you otherwise."

He moved closer, invading her space. She looked so tiny compared to him. Her scent filled his nose. Vanilla and coconut shampoo, some mixed-fruit body wash, and just Shay. His dick began to harden.

He backed off, taking the blanket. It was soft and fuzzy. He snorted a laugh as he wrapped it around his waist.

"Covered."

She turned and backed away to put more space between them. "Apology accepted. I don't hold grudges."

Her mouth said one thing but he could see the hurt in her eyes. She didn't seem pissed but he'd obviously caused her to cry. There was no denying that. "Will you sit with me? Give me a chance to make this right? Please?"

"Only because you asked nicely." She waved to her couch. "And your kind doesn't say please often."

"My kind?"

"You're a dominant with alpha blood. I guessed you would be, since you and Arlis are half-brothers. You share a mother, and she was an alpha female. Most guys like you are too arrogant to think they ever did anything wrong. An apology implies you're admitting it."

Arlis was right. Shay had backbone to speak to him that way. He sat, and she planted her little ass on the coffee table instead of next to him. Her gaze kept flicking to his chest. She might be upset, but she was still attracted to him.

He leaned forward, invading her space again. She sat up straighter, and Trayis hid his smile. Those few inches she'd just given herself wouldn't help her.

"I've never taken a virgin to bed before. It unsettled me."

"I said I accepted your apology." She began to avoid his gaze again, looking at the cushion next to him, the arm of the couch, and even the old hardwood floor between them.

"Shay?"

"Yes?"

"It's polite to look at someone while they're talking to you."

Her gaze snapped to his, and he saw a flash of anger there. "I'm looking. Happy?"

"Would you like to slap me?" He cocked his cheek her way. "It might make you feel better."

She clasped her hands together and shoved them between her slightly parted thighs. "No. I don't want to hit you. That's not my way."

"You're part Lycan. They enjoy a little violence."

"But I'm mostly not." Her gaze dropped again. "Do you want to know what I inherited from my dad? My hearing is good. I heal fast for a human but not as well as a Werewolf." She sighed. "I can pick up vibes if someone's throwing them out. My senses are keener, I can feel it most of the time when someone is close to me. That's it. Oh—and I can eat without gaining a bunch of weight. I didn't realize that until I got into watching a lot of human shows. They always complain about how eating a sliver of pie or whatever adds five pounds to their ass. I've eaten plenty of pies without having to buy larger pants.

"I'm not old enough yet to know if my aging will slow. I'll find out in a few years, I guess. I don't even *look* like my dad. My foster mom says I'm almost an exact replica of my mother, right down to my short stature and small bones. I got her dark blonde hair, light brown eyes, and her features. Plus a ton of human weaknesses."

"There's nothing wrong with being so human."

Her head snapped up and she glared at him. "Are you kidding?"

"No."

"Now you're being *too* kind. Great." She lowered her chin. "I forgive you. You wigged out because I didn't tell you I'd never slept with a guy before. I get it. You think I had ulterior motives. I didn't. But it's all good. I'm not even going to tell my best friend what happened, okay? And Arlis will never find out."

"Why do you think I'm being kind when I tell you there's nothing wrong with you?"

She stood, avoided touching him, and put the coffee table between them. She paced the small space. "You don't know what it's like growing up in a pack when you're the weakest member." She stopped, sighed— and began to pace again.

"Tell me."

"Sylvia had to homeschool me. The other kids and parents didn't want me at Diego's house. He's the teacher for the pack. All Lycan kids go there. Just not me. He had to send my homework home, and my foster mom helped me learn everything."

"Why?"

She sighed. "The parents believed I would hold their kids back if they had to 'adjust to my flaws.' Being physically weaker translated to them believing I'd have problems learning how to read and stuff. It was all stupid. But the other instructors agreed. On day one of outdoor pup training, I couldn't keep up when they had us running together. I was four, and everyone just left me behind. I wasn't fast, my reflexes were crap. I even got lost—my sense of direction *sucks*. There wasn't a day two. I was banned from returning. The others got to learn our territory, run and play together as they were taught to fight to defend themselves...but me?" She turned and flashed him a bitter look. "In our teens, Marcia taught me how to fight well enough to be able to defend myself against a human. That's the only training I've received. And she and Rod were, and still are, my only friends." She snorted slightly. "Let's just say I have a real love of books. Not that reading's a bad thing. It isn't. But books are my life. My adventures."

He ached for her. It must have been so lonely. No pup should be ostracized that way.

"My foster siblings were great. Don't get me wrong. Sylvia and Dean birthed three kids, then a big gap, before having their last two. The older ones began to mate by the time I was five. Marcia is my age, and Rod's a year older. They kept me sane by playing with me and spending time with me, but they were also busy a lot of the time. Going to a school room I couldn't attend. Outdoor pack training that I was banned from. My foster family loved me...they didn't have to take me into their home, yet they did. It was my safe haven, but I was lonely. The other kids teased me; some of them were flat-out cruel. Most of the adults were, too."

"Because you're too human, or from what happened to your parents?"

She shrugged. "Both. It doesn't matter." She retook her seat on the coffee table and stared at her hands laced together. "I used to dream that my Were side would kick in when I hit puberty, like some other late bloomers, and I'd become some super badass. Make them all sorry for the way they'd treated me and finally be accepted." A sad smile curved her lips but it disappeared fast. "That didn't happen. I can't shift at all. Not even a hint of claw. No fangs."

He wanted to hold her. "Shay."

She refused to look at him. "You want to know how I made it to my age a virgin?" Her shoulders slumped farther.

61

"You don't have to tell me." He had a feeling he wouldn't like the answer, judging by her defeated posture.

"No. You should know. My dad got my mom pregnant right off the bat. Two-week vacation and he came home with a pregnant mate. Everyone in the pack fears I'm just like her. That I'll get pregnant if they fuck me even once, and they'll be forced to mate me. Some even think I'll overdose on pills the way she did, and take my mate out with me. And if that's not enough to keep everyone away, they think I carry weak genes. My father was one of the strongest enforcers in the pack. But he bred with my mom...and got me." She kept her chin tucked, eyes closed. "*Nobody* wants the kind of child I was."

She was breaking his heart. "That's bullshit. You're half Lycan. If you mated and had a child with a full-blood, your child *would* shift."

"They don't care about statistics. I'm viewed as so weak and pathetic, they don't see me as *any* part Werewolf."

Unable to stop himself, Trayis reached out and grabbed her. She gasped as he lifted her and sat her across his lap. He wrapped both arms around her waist when she tried to get away.

"Hold still," he ordered.

She stopped struggling and, after a pause, relaxed in his arms, resting her cheek against his chest. "And now you feel sorry for me."

"No. I'm pissed that you live with a bunch of idiots who didn't raise smarter pups, and that my brother didn't rain hell on his pack every time they mistreated you until it stopped for good."

She shook her head. "Thanks. Anyway...the only time guys approach is when they want blow jobs or anal sex. No worries over a condom breaking...not that they'd wear one. My vagina is about as appealing as the plague, to be blunt. Plus, there's the being-treated-like-shit-my-entire-life thing. Not exactly a turn-on, you know? Even the ones who didn't taunt or tease me, still kept quiet and allowed it to happen. The only boy who ever stood up for me was Rod. And he's like a brother."

He rested his chin on the top of her head. He was so mad he wanted to snarl, imagining what she'd endured. The urge to beat every male in her pack who had ever approached her as if she was something to use for their own selfish pleasure had Trayis wanting names, so he could track them down.

He'd noticed she hadn't mentioned them wanting to perform oral sex on *her*. That explained how she'd reacted to his mouth on her pussy. That had to have been a first for her, too.

Now wasn't the time though to seek vengeance. So he tried to lighten her mood. "You said 'vagina.'"

She put her hand on his chest and lightly tapped him. "Don't make me laugh. I'm trying to be serious. I picked you because you were nice to me, Trayis, and I'd had fantasies about you for years."

His dick stirred. "What kind of fantasies?"

Now she did laugh slightly. "Well, I read a lot, remember? And I'm not confessing anything about *you*. But suffice to say, the only romance in my life is written by authors. I may have been a virgin, but I certainly know what my clit is. I've gotten myself off plenty. I just never dared to buy things. And...I wasn't using you, Trayis. Not the way you accused me of. I just didn't want to die a virgin, and it's likely I would have, living here. I've always been attracted to you, and since you live in Alaska, you were a safe choice. Was that wrong?"

"No."

"Werewolves are into casual sex. I truly didn't think you'd get upset."

He snuggled her closer, liking how she fit on his lap. He'd never been one to cuddle a woman, but it felt nice. "It just surprised me. Did you eat?"

"I had a frozen pizza."

"That's not real food."

She laughed. "You sound like my foster mom."

"She's wise." He ran his hand down her back. "Are you still experiencing any dizzy spells?"

"No."

"Did I hurt you?"

"I'm a little tender but that's to be expected. You're not exactly small down there."

She was, though. "You should show me. I don't smell blood, but I'd feel better if I made sure you were healing."

She tensed in his arms. "Are you a doctor?"

"No."

"Then you don't need to pretend you're my gynecologist."

He smiled. "What if I want to?"

She lifted her cheek off his chest to stare at him, looking more than a little confused. "Are you hitting on me ?"

64

That confusion broke his heart all over again. She was a beautiful woman who apparently had no clue what she did to men. "I want to get you out of your kitten-covered pajamas and have you spread your thighs for me again. Remember the last time? I bet I can make you forget all about being sore. I have a magic tongue." He winked.

She blushed. "Why? I already forgave you. You don't need to make anything up to me."

"You think that's why I want to lick your pussy until you cry out my name?"

"Men don't *really* like to do that."

He reached up and slid his hand into her hair, getting a good hold. "You've never *known* any men, doll. Just a bunch of morons who are blind and too stupid to live." His gaze left hers to glance up at the loft. "Tell me it's bigger up there than it looks."

She shook her head. "It fits a twin bed and a narrow dresser."

"Why'd you pick such a tiny home?"

"To avoid running into pack all the time. It was the only cabin livable but still safe."

He hated that answer but hid his feelings on the matter. "Do you have more condoms?"

She shook her head. "I gave you the only ones I had."

"Let's go back to my place, then. We have three left. Pack a bag. You're sleeping with me tonight."

Her lips parted, and he saw indecision in her eyes. More confusion, too.

"Shay?"

"What?"

"When a man wants to make things up to you, give him a break by saying yes. I promise this time things are going to be much better." He smiled. "You're not a virgin anymore. Nothing to freak out about this time."

She nodded. "I'll get an outfit for tomorrow."

"How brave are you?"

"Very. I went after *you*, didn't I?"

Damn, she was cute. "I don't look like your pack while shifted into my other form. I'm a lot bigger, have less fur, and I'm shaped a bit different. It would be faster if you rode my back. Ever gotten a ride before?"

"No."

"You're about to. I'll be waiting outside. Just climb on my back." He lifted her off his lap and set her on her feet. The blanket fell to the floor, and he knew she noticed his stiff cock.

"This is how much I want you, Shay. Hurry up."

He strode out of her cabin to the porch and grinned, before letting go of his skin and landing on all fours.

Chapter Four

Shay couldn't say Trayis hadn't warned her. It was just that she'd thought he might be joking about the ride. The beast on her porch was far larger than any Werewolf she'd ever seen. She dropped the small backpack and crouched next to him, taking in every detail.

His head was large with a shorter muzzle. He had pointed ears like a wolf but he didn't really look like one otherwise. He was far scarier in appearance. Golden eyes regarded her as he lowered his head and twisted it a bit.

She reached up and lightly raked her fingernails between his ear. His fur felt soft but a lot thinner than that of anyone in her foster family. They were the only ones she'd touched before while shifted.

Her gaze ran down his body. His front legs and chest were more muscular and their shapes almost human. He lifted one of his paws and she looked it. He showed her a deadly set of claws, the toes more closely resembling fingers. They were longer and thicker than a normal wolf's toes. She also took note of the way he moved. His limbs were more flexible than a full-blooded Werewolf's. It would make him deadlier in a fight between the two.

"Amazing."

He growled low but it wasn't an angry sound. She stared into his eyes.

"I said that out loud, didn't I? You *are* amazing. I don't know why the pack fears you like this. They're probably jealous." She grabbed the backpack and put it on. "I thought you were joking about the ride but you're totally big enough and then some."

He moved closer and bumped against her. The line of his back reached a bit higher than her waist. "I'm going to have to climb up."

He held still as she threw her leg over him and got settled. "Does it hurt? Am I heavy?"

He huffed and shook his head.

She bent forward and wrapped her arms around his neck, careful not to choke him. He moved slow going down the porch steps to the ground, and then padded into the woods. She was impressed with how easily he seemed to carry her.

"I could walk." She had put on slip-on shoes.

He picked up the pace instead of stopping to let her off. She heard voices, and Trayis changed directions, avoiding the sentries. It didn't take long for them to reach his trailer. He sat up on his hind legs and she laughed, sliding down his back. She managed not to land on her ass. He shifted to skin fast and stood, smiling at her.

"I want you to know I've only let pups do that before. You're the first woman who's ridden my back." He grabbed her hand.

That was sweet. He had given her a first for him. Her smile widened. This was the person she'd imagined Trayis would be when they were alone. Nice, a bit playful, and endearing. He opened the door and let her enter first. Lights had been left on inside. He locked the door behind them, helped her take off her backpack, and strode down the hallway with it.

"Bed, Shay. Naked."

She blew out a breath and followed. "You're showing off that alpha blood. So bossy."

He chuckled, tossed her bag in the corner where he'd been when she'd woken earlier, and turned to face her. "Well, that shouldn't be a surprise. I'm used to giving orders."

His words penetrated and her heart raced. "Meaning?"

His smile faded and he just peered at her.

"You said you're used to giving orders. What does that mean?"

He still said nothing, but his eyebrows rose a little.

"What position do you hold in your pack, Trayis?"

"You don't know?"

She shook her head. "I handle pack correspondences for Arlis, but you're his half-brother. Your pack doesn't go through official channels to contact him because of your relationship. Most packs love to document everything with paper or emails. You just call each other on the phone. Sorry...your *clan*. Which I always thought was strange, since Vampires have nests... Anyway, I know you live in Alaska, that you share the same mother with Arlis but have different fathers. Yours was a Vampire. Arlis told me that. I'm not exactly in the loop when it comes to gossip, since most of the pack avoids talking to me. Are you an enforcer?"

"Does it matter?"

She had to think about that for a moment, before she said seriously, "I really *was* out of line by daring to approach you if you're an enforcer for your alpha. My ranking is too low. Maybe it doesn't matter, though, since you're not a member of my pack?"

His grin returned. "You really don't know my status, do you?"

That uneasy feeling returned. "No."

"Undress, Shay. Now." The golden streaks in his eyes brightened.

"But now you've freaked me out."

He approached her and gripped the bottom of her top, tugging it up her body. She lifted her arms to help. He kept that smile in place as he sat on the bed, pulled her closer, and shoved his thumbs in the sides of her pajama bottoms, pushing them down her thighs. A low growl rumbled from him.

"No panties? I'm shocked, doll. And turned-on."

She lifted each foot as he removed her bottoms, holding on to his broad shoulders to keep her balance. It still bothered her that he hadn't answered her question. *Was* he an enforcer? If so, she was way beneath him in hierarchy. It probably didn't matter, though, since they were just having casual sex. Any chance of a future with him wasn't an option. Not that she thought he'd ever want to make what they had permanent. She'd never find someone who'd consider her for a mate...unless she left the pack to marry a human.

Trayis sniffed. "I'm glad you're not still bleeding. I worried about that."

"I heal faster than a human. I'm good."

He pulled her between his spread thighs and it put them almost face level as he leaned in closer. She closed her eyes, loving the way it felt as he brushed his lips over hers. Trayis was surprisingly gentle. He applied a little pressure, and she opened to him, his tongue sweeping into her mouth.

He teased and tormented her with the way he kissed. It reminded her of what it had felt like when he'd fucked her earlier, after the pain had faded. She moaned, sliding her hands up and down his back, lightly raking her fingernails over his shoulder blades. There was something amazingly sensual about touching him.

He cupped her ass, hauling her even closer, until their bodies were pressed together. His skin was hot and firm. She loved the feeling of being flush against him. She inhaled his scent. Everything about Trayis drew her, excited her, and made her long for more. She gasped when he broke the kiss, lifted her off her feet and turned. She landed on her back on the bed, and he came down over her.

His mouth reclaimed hers, and he adjusted his body, using one hand to nudge her enough to let her know what he wanted without words. She spread her legs wide, wrapping them around his waist. Once she did, he arched his chest off hers enough to slide his roaming hand to her breast.

She moaned louder as he lightly pinched the taut nipple, sending a jolt straight to her clit. He maneuvered his hips, his thick, hard cock rubbing against her slit and clit. She was already wet. Her nails dug into his skin.

He tore his mouth from hers. "Throat," he demanded, his voice inhumanly deep.

She twisted her head to bare it, remembering the last time he'd bitten her. He didn't sink his fangs in this time, but instead left hot, wet kisses that trailed from her shoulder up to just under her ear, before he retraced his path. Her belly clenched and the ache to have him inside her grew stronger, until she realized she was grinding her hips against his cock, desperate to come.

"You're so fucking hot, doll."

His fangs nicked her skin, and she moaned louder. "Yes!"

He still didn't bite, though, instead grinding his cock against her clit. She tensed under him, moaning his name. He stopped playing with her breast and slid his hand down her side to her hip—and then pulled away.

She opened her eyes as he lifted completely off her, feeling bereft and aching. She'd been right at the edge of a climax. He fumbled for something, and she watched as he tore off a condom packet, used his mouth to tear an edge before he rolled the condom over his cock. He returned to her, pinning her under him again.

"Wrap around me and hold on tight," he demanded.

She clung to him as he adjusted a bit until he could slide his cock inside her slowly. He took his sweet time, letting her body adjust.

It was a completely different experience. There was no pain. Just a sense of being sensually stretched to fit his wide girth and completely filled. Then it felt incredible as he drove into her deeper and began to thrust at a slow, steady rhythm.

Her nails sank into his skin and she threw her head back. "Trayis!"

He growled in response, fucking her a little faster and harder. He lowered more weight onto her, his body rubbing against her clit.

Ecstasy exploded inside Shay.

He snarled and buried his face against her throat, arching his back and increasing his pace. His fangs sank into her throat—and she cried out his name again as an unexpected second orgasm slammed through her. His body jerked, *hard*, the mattress under them made a weird pinging noise, and wood snapped somewhere.

Trayis stilled, both of them breathing hard.

He eased his fangs out of her flesh and licked her skin. "Fuck," he rasped. "I didn't mean to do that."

"It's all good," she panted, still clinging to him but not as tightly. Every muscle in her body grew lax and she suddenly felt sleepy.

"You're too little to be bitten this much."

"Multiple orgasms. No complaints from me," she admitted, glad he couldn't see her flaming face.

He chuckled and licked her throat again over the puncture marks. "Am I too heavy?"

She knew he was supporting some of his weight. "It feels good. I like being under you."

"I like having you here. No pain? Was I too rough?"

"I loved it." She had a bad feeling she was starting to love *him*. She kept her eyes closed when she felt him lift his head, afraid he might see too much emotion in them.

"I'd planned to go down on you."

"Still no complaints." She smiled.

"Look at me."

She hesitated, reminding herself that they'd never have a future, and to not hope for one. He'd return to Alaska in a matter of days, the way he always did, and be gone for years at a time. He'd find a strong mate, one like him, or maybe a full Were.

It was just casual sex. Her heart would be broken if she allowed herself to fall in love.

"Shay?"

She opened her eyes and peered into his eyes. The gold had faded, no longer so bright, but they were still intensely beautiful. "Yes?"

"You need to eat, doll. Real food."

"Why do you call me that?"

"Doll?"

She nodded.

"You remind me of one. It's not an insult. You're petite and adorable."

She scrunched her nose at him. "I'm not petite."

"You are compared to most women I know. I need to deal with this condom."

He chuckled as he slowly withdrew his cock, easing his weight off her as well. He crawled down the bed and got up. She lifted her head to admire his ultra-fine muscular ass as he walked out of the bedroom and into the tiny bathroom beside it.

She sat up and gripped part of the bedding, covering her lap. She heard the sink running, then he returned...frowning when he saw her.

She didn't understand what she'd done to cause that look. "What?"

74

"Hiding?"

"I'm not a shifter, Trayis. Sorry." She shoved off the covers to expose herself again. "Nudity isn't normal for me. I'm a bit shy."

He sat on the bed next to her and stretched out on his side, using his bent arm to hold up his head. "I knew that already. You blush a lot."

She shrugged. "I don't let it hinder me. I still face things head on."

"Like coming after *me*. That took a lot of courage."

"It did."

"Are you lightheaded? Dizzy?"

"Sleepy, but I usually get up at three in the morning, so it's really late for me."

"Why so early? You work in the office, right?"

"I do most of my work before anyone else arrives. The office is officially open for staff at eight. He comes in around nine. It gives them an hour to get ready for the day before he arrives. That's when I return home to type out letters for him. I have a laptop in my cabin, with internet. I send them to his email to read over. But sometimes I go in while he's at the office, if I need to print stuff out for him to sign and send by courier."

"Why don't you work the day shift?"

"I make certain members of the pack uncomfortable, if they come in to see Arlis."

His features hardened and the color of his eyes darkened. "Arlis allows that shit?"

"No, I *asked* for it to be this way, Trayis. It's more comfortable for me, too. I wasn't kidding about how some of the pack aren't accepting of

75

me. They view me as an outsider; I'm not included in anything. If things get loud enough in Arlis's office, even I can overhear what's being discussed. I'm not trusted by some."

"Trusted with what?"

"The enforcer meetings. They discuss the safety of the pack and outside threats. The sentries come in to give reports to Arlis, too. They see a lot of things that should be kept private. They'd rather I didn't hear."

"Like?"

She shrugged. "Who's fucking who. Things like that. Darlene, his secretary, once told me about two men pursing the same woman to test a mating. The sentries had caught her having sex with both men at different times. I wasn't given names, but it could have turned into a death challenge over the woman. Arlis put a stop to it before the men found out about each other. The point is, Darlene overhears things in the office, and most of the pack don't want me to have that kind of information.

"But Darlene is always nice to me. She's the one who explained that, since I might hold grudges against certain pack members, the sentries were worried I'd let information slip."

"That's an insult to you. You're honorable, Shay."

"I'm also mostly human and a lot of the pack have treated me like shit. I understand their concerns, Trayis. I don't take it personally. They'd have a lot more to worry about if I were bitter and petty. Luckily for them, I'm not. They just don't realize it."

He sat up and reached over, playing with her hair. "I'm offended *for* you."

"Don't be. It's not worth the stress it causes. I focus on being grateful instead."

"For what?"

"I'm a part of the pack, even if some don't like or acknowledge it. Working for Arlis gives me status. As a child, I was just a burden. Now I earn my keep. For a long time, I was also worried about the future of my foster parents. I know they're looking forward to alone time after their children are mated...you know, being able to have sex wherever they want in their own home without worrying about someone catching them. But in our pack, girls don't leave the protection of their parents' homes until they either find their mates or move in with a male member of their family, the way Marcia did with Rod. He offered to let me move in, too, but I couldn't do that to him. His future mate wouldn't have liked having me around, since I'm not a blood relation. And depending on who he chooses, she could also dislike humans. Marcia will be out of Rod's hair soon, when she takes a mate. But Arlis understood my unique situation. He's allowed me to live on my own in my cabin. I'm exceptionally grateful."

His eyes flared golden and his fingers stopped playing with her hair. "Unique situation?"

She held his gaze. "I'll never have a mate."

"That's bullshit. You're young and have plenty of time to find one."

She broke eye contact. "Of course."

His fingers stabbed into her hair and he fisted it at the back of her neck, forcing her to look at him again. It didn't hurt, but she couldn't resist, either. Anger glinted in his gaze. "There's not a *damn* thing wrong with you. You're beautiful, sexy as hell, and sweet, Shay. Anyone would be lucky to claim you."

She wanted to break the tension, but she also didn't want to lie. "Plague vagina, remember?" She smiled slightly. "There's not one Werewolf here or in the nearby packs who'd look at the history of my parents and risk taking me on." She reached back and tapped at his fingers in her hair, and they relaxed slightly. "Fact of life, Trayis. I accepted it long ago. The sun will rise and set, and I'll die alone. I'm at peace with it. I'll never mate a Werewolf, and I refuse to live amongst humans. I tried to date a few. I'd be happier alone than I would with one of them, and anyway, it would be too much to ask Arlis to accept a pure human into the pack if I married one. Plus, I do faintly carry the Werewolf scent. I'd put any husband in danger in the human world, if someone came after me, thinking I'm a rogue."

Trayis stared at her intently for a long moment. Then he growled, looking angry still, but he released her hair. "Food. I'm feeding you." He got off the bed and stomped out of the bedroom.

She sighed and followed him into the kitchen. It would have made her more comfortable to put on clothes, but since he hadn't, neither did she. Shay figured she'd said and done enough to remind him of just how different she was from the women he must be used to.

Trayis fixed them both roast beef sandwiches, heavy on the meat. Shay hovered near him, being entirely too quiet.

He wasn't certain what had set him off more—his anger at her pack for making her feel unworthy of a mate, or her acceptance of such bullshit. He also wanted to have a severe talk with his brother. That Arlis had allowed his pack to treat her this way, for so long, wasn't acceptable.

He turned, thrusting a plate at Shay. She took it, staring at him with those doe eyes of hers. A small smile played at her lips and some of his rage faded. She didn't seem to feel aggression the way he did. He needed to remember that.

He was also still worried about the blood he'd taken. "Eat it all," he ordered. "Do you want a beer, milk, or water? It's all I'm stocked with."

"Milk. I can get it."

"Sit at the table. I know where the glasses are."

She turned and put her food on the table, taking time to toss down two dish towels over the bench seats for them to sit on. Her attention to such details amused him. She took a seat on one.

He poured her milk, snagged a beer, and sat across from her, since the table wasn't wide enough to accommodate them both on the same side. He took a bite of his sandwich and watched her eat. She took small, dainty bites. Everything about her was too fucking cute.

It bothered him to notice that particular word kept springing up in his mind.

He finished his food first and drank his beer, relaxing back against the seat as he watched her. His gaze kept going to her breasts. She had beautiful ones, full and high, and his dick hardened again. He ignored his reaction since she yawned, looking tired.

She stopped chewing and drank some of the milk. "I'm full. I can't eat as much as you do."

79

He wasn't happy that she'd barely eaten half of the sandwich. "You need sleep."

"Do you want me to go home? You still look mad."

He wiped the expression off his face. "No."

She propped her elbows on the table and crossed her arms, effectively blocking his view of her tits. "No, I shouldn't go home, or no, you're not mad?"

"Both.

"Okay. But you're not exactly happy, either. A penny for your thoughts?"

"It's been a long day. I got up early, too. I wanted to familiarize myself with the territory again and went for a run. We're both just tired."

She didn't look convinced.

"I'll probably wake you in the night."

That drew a smile from her. "Sex? I'm all for that."

His dick hardened even more, but he didn't want to wear her out. She'd only had sex twice, and she wasn't fully Lycan. "Go to bed. I like the right side. I'll join you in a few minutes. I have to call Alaska to check in with my clan."

"Do you like your alpha?"

She truly had no fucking clue he led his clan. It stunned him. He was used to women coming after him because of his status, but not Shay. She'd just wanted *him*.

He'd accused her of it, though, thinking she was trying to trap or guilt him into mating her.

"The clan leader can be an asshole, but he never takes himself too seriously," he finally stated.

She smiled and scooted off the bench, grabbing her plate. He reached out to stop her. "I'm going to eat the rest of that."

She laughed, releasing the plate. "Big shocker. You're huge."

He watched her slowly walk down the hall to the bedroom, his gaze locked below her waist. She might be small in stature, but he loved her heart-shaped ass. It had some meat on it.

Still staring, he picked up the rest of her sandwich—and paused.

It was the first time he'd ever eaten someone else's food. Hell, he'd thought that was a bit gross before. Now, he took a big bite, not minding at all.

He probably *should* call home, but his clan would contact him if there were any problems. He felt secure that they'd handle things while he was gone. Trayis finished eating, cleared the table, and retrieved his cell on the couch where he'd left it, just in case. No missed calls. He turned on the ringer and flipped off the lights, ending up in the bedroom quicker than he'd planned.

Shay was curled up in a small ball near the edge of the mattress, already asleep. She had to have been exhausted. He stepped back, flipped on the bathroom light since she probably couldn't see in the dark, and turned off the bedroom light. He got under the covers and reached for her, pulling her against him. She fit perfectly in his arms as he curled around her, breathing in her scent.

It would be so easy to keep her. Just take her to Alaska. *His* clan would accept her. Of course, there might be some problems with a few of the single women who'd tried to seduce him into making them his mate. Would they be mean to Shay?

He wouldn't stand for it. He wasn't Arlis. That shit would be dealt with swiftly and harshly.

His train of thought stunned him. He wasn't ready for a mate. The very idea of it left him feeling uneasy. And he wasn't in love with Shay. Drawn and protective toward her, sure. But they didn't know each other well enough for him to be contemplating bonding to her forever.

Though...he couldn't discount the fact that he'd taken her blood during sex—twice. Something he never did. It could be some dormant Vampire bullshit instincts popping up. Regardless, she was in his veins, literally.

He ignored his throbbing dick as he got more comfortable, adjusting her a little in his arms to make sure she would be, too. She rubbed her cheek against his arm that had become her pillow. In her sleep, she wiggled her ass, teasing him, since that's where his dick was nestled against.

He bit back a growl. Even that was fucking cute.

He closed his eyes and pushed all thoughts from his head.

Sleep. That's what he needed. And to stop sinking his fangs into Shay. He hadn't meant to do it a second time, but damned if he could resist. He was mostly Lycan...but with Shay, all he wanted to do was bite.

Chapter Five

Shay let herself into the office and flipped on the overhead lights. Her thoughts were on Trayis. The night she'd spent with him had been terrific. He hadn't been kidding about waking her up. She just didn't expect it would be with her thighs spread wide by his hands while his tongue licked at her clit. He could do remarkable things with his mouth.

They'd used condom number three after he'd made her come then flipped her over onto her hands and knees. He seemed to enjoy that position most.

Condom number four had been used in the shower. Trayis had pinned her against the wall, and now she knew how amazing sex could feel while vertical.

Arousal flooded her just remembering the sexy guy standing there under the hot water, pounding into her body wrapped around his, and how hard she'd come.

Trayis hadn't been mad when she'd seen the time and told him she needed to leave for work. What she *hadn't* mentioned was that she should have been there an hour before. It wouldn't really matter to Arlis, since it wasn't a common occurrence. He wasn't an asshole about people taking days off or occasionally being late. No one would even know unless she wasn't there by the time the office officially opened.

She set her laptop on the corner desk she used, opened it, and turned it on. No one had run into her and Trayis when he'd escorted her to her cabin. She might have brought clothes to his trailer, but she'd forgotten her laptop.

It made her melt a little inside when he'd offered to stick around and walk her to the office. Trayis was just so sweet. She'd said no, though. It was one thing to make it from the trailer to her home without being spotted together. The office sat where the majority of pack homes were located. No way would they have made it through there without running into someone.

The door behind her banged open, and she startled, spinning. Tegan stormed in with a scowl. "Oh. It's *you*. You didn't show up on time this morning. I figured you weren't coming in."

"I overslept."

He sneered.

She translated that reaction to his well-known opinion of humans. He probably thought lateness was just one more of her flaws. It didn't matter that she'd never been late before. "Now you've established that I'm not an intruder. Patrol on." She gave him her back and opened a cupboard, grabbing the instant coffee she stored there. Her mug, too. She turned on the tap, filled the cup, and popped it into the microwave.

Tegan hadn't left. "What are you doing?"

"Making instant coffee. Never seen it done before?"

"Why not use the coffeepot like a normal person? It's easy. Any moron could figure it out."

She closed her eyes and slowly counted to ten. The microwave dinged. She opened a drawer to grab a spoon, snapped off the top of her instant-coffee tin, and removed the cup from the micro.

The sudden sense of him behind her, *close*, hit Shay. She ignored it by putting two teaspoons of coffee into the mug and stirring the contents.

"That's not right."

"It's good." She closed the microwave, tossed the spoon into the sink, and faced the sentry. A mere two feet stood between them. "Why waste an entire pot of coffee since I'll only have one cup? By the time everyone else arrives, they'd just have to dump it to make fresh. That would be wasteful. May I get to work now?"

He didn't budge. His dark brown eyes narrowed. "You're tight with Marcia. Did you know she was fucking Kale?"

Joy leapt in her heart. It had worked! Her best friend had gotten her man. "Really? Are you sure?"

"She's been at his place since yesterday, when they left the celebration together, and I could hear them going at it from a distance. Why now? She's not his type."

Understanding dawned. Tegan and Kale would both want the enforcer position that was opening. Only an egotistical ass would see a plot in her friend hooking up with a hot guy. She'd never liked Tegan.

"She's *not* his type," he repeated.

His words angered her. He meant it as an insult to her best friend. "That's the second time you've mentioned that, and I'm confused, Tegan. Marcia's very pretty and has a great body. He's a man. Figure it out. Even I can."

85

He took a step closer, invading her personal space. "She's also a dominant. Any chance she's looking for a mate? That she's considering Kale?"

She took a step back and bumped the counter. "You said it yourself. They left the celebration together. Everyone tends to look for a sex partner at those things. People like to hook up."

"But how does she feel about Kale? Could he talk her into mating him?"

She wouldn't betray Marcia's confidence and give Tegan ammunition against her best friend if things didn't work out with Kale. "How would I know? We don't talk about guys. Why don't you go ask her?"

He snarled and lunged. His hand was suddenly wrapped around her throat. He didn't squeeze but he had a great grip. The mug in her hand crashed to the floor, splashing hot liquid on her foot and her pants. She instinctively jerked her leg and tried to twist away.

"I don't believe you. Is he planning on mating her?" His hold tightened, and he pressed his much larger body against hers to pin her in place.

She stared up into his eyes. "I don't know. Get your hand off me!"

His nostrils flared, and she saw an emotion she couldn't identify flash across his features before he lifted his upper lip to show off his teeth. "Bullshit! You're her best friend. Are they working together to help him win the open enforcer spot?"

"You're talking crazy," she ground out. "Get your hand off me and back away, Tegan. You sure as hell won't make enforcer if I tell Arlis about this. I won't even have to if you leave a bruise. Law breakers get punished instead of promoted. You're not allowed to touch me. Let go, or you won't even keep your sentry position. How does picking up trash sound?"

"Bitch!" He released her and backed off. "You have everyone fooled, don't you?"

She glanced down at the mess on the floor before looking at him. "I have no idea what you mean."

"You act stupid, but you're actually a scheming bitch. You've always had it out for me. Did *you* talk Kale into going after Marcia, since it might impress Arlis if he could win over a dominant bitch? Or maybe you and Darlene plotted this out together. *That* bitch hates me too."

"I don't think about you at *all*, Tegan. And I have no idea how Darlene feels. We're not exactly friends. Just co-workers. I've never had a single conversation with Kale. Saying hello or waving to him when we cross paths is the extent of our interaction. I also don't care *who* replaces Ted. You need to leave, *now*."

She moved to the closet and found the broom and dust pan. It was difficult to ignore him as she cleaned up the glass, and then used wet paper towels to soak up the spilled coffee. She threw them in the trash, washing her hands.

"Those two have never hooked up before. It's pretty suspicious."

She walked over to her desk and took a seat. She grabbed her mouse, moving it to wake the screen, and opened her email to read incoming pack correspondence.

"Don't ignore me!"

She turned her head. "I don't know why you're still here. I can't help you with whatever is going on in your head. Maybe you should go talk to Doug. *He's* the pack therapist, not me. I have work to do. And so do you. Patrolling, remember?"

"You're Marcia's best friend. The bitch protects you. Tell me what her and Kale are up to."

"I. Don't. Know! They're probably just having a good time together. You're being paranoid."

"No. You're lying. You two are *always* together."

"Not since yesterday before lunch. Believe it or not, days sometimes go by when we don't speak. Marcia also doesn't share details about her sex life with me."

"Liar," he snarled. "You just want me to lose my chance to become an enforcer for...what? Because of that time I shoved you off that rock into the river?"

"I'd forgotten about you pushing me into the water until this very moment. It was like twelve years ago. Get over it. I have. I'm not plotting against you, Tegan. I also can't tell you why Kale slept with Marcia—*if* they even had sex. I'm taking your word for it, since I haven't spoken to Marcia. Kale was probably horny and Marica said yes. Just a guess. Ask *them*." She faced her computer. "Now seriously, I have work to do."

She heard a click and whipped her head around. He'd locked them in instead of leaving. Her finger went to the mouse and she glanced at her screen, quickly connecting to the security office instant-messenger account. "What are you doing, Tegan?"

He grabbed one of the tables, shoving it in front of the door. "Getting the truth outta you. I'd hate to hurt you—but I will. You're going to tell me what those two are planning."

She typed in a swift, short message to security.

She'd barely tapped send before Tegan hauled her out of her chair and slammed her onto her back on the desk beside her laptop. He shoved the lid on it closed with his free hand, lifted it off the desk and put it on her chair. Then he kicked the wheels and the chair rolled away.

He bent over her, getting in her face.

"There're a lot of ways to make people talk without leaving marks," he hissed, smirking. Dominant vibes blasted at her and fur sprouted along his arms, neck, and face where his shirt didn't cover his body. "Is Kale taking Marcia for a mate to fuck me over? Do I need to claim a dominant female myself to even the odds?"

"I don't know!" she shouted. "Have you lost your mind?" There was a crazy look in his eyes, and it petrified her.

"I *want* that fucking spot," he snarled. Saliva slowly dripped onto her throat from his open mouth, from the fangs he displayed. "I know Kale is willing to do anything to win it. So am I. I will fucking *hurt* you, Shay. Tell me what they're plotting. Last chance. Do I need to take a bitch for a mate before he does? Is that what he's doing?"

Real fear swamped her. "*I don't know!*" she repeated, quieter now, but firmly. "Please calm down, Tegan. Think about what you're doing. Just let me go. I won't tell anyone. Take deep breaths." She used her calmest voice, holding his gaze. He really *had* lost it. She had no idea why. He'd always been a bit of a bully and an asshole, but this was way out of line, even for him. "Please..."

He snarled and his gaze went to her mouth. "I bet Marcia wouldn't be in a mood to mate that shithead if she was grieving your loss... You're like her fucking *pet*."

Now he was threatening to *kill* her? She prayed that someone at security had gotten the message and help was headed her way.

His phone beeped, but he didn't reach for his hip, where it was clipped. She really hoped that was an alert going out that something was happening at the office. It might scare him if he realized pack would be arriving soon. He'd have to let her go...

"You should check that," she urged. "You're on duty."

His dominant vibes increased. Any fully submissive Werewolf would have been whimpering by now, unable to think beyond the terror he'd instilled. She felt grateful for once that she was so human.

"Tell me the truth!"

"I haven't talked to Marcia! I didn't know she'd slept with Kale until you told me."

Someone tried to jerk open the door across the room.

Tegan whipped his head in that direction, just as someone kicked from the other side.

He released her and jumped back.

The door came open on the second kick, hitting the table, but whoever was out there had to shove their way inside. The table flipped, crashing to the floor.

She was never more grateful to see an enforcer in her life as Pete stormed in.

"What the fuck is going on? We got a message that said S.O.S office."

"The pathetic bitch locked the door and blocked it, begging me to fuck her," Tegan snorted. "Thanks for saving me. She was offering to suck my dick...and damned if I wasn't considering it."

She slid off the desk, shaking. "He's lying."

A second man rushed through the door. Martin, the alpha's head enforcer and best friend, came toward her and gently held her upper arms, sniffing. A snarl tore from him, and he glared at Tegan. "What the fuck? She's terrified."

"A misunderstanding." Tegan shook his head. "She hit on me. I wasn't interested. I might have yelled a little. That's all."

Martin bent his knees slightly, lowering enough to peer into her eyes. "What happened, Shay?"

"I just told you!"

"Shut the fuck up, Tegan." That was Pete.

"*He* was the one who locked and blocked the door." She hated that she was shaking. "He—"

"The bitch is lying!" Tegan snarled. "I wouldn't fuck her so she's trying to pin shit on me to get even. You're pathetic, Shay!"

"What's going on here?"

Arlis's sudden presence could be felt by everyone, since their alpha's angry vibes flooded the room. "Shay? Get your hands off her, Martin."

The enforcer released her and stepped to her side. "We got an alert. The door was locked and the table on the floor was against it. Shay reeks of fear—and Tegan was in here with her. I'm trying to find out what happened. I was just trying to soothe her."

Arlis approached Shay. He gently cupped her chin. "What happened?"

"Why are you asking *her*? She's already tried to lie. The bitch is crazy! She hit on me then tripped some alarm before I could get away from her!" Tegan shouted.

Arlis shot him a deadly glare. "*Silence.* Now. You talk again, and Pete is going to break your jaw. I smell her fear. She also would *never* fucking touch you. You've always looked down on her." Her alpha met her gaze again. "What did he do, Shay?"

Tears filled her eyes but she blinked them back. "He came in here going on about some crazy plot, and he thought I'd know about it. He said Kale and Marcia are together. I haven't talked to her since yesterday, so it was the first time I'd heard about it. He put his hands on me and made threats, wanting the details of some plot that doesn't even exist. He thinks if Kale mates Marcia, you'll chose him for the enforcer position. He's lost it, Arlis."

Arlis released her and gently nudged her toward Martin. "Take care of her and get her home."

"She's lying!" Tegan hissed.

Arlis moved fast, grabbed Tegan by his throat. "What the fuck? You smell weird. Did you take something?"

Martin quickly came forward and lifted Shay into his arms. It surprised her, but she didn't protest as he carried her out of the office. She heard a loud snarl, and then something crashed inside the office. Martin kept walking, and she tucked her head against his chest, closing her eyes. He was a mountain of a man, but she wasn't afraid. She knew the enforcer wouldn't hurt her.

"It's going to be okay, Shay. Arlis will fuck him up good. I'm almost sorry it's not going to be *me* doling out his punishment. And Tegan never stood a chance of taking over for Ted. He's not suited for the position. The only reason he even became a sentry is because it would have made him meaner if he'd been assigned a lesser job."

"Thank you for coming."

"It's what we do. Protect pack. It just shouldn't be from each other. Arlis might kill him for this. But don't feel bad if it happens. Any asshole who'd attack a woman deserves it…but especially you."

"What did Arlis mean when he said Tegan smelled weird?"

"I picked up on that, too. His scent is wrong for some damn reason."

Voices drew her attention, and she opened her eyes, seeing pack members gawking as Martin strode past them with Shay in his arms.

"I can walk, Martin. We're making a spectacle. They'll gossip and come to the wrong conclusion, seeing you carrying me. Especially when you're not mated."

He snorted. "I don't give a fuck what they think. You're still shaking. And no offense, honey, but you've got those short legs. I want to get you home and return to the office ASAP, to see if anything is left of Tegan. I never liked that prick. He was forever in trouble as a youth, and I can't tell

93

you what a headache it was trying to make something of him. Not that I thought it would work. He had his chance, and he blew it this morning. Good riddance."

"He was acting insane. I don't know why."

"I can guess. Someone broke into the medical storage last night and drugs are missing. I think Tegan probably took them, judging by how he smelled. I know he's been stressed lately, but fuck. What kind of male takes drugs to deal with shit?"

Shaw saw Sylvia rushing toward them, jogging to catch up with Martin's brisk pace. "Are you hurt, baby?"

She met her foster mom's worried gaze. "I'm fine."

"What happened? Can you stop, Martin? I want to check her over."

"Nope. I need to get back. I'm taking her home. Keep up if you want to know the details."

"I'm okay," Shay repeated.

No one spoke until Martin reached her porch and set her on her feet. "You're safe now. But stay here, Shay. I'm sure Arlis will check on you later today, or Ginny will." He took off running back the way he'd come.

"Baby, what happened?" Sylvia started pulling at her shirt, trying to inspect her body. "I don't smell blood. Did someone hit you? Hurt you?"

Shay grabbed her hands. "I'm *fine*. One of the sentries decided to go insane, and I was his target."

Pure rage flashed in her foster mother's eyes. "Did some bastard try to make you blow him? Did he use his vibes on you?"

"No and yes. No blow job attempts were involved, but lots of vibes. It's a long story."

"I'm going to make you breakfast and you're going to tell me everything." She pulled Shay to her front door and pointed at the lock.

Shay punched in her code and opened the door.

"Have you talked to Marcia? I've called her twice since last night, but she hasn't responded. Call her now. She's going to flip if she hears Martin was toting you around in his arms in front of the pack. She'll think the same thing I did—that some asshole tried to force you to your knees."

Shay sighed. *Great. Everyone in the pack will probably assume that, too.* She'd call Marcia, but if she was still with Kale, her bestie wouldn't answer. No way was she going to be the one to break the news to Sylvia about why her daughter wasn't returning calls.

Kale might be Marcia's dream mate, but her parents thought she'd do better with a submissive Werewolf. It was a topic that had already caused many arguments over family dinners.

It meant Shay would have to dodge big parts of her explanation of what happened with Tegan in the retelling. Which she would do. Shay didn't want to watch her foster mom flip out even more.

* * * * *

Trayis smiled when he entered the alpha house. The strong smell of coffee, bacon, and other foods filled his nose. He enjoyed having breakfast with his half-brother's enforcers and their mates. It was something he'd considered doing many times with his own clan. He liked the way they all joked and teased each other. It was also a less stressful

95

way to discuss any issues they had to deal with before going into the office.

Two other women helped Ginny in the large kitchen. She smiled when she saw him, rushing his way.

He gave her a gentle hug. "Where's the baby?"

"Sleeping. The twins are already at school. Arlis will be down in a minute. He had to take a shower."

"He actually stayed in bed until after the sun rose? Having a new baby must be wearing him out," he teased.

She rolled her eyes. "He had to wash off some blood. Do you want coffee or juice?"

"Blood?" His good mood dimmed. "What happened?"

"A sentry decided to give my mate a reason to remind him who's in charge...and why rules shouldn't be broken."

Trayis understood. It happened at times. "Coffee, please. I can get it."

She spun away. "Sit at the table. I'll bring it."

Arlis came down the stairs and grinned. "You made it!" He hugged Trayis and led him to the table, where others already waited, even pulling out his chair.

Trayis saw the state of his brother's split knuckles. They'd stopped bleeding but the freshly healing wounds looked angry. "What in the hell did the sentry *do*? That looks like a serious beat down."

"I'm retiring." Ted raised his hand.

His mate, Donna, seated next to him, smiled at Trayis. "I want him to finally spend more time with *me*."

Arlis plopped into the seat at the head of the table next to Trayis. "Tegan was never in the running, but it seems *he* believed I might choose him to replace Ted. He's egotistical, can be pretty reckless on a good day...and on top of that, he took some drugs."

"Drugs?" The very idea shocked Trayis.

"He said it was to steady his nerves and to calm him, but it did the opposite. He fucked up bad, and I had to punish him. He'll heal in about a week but the down time will be a good lesson. I demoted him to outer patrol. That way, he'll have no interaction with the pack for six months. He's also paying for the drugs he stole from our healer."

"He's a moron," Martin muttered. "I would have killed him in your place."

Arlis unwrapped his silverware. "I know your patience is long gone when it comes to Tegan. Wasn't he the one always in trouble during training?"

Martin gave a nod. "He's stupid and a bully. That will never change. You still see potential because he hides his true nature around you. That one has none."

Arlis sobered. "This is his last chance. Next time, I'll kill him. I also called Graves, to fill him in."

"Where *are* Graves and Micah? I haven't seen them since I arrived," Trayis asked of Wen's cousins.

"Graves is hunting a small group of rogues that have been making trouble about a hundred miles from here. Micah went with him as backup. There's supposed to be seven of them, from what we've heard. They're committing petty robberies, threatening humans, and generally being assholes."

Pete snorted. "They're disguised as a motorcycle gang. The cops are all over them."

"And they're stupid," Martin added. "It's only a matter of time before they slip to reveal what they truly are. But the brothers will clean up that mess. Of course, I wish Graves were here right now." He shot a grin at Arlis. "He'd pay Tegan a visit even if you didn't ask him to. Nobody does that shit kind of shit in this pack without Graves having a painful chat with them—and usually leaving them not breathing."

Trayis frowned. "What in the hell did this Tegan do while he was high?" He had a hard time imagining killing one of his clan. The offense would have to be terrible to warrant death. It was stupid for a Lycan to take drugs, but the male was probably young enough to make those kinds of mistakes.

"He went after a pack member, trying to gain information from her." Martin said. "Dumb fuck. As if that girl would know anything that might have given him an advantage."

"Tegan's only suffering some broken bones and facial injuries, since he didn't harm her." Arlis kissed his mate on the cheek as she brought him a plate of food. "Thank you, Ginny." His gaze fixed on Trayis. "I'd have killed him if he'd done more than frighten her."

"I still think we should have killed him."

Arlis stilled, watching Martin. "Do we have a problem? Are you questioning my decision?"

Martin shook his head. "No, Alpha. I just hate that bastard. That's all. I'm still pissed. She's so fucking tiny. It offends me that he'd target someone as weak as Shay."

Trayis stiffened, everything inside him going tight with shock. "Shay?"

Arlis dug into his food. "She's fine. As I said, I'd have killed him if he'd hurt her. She's under pack protection. I reminded Tegan of that fact as I snapped his bones. He goes near her again, and he dies."

Fury filled Trayis. "What did he do to her?"

Everyone in the room froze.

Arlis stopped eating and cocked his head, narrowing his eyes at Trayis. His nostrils flared. "You're throwing off vibes, brother."

Trayis got a handle on his emotions. "I apologize."

"Damn," Ted chuckled. "That sent a chill down my spine. The hair on my arms is still standing."

Arlis arched an eyebrow at Trayis, his expression wary.

"I'm not used to containing my anger the way you do." Trayis glanced around the table. "VampLycans aren't as sensitive to emotions as you are. We throw off vibes without giving it a second thought."

Arlis smiled but it looked forced. "Understandable...but I'm more curious as to why you'd react that strongly to Shay being mistreated."

"I spent time with her. I mentioned that. She told me about some of the problems she's faced in the past."

"She's defenseless," Martin agreed. "She always stirs my protective instincts, as strongly as if she were still a young pup."

Ted nodded. "Me too. I even find myself softening my voice when I speak to her in the office. I'd feel like shit if I accidently startled her by sounding too gruff."

Reese added, "I assigned more patrols around her cabin than for anyone else staying on the outskirts of our living area. No humans would ever get that deep inside our territory without a sentry catching them, but I do worry about her falling or getting hurt. She's so frail. What if she tripped and broke her leg?" His expression grew serious. "I still think it was a bad idea to allow her to live out there on her own."

"We've discussed this many times." Arlis sipped his coffee. "She's an adult. Not actually a pup. We need to give her a sense of independence while still keeping her safe. It makes her happy, and she deserves what little happiness she can find."

Trayis didn't like the way they discussed Shay. He kept his silence, though, and ate the food placed in front of him without really tasting it.

"I think we should invite some half-breed males to interview for our pack." Martin paused, looking thoughtful. "We might find one who's attracted to her, who also has a fondness for his human parent."

Ted nodded again. "Some would be desperate enough to take her on in exchange for acceptance. It's rough for half-breeds to find acceptance into a pack."

"I suppose I could tell her she's needed in the office when we bring in potential mates." Arlis paused. "But we couldn't let her find out why they're really there. She's too proud. And of course, I'd have to make it a

100

condition with the half-breed that he never reveal we let him in because he was willing to mate her."

"It would make everyone's life easier," Ted reasoned. "She'd have someone to protect her instead of all of us worrying constantly."

Trayis clenched his teeth and pushed down his anger until he could speak without betraying how he felt. "Someone should mate her because they *care* about her. Not to gain entry into your pack."

"The situation isn't ideal, but at least she'd have a mate." Arlis shrugged. "No one else in our pack wants her, Trayis. I was hopeful for Rod, but he's only shown interest in Weres."

Trayis remembered the name from talking to Shay, but wanted to make sure they were talking about the same male. "Her *foster brother*?"

"That's the one. He's protective of Shay, even though he's got a very passive personality." Arlis finished his breakfast. "I hoped he'd be drawn to her despite her flaws...and hell, she makes even the most submissive males feel close to dominant."

Ted laughed. "True. Graves avoids crossing paths with her because he's afraid even the sight of him will scare her."

Trayis frowned. "Rod is a submissive Lycan? Shay said her foster siblings defend her."

"Marcia is the most dominant one in that generation. That's Rod's younger sister." Martin grinned. "He'll do whatever Marcia says, or she'd kick his ass. He's more afraid of *her* than most of the idiots who target Shay."

More chuckles sounded around the table. Each and every one grated on Trayis's nerves. The urge to go check on Shay rode him hard, but Arlis had said she was physically unhurt. He had to trust that.

He needed to stay calm, keep his emotions under control—but he fully planned to go visit her as soon as he could.

"I forgot that tonight is when the other alphas and their mates join us for dinner. It's something we try to do every few months with our neighbors, to keep relations solid. It's our turn to host. Dinner is at six." Arlis's gaze locked on Trayis. "Are you in?"

"I'll pass, if you don't mind." Alphas tended to get their hackles up when Trayis was around, as if he were a threat.

Arlis grinned. "I figured, after the last time I invited you around the other packs."

"What happened?" Ginny glanced between them.

Martin chuckled. "A fuckload of posturing. They get a whiff of Trayis and they can't relax."

"VampLycans tend to have that effect on most alphas," Reese added, smiling. "They don't know how laid-back Trayis is."

"Or they bug him to form an alliance," Ted snickered. "Too stupid to figure out a war between packs would mean he'd help us hand them their asses, instead of the other way around."

"I'll eat in the trailer." Trayis immediately decided to invite Shay to have dinner with him.

Ginny drew his attention by whipping out her cell phone and texting something. "I just told the caterer to send enough food for four more, and to separate those portions from the rest. I'll have someone bring your dinner, Trayis. There's no reason you should have to cook or miss out on such great food. The kitchen in the trailer is tiny."

"Thanks. Why four?"

"The caterer is human, and you know they eat so little. I won't ever make that mistake twice. I just times the actual number of guests we've invited by four, and give the caterer that number. It's not like they stick around to serve it and do a head count."

Arlis leaned over and kissed her. "You're doing a great job, sweetheart."

"You mean when I order enough food to actually feed our guests?" She winked at Trayis. "Rookie mistake I made the first time we hosted. It was incredibly embarrassing to realize there wasn't enough food."

"We ordered pizzas. Everyone loved it. Besides, you were suffering morning sickness with the twins at the time. They understood." Arlis's tone softened. "I should have planned that event instead of you."

"It's my job," she reminded her mate.

"Sweetheart, it's *my* job to take care of you, first and foremost."

Trayis leaned back in his chair, watching as his younger brother and his mate continued to chat. Envy was an emotion he rarely felt, but the love bond between them was extremely strong.

It made him think of Shay.

She'd have a hard time stepping into the role as his mate; he could see himself trying to soothe her if she hosted a party, only to realize she hadn't ordered enough food for all the guests he'd invited.

Fuck. He reached for his drink, wishing it were something a hell of a lot stronger. The idea of taking her home to Alaska appealed to him far too much.

Chapter Six

Shay had survived the ordeal of buying condoms. She had to hit a well-known superstore to do it—also grabbing a bunch of other things to hide the box in her cart—but the checkout clerk hadn't given her a raised eyebrow or commented on it.

That wouldn't have been the case if she'd purchased condoms from the pack store. Within half an hour everyone would know and be wondering why. It would put a huge target on her back to be the topic of jokes or worse, they'd start speculating on who she had bought them for.

The Bitch Trio had seen her leaving the picnic with Trayis and might put it together. They'd gossip hard, twisting any details they made up into something to embarrass her for years to come.

And a promise was a promise. She wasn't going to break her word to Trayis to tell anyone about them, even if it meant leaving pack territory to venture into the human world to shop.

She pushed the cart to her car in the parking lot, feeling relieved. That hadn't been so difficult after all. Trayis may not want to have sex with her again, but she'd be prepared if he did. She'd also bought some sexier pajamas, still feeling a little regret over him seeing her in the kitten ones. They'd been a gag gift from Marcia on her twenty-third birthday months before. The thing was, she loved how soft and comfortable they were.

Shay fished out her keys to unlock her trunk, dropped the bags inside, and closed it. She turned, looking for the nearest cart corral. She spotted one five parking spaces over and headed toward it.

The hair suddenly rose on her arms, the feeling of being watched striking hard. She froze, glancing around.

A young man with dark brown hair, piercing eyes the same color, stepped out from between a van and a large SUV in the next row. He locked gazes with her, and his nostrils flared. She realized the light wind was hitting her from her right, the flow of air traveling his way. The fact that he seemed to be smelling her put every fiber of her being on alert.

He wasn't human. It was daytime...which only left one option.

The man approached slowly. She should have fled to her car, and would have...but there was something familiar about him. He wasn't a part of her pack, though.

Five feet from her, he stopped. Cars cruised past them, hunting for open parking spaces. She was safe in public. No way would he attack or cause a scene.

"I'm not rogue," she informed him.

He studied her. "You're a half-breed."

"Yes. But I belong to a pack. You can move along. I'm not committing a crime."

He just frowned at her.

"What?"

"You're the first one I've ever seen."

He seemed more curious than threatening as she studied his face. It was tough to tell the age of Werewolves, but she'd guess he was anywhere between sixteen to early twenties, considering the way he dressed. He had big bones but looked as if he hadn't grown into them yet, with his thin build. No animosity showed in his expression. He blinked, simply watching her back.

A thought struck her. "Are you a half-breed? Do you belong to a pack?"

He jerked as if she'd slapped him. "No. And yes, I belong to a pack. Why would you ask me that?"

"No offense, but you seem to be wandering around aimlessly in a parking lot. I was just making certain you didn't need help."

"Help?"

"Yes. Like money. An introduction to my alpha to see if he could find you a home. I'm willing to do that if you need help."

"You think I'm some homeless rogue?" Anger flashed in his eyes.

"You don't look it, but if there's one thing you should already know, it's that looks are deceiving. All these humans around us aren't aware that we're different from them. I didn't mean to insult you. I apologize. I'll be leaving now." She pushed the cart between the metal rails and turned, only to find him blocking her path to her car.

"You don't seem crazy to me."

She frowned. "Is that what you've heard? Half-breeds are all nuts? I'm sure that some are, but I was raised with a pack."

"That's pretty rare."

She shrugged, figuring he must be from one of the three packs bordering hers. They weren't big on humans. "Alpha Arlis took me under his protection."

He paled.

"Are you okay?" She felt alarmed at his response.

"I know who you are now." His gaze scanned down her body slowly, and then back up to her face. He curled his lip up in disgust.

She glanced around, seeing humans nearby, and acted without thought. She strode toward him and put her hand on his arm. "Close your mouth."

"Or what?" he growled.

"Or someone will see those canines you're sporting. Get control of yourself." She released him and took a step back. "How old are you?"

He hid his extended teeth and looked around. A faint redness showed in his cheeks, as if he were embarrassed by his slip. "Fifteen."

That was a tough age for boys. She remembered what Rod had gone through. Control had been an issue, with all the aggression that came naturally with hormones. She rubbed his arm to help ground him with touch. "Just take deep breaths. I get that you don't like me for some reason, but there're cameras in this parking lot and it's full of humans." She lowered her voice. "Focus on the contact. It helps. Air in. Blow it out. That's it. Again."

He opened his mouth and ran his tongue over his now human-looking teeth. The sharp points were gone. "Why are you helping me?"

"I'm not your enemy, kid. Regardless of what you've been told about half-breeds."

He jerked his arm out of her reach. "You *are* my enemy."

She backed away from him. "Whatever. I'm out of here. Have a good life—and be more aware when in public. My older brother had a hard time controlling his shifts, thanks to his strong emotions. He said closing his eyes and thinking about something peaceful helped. Try that method." She stepped around him, heading toward her car.

He suddenly reached out as she passed him and gripped her arm. It didn't hurt but he got a firm hold on her.

She turned her head, staring up at him. "Let go."

"You don't *have* a brother. You have no family at all, Shay."

It shocked her when he spoke her name, and the harsh tone he used. "How do you know my name?"

"I told you—I know who you are."

"How? Have we met before?"

He stepped back, releasing her arm. "No. But I've heard all about you."

Now she was confused. "How? From who?"

"You have no fucking clue who I am, do you?"

"No. Should I?"

"If you had family, I guess you'd call me your uncle. Not that I'd ever claim you."

She nearly dropped her purse in astonishment.

He seemed familiar because she'd seen pictures of her *father*. The kid standing in front of Shay had her dad's eyes and cheekbones. The mouth was different, his hair a lighter shade of brown, but the resemblance could be seen after she knew to look for it.

"My parents didn't share my existence with that fucked-up pack they were stuck in for a while. Your alpha may as well have banished them to

109

hell when he stationed them away from the pack and cut them off from everyone. Arlis did that as payback for saying he was an unfit alpha." He leaned in closer, glaring at her. "My mother had to give birth to me without a healer. My parents feared Arlis would steal me, and they'd lose a *second* son."

Still shocked, she did the math. He'd been born when she'd been about eight. Then his words penetrated. *"What*? Arlis wouldn't have stolen you! They also weren't cut off from the pack. Trust me. They had plenty of friends."

"Liar," he sneered. "You're the nasty result of what happens when an unfit alpha forces a great enforcer into mating, just because he stuck his dick in the wrong hole! My parents are still furious that Arlis got Marcus killed."

Shay felt like she'd been slapped. "Is that what they told you? That Arlis *made* my father mate my mother? You were lied to, kid. My father didn't even tell Arlis he'd mated my mom until *after* he'd brought her home from California. He loved my mother."

"You're a liar!"

"No, I'm not."

"You said you have a brother but you don't. That's proof that you lie."

"He's my foster brother. I actually have a few of them."

He scowled. "You're lying about my brother. Marcus was forced to mate an unstable human by his alpha, and he died as a result! My parents were punished for not keeping quiet."

110

She frowned. "Do you have a best friend?"

He frowned at the question. "Yes."

"Does that person know you better than your parents do? Do you tell your best friend everything?"

He hesitated...but then gave a reluctant nod.

"Dean and Sylvia grew up with my dad. They're the couple who raised me. They were best friends to Marcus from the time they could crawl. The three of them were inseparable. They told me the truth—all of it. I wasn't a planned pregnancy, but my dad loved my mom enough to mate her without getting permission first from his alpha. Arlis found out *after* it was done. My parents were tightly bonded mates. That's why he didn't survive her death. When he died, his best friends raised me— because *your* parents wanted me dead. That's why Arlis had to assign them to new duties away from me. He was trying to keep a toddler alive. There was even fear that they'd poison my food, since they ran the pack store. Think about that—I was two years old."

"That's not what happened—"

"It *is*. And as for your parents losing all their friends? Total bullshit. They talked over twenty pack members into trying to have me banished when I was still a few years younger than you, all because I couldn't shift. Do you understand what would have happened to me? *You* smelled what I am. So would other Werewolves. If you haven't figured it out, they wanted a thirteen-year-old girl thrown off pack land and out into the human world. My own grandparents basically tried to kill me, *again*. I wouldn't have survived a week. *That's* when Arlis sent them to live with

111

another pack. They just wouldn't stop trying to hurt me. And the sad part? Until the day they left, I still kept hoping they'd learn to love me."

"You're the reason they lost their son." He no longer met her gaze, though. "You can't blame them for that. You were and are a reminder of that pain."

She stepped closer to him, until he finally held her gaze. "I *can* and *do* blame them. I want you to think about something, kid. One day, you might fall in love with someone they don't approve of. God forbid it's a human. That's what happened to my father...your brother. He fell in love with my mom. Your parents refused to accept her. From what I was told by his best friends, they went out of their way to make my parents miserable. They refused to acknowledge their own grandchild, kept sending single Werewolf women to attempt to seduce my dad.

"It hurt him that his parents purposely insulted his mate and tried to drive a wedge between them. So imagine how a young human girl felt, having women throwing themselves at her mate, all the while, being told by her in-laws that she was ruining his life. She killed herself. And my father died *three days* later of a broken heart. She meant that much to him. You're a fucking Werewolf. You know he would have survived her death if she hadn't meant everything to him."

Shay blinked away tears. The kid said nothing, but he had paled again.

"You've been told a twisted version of the truth by your parents. But we're blood. That *means* something to me. You know where to find me if you ever want more of the truth, or just need someone who will accept you no matter what. I'll always welcome you. Don't believe me? Talk to

112

Sylvia and Dean, the two people who knew your brother best." Shay hesitated before asking, "Will you even tell me your name?"

At that, he backed away and fled.

She watched him disappear between the cars and wiped at her tears. It took her a few tries to open her car door, but she finally did, collapsing into her seat. She closed the door and locked it, letting the tears flow. People may have stared at her, but she didn't care.

She had an uncle. Once again, her grandparents had denied her family. It hurt…badly.

It took Shay a good fifteen minutes to pull herself together. She hoped he'd return, but he didn't. Finally, she started the car and drove back to pack territory.

* * * * *

Trayis knocked on Shay's door. He heard her moving around, and then she unlocked the bolt and opened it. Her eyes were watery, slightly swollen, and red. She'd been crying—again.

Rage filled him.

"That son of a bitch Tegan hurt you, didn't he? Where is he? Do you know? I'll fucking kill him myself!"

Shay's mouth fell open.

Trayis gently pushed his way inside the cabin, moving her back, and closed the door behind him. He didn't think, just acted on instinct by scooping her into his arms and cradling her there. The couch was the only surface to sit on, since her coffee table didn't look sturdy enough to hold their combined weight. He took a seat and held her on his lap even tighter, needing to comfort her.

"I've got you, doll. It's going to be okay."

She turned her head and lifted her hands, touching his shirt. He liked the feel of her small hands on him. "I'm fine."

"You've been crying. I didn't get many details except that some asshole came after you. I want to hear everything that happened."

"I'm not upset about this morning. I'd actually already forgotten about Tegan."

He was confused. "Then why are you crying?"

"I have an uncle."

"What did he say or do to you?"

"I didn't even *know* about him."

Trayis shifted her on his lap, turning her enough to see her face better. "How is that possible?"

"My grandparents had another son. He's fifteen years old, and I ran into him today in a parking lot." Fresh tears filled her eyes. "They told him horrible lies. I don't even know his name…"

He reached up and gently wiped at her fresh tears, trying to make sense of what she'd said. "What parking lot?"

She blushed and dropped her gaze. "I left the territory to buy condoms. I was hoping maybe I'd see you again, and we'd need some. It would have everyone gossiping if I bought them from the pack store. Usually only pack males sleeping with humans buy them there."

She'd left the safety of her pack to keep their seeing each other a secret—just as she'd promised—and then ran into a family member she didn't even know.

"Damn it, Shay. Did he threaten you? Hurt you? I don't want you putting yourself in danger."

She lifted her gaze. "He didn't threaten me or anything. I'm just upset. He thinks Arlis forced my father into mating my mom and...just a bunch of other bullshit. They made him seem like an evil alpha who would've kidnapped him at birth, and a lot of other crazy stuff."

He stroked her cheek. "I've learned a little about your grandparents. They sound like idiots."

"Dangerous ones. It was bad enough that they wanted me dead, but he's fifteen, Trayis. They've twisted his mind enough to hate this entire pack. What if their lies drive him to do something stupid? I'm worried. I tried to tell him the truth, but I think I hurt him more. I was just so stunned and angry! I blurted shit out."

He ached for her. She was too sweet. "You're more upset for this kid than anything else, aren't you?"

She nodded. "He reminded me of Rod when he was younger. He felt the world was against him because he was different from other boys, and he picked a lot of fights, trying to fit in. Rod isn't dominant *or* a great fighter. He could have been killed. What if my uncle picks a fight with Arlis because he's been lied to and thinks Arlis wronged his parents and my father? I called Arlis, but he was busy. I forgot about the alpha party tonight. Darlene said she'd get me in to see him in the morning. I need to

115

tell him what's going on, to make sure my uncle isn't hurt if he does something impulsive. He really doesn't know any better."

"Doll, you're breaking my heart." Trayis pulled her in close and hugged her, kissing the top of her head. "It'll be fine. Arlis wouldn't hurt a youth. It's going to be okay."

"My uncle *hates* me," she whispered. "You should have seen the way he looked at me. I had to calm him down in the parking lot. He was losing control of his body."

Trayis tensed. "Did he hurt you, Shay? Tell me." He wouldn't kill the kid—but he'd hunt him down and teach the youth a lesson he'd never forget about harming someone weaker. Especially Shay.

"No." She shook her head. "My heart hurts, but he didn't attack or anything. Just flashed some canines."

He relaxed. "It *will* be okay."

"I don't see how. They've made Arlis out to be an evil alpha, and I think I made things so much worse."

He wanted to fix it for her. Make her smile. The urge was so strong, it left Trayis unsettled. He stroked her back and held her even closer. "Do you know what you need?"

"Ten minutes in a room with my grandparents, where I shoot them with Taser darts and hold down the button while they flop around?"

He laughed, loving her sense of humor. "Besides that."

"What?" She looked at him.

Her eyes were so beautiful. "Come to the trailer with me. Spend the night. I'll take your mind away from this."

She hesitated.

He didn't like it one bit that she didn't instantly agree. "Come with me, Shay."

"I want to...but two nights in a row doesn't sound casual."

He knew that, too. "Come anyway. We'll have fun, and Ginny is sending catered food from their party to the trailer soon. I have a feeling it will be a lot. You need to help me eat it all."

She grinned. "Okay."

He smiled back, glad she'd agreed. "Go pack a bag. Don't bring the kitten pajamas. I like you sleeping naked."

A blush crept into her cheeks. "Good thing I *did* buy those condoms."

"Yes." He eased his hold on her and helped her to her feet. "Hurry up."

He watched her climb the ladder this time, up to the tiny loft she called a bedroom. Shay deserved so much better than living in a tiny home on his brother's territory.

He pictured her inside his home in Alaska. She'd probably like it. It was roomy, and his clan would treat her extremely well. He'd make damn certain of it.

He clenched his teeth, not liking where his thoughts kept straying.

Keeping Shay... It would be a bad idea to take her home with him.

Then again, she'd be better off there. No one would dare harm a single hair on her head or hurt her feelings. He'd beat the shit out of them for even thinking about it. His clan would welcome her with open arms, or he'd kick their asses so hard, they would change their attitudes—quick.

* * * * *

Shay worried as they made their way to the trailer. It was still daylight, and a time when a lot of the pack roamed. "Someone might see us together. Maybe you should walk ahead of me a ways."

Trayis surprised her by reaching out and taking her hand, instead. "I don't care if anyone finds out."

That stunned her enough that she stumbled. "They could get the wrong idea if we're seen together again. Some already saw us leaving the party yesterday."

"I don't care what the pack thinks, Shay."

Her eyes widened and she swallowed hard. The thought of the pack finding out her and Trayis were having sex, more than once, would be huge news. No matter what his position in his clan, he had some alpha blood. She was considered the weakest member of her pack. Tongues would wag. It could change how everyone viewed him.

She stopped walking, yanking her hand from his.

He turned, frowning.

"I can't do this."

"Shay?"

"I don't care if everyone thinks badly of *me*, but you're Arlis's half-brother. You'll lose respect if anyone believes we're more than just a one-time hookup. You go first, and I'll sneak in once I'm sure no one's around."

"Fuck that." Trayis moved fast, grabbed her, and scooped her into his arms.

She clutched at him, almost dropping her bag. "Trayis!"

118

"I don't care what they think, what they assume, or any *other* damn thing. We're spending time together. There are a lot of idiots in your pack, Shay. You're worthy of my attention—and I dare *anyone* to say otherwise. I'd enjoy making them bleed after the way you've been treated."

He resumed walking toward the travel trailer.

Shay didn't struggle in his arms. Instead, she settled the bag on her lap and wrapped her arm around his neck, before gently placing her free hand on his shoulder. "But what will Arlis think? It might upset him. He'd tell you to spend time with someone else."

"I'll deal with him if he has a problem with us."

She heard a noise and whipped her head around. Dread filled her. Martin walk down one of the trails.

He spotted them and hurried forward with a scowl. Trayis stopped.

"Are you hurt, Shay?" Martin glanced at Trayis. "What's going on?"

Before she could respond, Trayis spoke.

"I'm carrying her because she almost fled into the bushes to hide the fact that we're walking to the trailer to spend the night together," he announced. "We spent last night together, too. I asked her to do it again, and she agreed. But Shay's under the impression I give a fuck if anyone has a problem with that—I don't." He paused. "Now, should I put her down to fight you? Or are we free to go?"

Martin's eyes widened and his mouth dropped open. He paled a little.

Trayis shifted his stance. "Am I breaking some law that I don't know about, being with Shay?"

Martin snapped his mouth closed and his dark gaze fixed on Shay. "You're okay with him?"

She had to clear her throat. Twice. "Yes. We did spend last night together." There was no reason to hide that now, since Trayis had already admitted it. "I approached him at the party and made my interest known."

The enforcer glanced between them. "You two are..." It was Martin's turn to clear *his* throat. "I didn't see *that* coming. Not in a million years." Martin gave a sharp nod and stepped off the trail. "Have fun."

Trayis didn't move, though. "Are you going to report this right away or give me time to speak to Arlis in the morning? I'd like to know if I should expect our evening to be interrupted."

"Shay's an adult female. Who she spends time with is *her* choice. She made it clear she's willing to go with you. I have nothing to report."

"We'll be going then." Trayis continued down the trail.

Shay's heart pounded. Martin wasn't a gossip...but Trayis planned to tell Arlis.

She waited until they'd reached the trailer and he put her down inside. "Your brother will be upset, Trayis."

He locked the door and faced her. "He knows me. Knows I wouldn't hurt you. I don't see a reason for him to be concerned."

"That's not what I mean. I'm the lowest member of the pack!"

He sighed, took her bag, and rummaged for the box of condoms she'd packed. He withdrew them and tossed them down the short hall, toward the bedroom. "Doll, stop thinking that way."

"It's true, though. You've given me the impression you have some standing in your clan, like you're an enforcer or something. Your *own* alpha would tell you that I'm beneath you."

He closed the distance between them and put his hands on her hips. "Think like a human."

"You're a man. I'm a woman."

"Exactly."

"You're not human, though."

"I'm also not pack. And I see *you*, Shay. You are wonderful and beautiful and I like spending time with you. We have great chemistry. And anyone who has a problem with it really *will* get their asses handed to them by me."

"I just don't want you to suffer in any way, Trayis. What if your alpha hears about this? He'll question why you would choose to spend time with *me* instead of a full-blood."

He smiled. "Damn, doll. You should come with a warning label for being too damn sweet." He pulled her against his body. "Don't worry about that. It's not an issue. I can tell you with absolute certainty that the leader of my clan would approve of me spending time with you one hundred percent."

Shay sighed. She trusted him. "As long as you're sure there won't be any problems for you later."

"I want you naked." He eased his hold on her. "On the bed. Legs spread. I promised to distract you and make you forget everything. I keep my word."

121

Shay gave a nod and a smile and began to strip.

Chapter Seven

Shay wore one of Trayis's shirts as they sat next to each other on the couch. He'd unfolded a couple portable trays, and they ate as a movie played on a television screen that slid down from the ceiling. A shelf of movies had been supplied for them to decide from, and they'd chosen an action film. He'd also put on boxers to answer the door ten minutes before, accepting the delivered meal from one of the sentries.

"This food is amazing."

Trayis nodded, reaching over and rubbing her bare thigh. "I'm glad you decided to spend the night with me. Great food, good movie, and the best company."

She felt heat flush her cheeks, liking that he thought so. Spending time with Trayis made her happy. They'd already had mind-blowing sex before the food had arrived, so the fact that he now wanted to have a mini date with her, including dinner and a movie, was immensely flattering.

She still thought this felt like more than a casual hookup, especially since they were together two nights in a row, and that left her feeling a little confused. She didn't want to push him for answers, though. One thing was for sure—she'd miss him when he returned to Alaska.

Trayis released her leg and picked up his knife, cutting one of the steak medallions on his plate. He had already eaten his lobster tails. He laughed as the human actor on the screen shot someone.

She smirked. "You find that funny?"

"Of course. It looks fake."

"It seemed pretty gory to *me*."

"They wouldn't die that fast from being shot there."

She wasn't sure she wanted to ask how he knew that. "Do you use guns often?"

"No." He glanced at her and lifted his beer, taking a sip. "Is this movie too violent for you?"

"No. I like movies where someone who does someone else wrong gets their ass kicked by the good guy. Or in this case, gets *killed* by the good guy."

He winked, returning his attention to the TV. She ate, finished what she could, and leaned back. Trayis glanced at her. "There's dessert."

"I'm full."

"You're done?"

She nodded.

He lifted her plate off her tray and dumped her remaining food onto his own. She smiled. He could put away a lot of food. When he finally finished, he leaned back too and pulled her closer until she snuggled into his side. It was nice...comfortable.

The movie eventually ended, and Shay got up first and began to clear the dishes. She washed while he dried and put them away. The last delivery bag he put in the fridge.

"For later." He held out his hand. "Ready for bed?"

"Always."

He led her to the compact bedroom and turned to face her. "Are you getting sore? Be honest with me."

"I heal pretty quickly, Trayis, human side considered. I'm good. And you're pretty gentle with me."

He put his hands on her waist and drew her closer. She reached up, holding on to his shoulders, and he lowered his head. She loved the way his eyes turned more golden in color when he was aroused. She closed her eyes as his lips took possession of hers, opened to him and kissed him back. He lifted her off the floor and she wrapped her thighs around his waist.

A ringing sounded and he stilled, a growl coming from him, and his chest vibrated against hers. He pulled away and she opened her eyes, meeting his gaze.

"I have to get that."

She nodded. He put her down, stepped away, and walked to his cell phone. Another growl came as he answered it, putting it to his ear. "What's wrong?"

She heard a male speaking but Trayis walked away before she could make out words with her keen hearing, putting distance between them. He paced in the kitchen area.

"Fuck. We knew this was a possibility, that's another reason I came. But I'd hoped no one would be that stupid."

He listened more. She noticed his expression, how angry he seemed. She wondered what was going on.

"That's bullshit. We stand together. I'll be right there. Try to keep your cool." He ended the call and snarled, his eyes darkening.

"What's wrong?"

His eyes became all black. Even the whites of his eyes were gone.

"One of the alphas is posturing at my brother's party." Trayis's voice came out deeper than normal. "Fucking Lycans. They see a perceived weakness and want to start shit." He put his phone down. "Stay here. Lock the door after me."

He moved fast, yanking open the closet in the bedroom, and began to dress.

"Someone is going to challenge Arlis?"

"Some alpha prick named Frank is being a dick. I don't remember him."

"He rules about ninety pack members. He's not mated, and he took over six years ago after winning a challenge." She paused, still sick with worry for Arlis. "He killed his older brother Fred to take control of the pack, Trayis. The guy is a dick; he sent a condolence card when he found out Arlis had mated Ginny. He acted like it was just a joke but...I doubt it. He's old school. Ginny isn't an alpha bitch, which means he doesn't hold any respect for her—or *Arlis* for mating her. It's not a secret. He usually avoids the alpha meets though, sending excuses to decline the invitations."

Trayis glanced at her as he put on shoes with a confused frown. "Explain the alpha bitch thing."

"I keep forgetting you don't live with a pack. Frank is a hard-core believer in strength, basically. He killed his own brother because he felt Fred was too weak to lead. Ginny is strong, but she isn't the baddest bitch in the pack. He thinks less of Arlis for that because he's a jerk. It's the same reason some think I should never approach someone like *you*. I'm too weak for you. Do you understand?"

He stood from the edge of the bed where he'd sat. "I think I do."

"Frank probably thinks Arlis should have bred and mated better. But it's bullshit. They're true mates. Everyone knows that...but jerks like Frank would ignore an emotional bond for the chance to birth the strongest sons possible. Knowing him, he'd invoke the old breeding fight law if he could."

"Breeding fight law?"

"The elders tell stories about the days when packs were smaller because they were killed by humans and other predators. They lived nomadic lives and didn't wait to find true mates back then. Once they hit adulthood, it was pretty much a requirement to breed to build their numbers. Alphas would allow their packs to fight it out. You know, only the toughest ones winning the right to breed with each other. Guess they believed their chances of creating hardier pups would increase. I can totally see Frank making women fight to become the mother of his young, to make sure he got the strongest bitch in his pack."

"He *is* an asshole."

"Of the worst kind. I agree."

Trayis paused in thought. "The name Fred sounds familiar. Why?"

"He took in the survivors of Bufford's pack."

127

Rage crossed his features. "That bastard who attacked this pack before?"

She nodded. "Not all of the Weres with him were fighters; they had no idea what Bufford had planned. Once the pack was disbanded, they would have been rogues."

"I remember now."

She nodded. "Fred ran a good pack. Until his younger brother challenged him. You're going to go support Arlis and Ginny?"

"You bet your ass I am."

"Be careful."

He smiled. "I will."

"You need to shower first."

He inhaled deeply. "No. I'm not hiding you, Shay. Lock the door after I leave. Until I know what's up, only open it for me."

He left and she locked the door, staring at it as she bit her lip. She hadn't been born yet when their territory had been invaded. Bufford had wanted their land, but he hadn't challenged their alpha pair the way their laws commanded. He'd chosen to go about in a sneaky way, showing up in the middle of the night to attack without warning. Worse, he'd poached unhappy members from other packs to help him by promising them status if they fought with him. Many deaths had occurred.

What if Frank decided to pull that same move?

She mentally replayed every communication she'd dealt with from him. He was a complete ass.

Shay suddenly wished she were in her cabin. Unlike other pack members, she owned a shotgun and boxes of ammunition. The lack of claws didn't mean she had to be utterly defenseless.

A cell phone rang, and she jumped. Trayis had forgotten his. She walked over to it, staring at the lit screen. It said "Wen." She didn't touch it, though. Maybe that was Trayis's alpha. No way did she want to get him into trouble.

She paced up and down the length of the trailer, wondering what was happening. Part of her wanted to get dressed and go snooping. Then again, she didn't want to be around if a war broke out. She'd be killed unless she could get to her cabin and a weapon.

"Let everything be okay," she implored aloud.

* * * * *

Trayis walked into his brother's house without knocking. Conversation stopped as over thirty people turned his way. He spotted Arlis standing by the large fireplace looking pissed and a tense male facing off with him. He guessed that must be Frank. A few of his brothers' enforcers gave him respectful nods. He was glad they were there, since each alpha had brought a few of their best fighters, too.

Arlis smiled but it didn't reach his eyes. "Frank, you haven't met my brother, Trayis."

Trayis stopped next to his brother, almost close enough to touch him. He knew his eyes were showing his rage, that they'd be pure black.

The other Lycan alpha backed up a step, looking stunned. "What the *fuck*?"

129

"He's VampLycan. I know you were aware of him." Amusement filled his brother's voice.

Frank cleared his throat and took a step forward, posturing by flexing his shoulders. "I heard. I didn't know he was here."

"I dare anyone to demand I announce my visits to my brother." Trayis glared at the alpha. He let his claws slide out of his fingertips and lifted his hand, scratching just under his chin as if he had an itch, letting the prick get a good long look at them. He retracted them just as fast. "You're the one who challenged your brother six years ago, correct?"

Fear flickered in Frank's eyes but it disappeared fast. "I didn't know you kept up with local news."

"I make *anything* that concerns my brother my business. Not that I need to." He smiled, showing off his fangs. "I taught my brother how to fight myself. He can take care of his own problems...but I'm nosey. You're aware of how he became alpha, aren't you?"

Frank swallowed, glancing at Arlis. "Yes. He survived when his pack was challenged."

Trayis wanted to gut the asshole. "There *was* no challenge. Fucking cowards snuck in at night to murder members of this pack while they slept. Arlis personally killed over nineteen of those assholes. I got here as fast as possible, ready to tear apart any who lived, but unfortunately there were none." He sighed, glancing at Arlis. "It was disappointing." He gave his brother a genuine smile. "You should have at least left a few of them alive for me."

"Why would you involve yourself with this pack?"

Trayis snapped his head back to stare at Frank. "Because unlike some, I stand by my brother. And didn't anyone tell you that many VampLycans have family who live here? My clan is related to probably half of the members." He was lying, it was only a few, but he wanted the prick to stew on that.

Frank paled a little but again, he hid it fast. He was good at masking his emotions. "I didn't know."

Trayis nodded. "Over fifteen VampLycans came with me after we heard about the last attack. A couple GarLycans tagged along, too. It gets boring in Alaska. We're always eager to band together for a good slaughtering of assholes who fuck with family." He remembered what Shay had told him about Frank—and he wanted to make one thing damn clear. "And my family means *everything*. Though, I haven't yet been fortunate enough to find a true mate the way my brother has." He glanced at Arlis. "Where is your precious mate? I'd love to say hello before I mingle. Ginny's the best."

Arlis grinned. "Look near the kitchen."

He nodded, gave Frank one last warning glare, and made his way to the kitchen area.

Ginny looked nervous, standing next to a few of the enforcers' mates. They were surrounding her in a protective group. She spotted him, and instant relief showed on her face. He walked toward her, blocked her view of the other guests.

"Calm down," he urged, keeping his voice low.

"Frank was making threats," she whispered. "I think us having another baby made him realize that with three sons, this pack would be

131

harder to take after they grow up. He's been insulting us and acting like he's ready to challenge for our territory."

"I know. It's taken care of. Smile. Frank is currently trying not to shit his pants. It seems his brother forgot to tell him to never fuck with Arlis before he died."

Ginny smiled, seeming to calm. "I know Arlis could win in a fight but…"

"You don't want a pack war. You've got three vulnerable children to think of." He nodded. "It's fine, little sister. I just let that prick alpha know the consequences of an attack." He winked. "I'm terrifying. I even gave him the freaky eyes."

Ted's mate, Donna, raised a brow. "Freaky eyes?"

Trayis let his eyes turn utterly black.

She gasped and jerked back.

He laughed, letting the black fade out. He smiled wider. "Scary, isn't it?"

"You've got amazing control." Donna stepped closer, releasing a deep breath. "Neat trick."

Ginny laughed. "Did you throw him some vibes?"

"No. I kept it under control. Words were enough."

"I could hug you."

He opened his arms. "Go ahead. I know I'm an amazing big brother."

Ginny stepped into the circle of his arms and squeezed him tightly. Then she sniffed, her head jerking up. Her eyes widened and her mouth fell open.

He'd forgotten. "About that...we'll speak of it later."

She frowned. "Shay?"

"What about Shay?" Donna stepped closer, sniffing. It was her turn to gasp.

"We're seeing each other. This is *not* the time to discuss it."

Ginny's expression remained concerned. "Does my mate know?"

"I'm not sure if I was close enough to him. And we haven't spoken of it."

She nodded. "Shay's a gentle soul, Trayis. Don't hurt her."

"I would never." He offered Ginny his arm. "Let's go say hello to the other alphas and their entourages. I want everyone to know I accept you as my brother's mate, and that I'd take it personally if anyone even *thought* about harming you."

Ginny put her hand on his forearm and nodded. He led her away from the enforcers' mates.

"You realize everyone is going to know about you and Shay by morning, don't you?" She kept her voice soft. "I love these women but they gossip like crazy."

"I don't care if the entire pack finds out."

"Good thing, because they will. What are your intentions?"

He laughed, glancing down at her—then stopped at her stern expression. "Did you honestly just ask me that?"

"I did." She smiled slightly. "I'm the official alpha bitch. It's my duty to look out for all the female members. That especially means Shay."

"I like her. We're spending time together. Don't make too much of it."

Her smile died and a few worry lines took its place. "Not many people have been kind to Shay...so the ones who are, she's completely devoted to. I have no doubt she'd throw herself in front of a Werewolf in a mindless rampage, even knowing she'd only slow them down long enough to tear her apart, if it gave the few she loves time to shift to better protect themselves. She'd already die for *us*—but *you're* the one man she's been intimate with. Think about that, Trayis. She loves with everything she is when someone allows her to get close. Do you understand what I'm saying?"

He had a feeling he did. "I don't want to hurt Shay."

Another alpha approached. "Trayis."

A flash of memory hit of meeting the man before. "Hello, Allen."

"You remember me. I didn't expect you here."

Trayis pulled Ginny closer to his side. "I had to meet my newest nephew, and seeing how big the twins have grown has shown me how remiss I've been in not visiting as often as I should. I'm not making that mistake again."

Allen nodded, not looking surprised. "Family is important."

"Yes, they are. How's your pack?"

"Good. We've had a great year. Three new pups were born. Six matings happened. On the business front, we opened a store..."

Trayis went on auto pilot, pretending to continue listening to Allen as he glanced around, finding Arlis. His brother remained by the fireplace but now he spoke to Gill, another alpha. His body language looked relaxed. Frank was at the bar, downing a shot.

Trayis hid a smirk. The prick had been put in his place and knew better than to fuck with his brother's pack. He watched the Were speak to the elder Lycan female behind the bar and saw anger glint in Yasha's eyes.

"Now I'm hoping to talk her into mating me," Allen finished.

Trayis forced a smile as he gave the alpha his full attention again. "I wish you luck with that."

"I'm determined. No one can resist me for long. Of course, I *would* have to choose the only woman in my pack who doesn't want to be the official alpha bitch."

"One of life's strange twists." Trayis cleared his throat. "I'm glad your pack is doing so well. If you'll excuse me, I need to get a drink. My throat is dry." He glanced at Ginny.

She let him go and nodded, telling him she was fine on her own. He looked over her shoulder, seeing that the enforcer mates were nearby. Her little personal protectors. He motioned for them to return to her side. They didn't hesitate. He strode to the bar and smiled at the bartender.

"How is my favorite elder?"

Yasha grinned in genuine pleasure. "I'm doing great. It's good to see you, handsome. What can I make for you?"

He winked. "Just a beer, beautiful."

She turned, opened one of the mini fridges, and grabbed his preferred brand. She twisted off the cap for him and passed it over. "You charmer. Too bad you're way too young for me."

Frank stepped closer, glancing up and down Trayis. "How old *are* you?"

Trayis took a sip and swallowed. "Just a few hundred years."

Frank seemed startled by that news. "I thought you and Arlis would be closer in age."

"Obviously we don't have the same fathers. He's full Lycan. I'm not."

Frank curled his lip. "Yes Your mother bedded a Vampire. *Disgusting.* The bitch must have been desperate."

Trayis had put the beer down and moved before the prick could even react. In an instant, he had Frank pinned to the wall by his throat, claws out. "Listen to me well, Frank. You're an ignorant asshole. I'll rip your fucking head off and shove it up your own ass the next time you talk shit about my family. My mother was the victim of a mind and body rape by a master Vampire—but she survived, birthed me, and then was able to meet her true mate. That was Arlis's father. This is the only warning I'll give you to *never* disrespect my family again by words or actions. Do you understand me?"

Frank couldn't respond since he'd turned deep red, unable to breathe. Trayis knew everyone had stopped speaking, and he could sense them watching. He eased his grip enough for the alpha to gasp in air and then dropped him, backing off a couple feet.

"Problem?" Arlis came up to his side.

"Frank needed a history lesson...and to learn not to insult a VampLycan's mother," Trayis snarled.

Yasha smirked. "It seems Frank didn't know how VampLycans came into existence. But Trayis set him straight. Did you know VampLycans hunt and kill Vampires who force our women to breed? They've also killed Werewolves who've sold our women to Vamp assholes. It's illegal to create VampLycans if it's not consensual for both parties."

Frank reached up and touched the bleeding scratches around his throat. "I'm a guest here, and this is how I'm treated?"

"Don't." Arlis allowed his voice to deepen and he threw major vibes. "You came into *my* house, tossing out threats and insults. The only reason I'm not dragging your ass outside to challenge you is *because* I'm a good fucking host. You haven't been an alpha for long, Frank. Six years isn't shit as far as experience goes. I've let some of your insults slide with that in mind. But you have a lot to learn. Do you want a fight? If so, let's do it alpha to alpha—the *honorable* way."

The other alphas approached. Trayis tensed, prepared to battle at his brother's side, but they made their support known by standing next to Arlis and glaring at Frank.

"Your brother earned my respect," Allen stated. "You have not so far, Frank. We enjoy the peace between our packs. Fuck with one, you pick a fight with all of us."

The other alphas nodded their agreement, throwing their own vibes at Frank.

He paled, glancing at each of them.

Gill spoke next. "You have two choices, Frank. Be an ally or an enemy. I know damn well I sent you copies of our alliance contracts when you became alpha, and so did the others. You agreed to all terms just the

137

way Fred did. We have stable, established packs that are flourishing. No one wants a territory war. You should have challenged for a different pack if you're ambitious enough to think you could take over neighboring territories. It won't happen with *yours*. And we have enough enemies without fucking each other over."

"We weren't pleased with the *previous* attack on this pack," Allen added. "Those cowards snuck in without warning. At least Bufford rid us of the troublemakers in our various packs by recruiting them. No one misses any of those pricks. But we all lost friends and family during that attack. It was a learning experience we're not willing to repeat. We're stronger together; peace means safety to the ones we're sworn to protect."

"You don't find him a threat?" Frank jerked his chin toward Trayis. "He's a *VampLycan*! What if Arlis decides he wants his brother nearby permanently, and a bunch of those bastards take our territories? We need to band together to get Arlis out!"

Trayis was already regretting not killing Frank.

But Allen just laughed. "You're showing your youth and stupidity. The only way to bring the VampLycans down on your pack is to fuck with one. Arlis is honorable, he's not greedy...and who in the hell do you think talked us all into sitting down to write out peace terms? We have sentries protecting our borders from humans, rogues, and Vampires. *Not each other*. In a crisis, we want to know we can count on help from our neighbors—not get attacked by them."

"Your thinking has been tainted by your fear, Frank." Gill glanced at Trayis then back at the alpha. "I too saw Arlis's close association with the

VampLycans as a threat at first. Knee-jerk response. Then I allowed myself to push past my fear to see the truth. Arlis survived an attack to his pack and mourned the losses. His grief was great. He could have asked the VampLycans to wipe every last one of us out, but instead he called for meetings, making peace with all the packs that surround his territory."

Damon, the last alpha there, chuckled. "Trayis hasn't killed *me* yet, and I'm an asshole who likes to push his buttons. He's a good guy who gives warnings when you go too far. You've experienced that yourself tonight, since your head is still attached to your body. Not to mention, he respects the fuck out of Arlis, which means he adheres to the peace terms his brother has created...as long as we keep up our end of the deal.

"My pack is the closest to the city. A large enough Vamp nest moving in could become a threat. And guess what? Nests have no qualms about fucking with packs. Those motherfuckers are *terrified* of VampLycans, though. I've used that threat more than once when Vamps have encroached on my border." He winked at Trayis. "Thanks, buddy. It's very effective when I tell them I have you on speed dial."

Trayis couldn't help but grin. "You *are* an asshole. I also never gave you my number."

"No need. I have Arlis's. I know you'd help me out, because if they started targeting *my* pack, it's reasonable to assume they'd fuck with your brother's, too. You'd never allow that to go down. Am I right?"

Trayis nodded. "My clan would definitely deal with the problem."

Damon's expression sobered as he glowered at Frank. "You have a lot to learn as an alpha. My father taught me a lot before he stepped down. His mistakes—like being an asshole to his neighbors—were things I learned *not* to do. We're stronger together than apart, being dicks to each other. Maybe you missed out on all that great advice and wisdom when you killed your brother. A smart alpha learns fast and adapts. Be smart, Frank. Or be dead. Either way, you're not fucking up what we've accomplished."

Arlis crossed his arms. "We're united, Frank. You're either with us or against us, but coming in here blustering and making threats isn't going to fly. Got it?"

Damon added, "And don't even think about seeking out our pack troublemakers and making false promises to follow you. I remind my pack that I'd fucking rip their limbs off one at a time to drag out their agonizing deaths if they ever betrayed me."

"I just tell mine I'll kill them in a heartbeat if I suspect they're plotting to attack another pack behind my back," Allen mused. "I'm sure I can replace them with any of your members who are tired of your shit, Frank."

Frank looked furious. "Are you threatening to take my pack?"

Allen snorted. "Not unless you start shit and leave us with no recourse. Nobody here wants a war except *you*. I'm with Damon on the VampLycans. Trayis is cool. So are the other VampLycans who visit."

Gill nodded. "You attack Arlis, he's not going to have to call the VampLycans. I think I can speak for Allen and Damon when I say we'll consider it a declaration of war against all of us."

"Damn straight," Damon growled.

Allen nodded as well.

Gill glanced at Trayis. "There won't be anything left for you to kill by the time you arrive, if you ever get that call. We'll have already handled the problem."

Frank began to sweat, the scent of fear and anger rolling off him. "I apologize," he said tightly. "I don't want a war."

Arlis turned to Yasha. "We need drinks."

Yasha grinned. "I'm pouring rounds now."

Trayis relaxed. His brother was a great alpha who'd built strong bonds with the other pack leaders. They'd stood together against Frank's bullshit. He hadn't been needed after all...but he decided to stick around just a little longer. It was better to be safe than sorry, since he didn't trust Frank at all. The Lycan had no honor, and he was also a total idiot.

Chapter Eight

Trayis remained until the last alpha and his enforcers left. Arlis stood at his side on the porch until they got word that all parties had left the territory from the sentries.

His brother sighed. "Frank's going to be a problem. He's been set straight...for now. But I see future shit happening once the fear fades. Stupid is like that."

"Agreed."

Arlis turned to face him. "Now...do you want to explain to me why Shay's scent is all over you?"

Trayis cocked his head, studying his brother closely. "I like her. We're spending time together. I respect the hell out of you, Arlis, and she's your pack, but she's also an adult. Are we going to have a problem?"

"Of course not. I just worry. She's not like other women."

"You mean because she's so human?"

"No. Because she's not anything at all like the typical alpha chasers. We both know the types."

He figured his brother had dealt with a lot of women coming after him, too, before he'd mated Ginny. Some power-hungry females were cunning, experienced at seduction, and coldly ambitious. "I'm aware of that. Hell, Shay doesn't even know I'm my clan leader."

Arlis appeared shocked for a moment, but then he sighed. "I can see how that happened. Shay is a bit distanced from pack gossip unless it's about her, and we don't have any official correspondence between my pack and your clan that she'd be privy to. It's all private phone calls with us. I'm just saying, Shay isn't the type to fuck and then walk away from. Her heart is fragile. You're going to bruise hers when you leave."

"I hope not," he said quietly.

"You're a good guy, Trayis. I know you'd never intentionally hurt her, but you *will* when you go home. I'd hate for that to happen."

"As if you or your pack can talk," he said, his anger sparking.

Arlis tensed. "What does that mean?"

"You were discussing a plan to *bribe* a half-breed into mating her and making it sound like she's some fucking child who needed a caretaker. That's screwed up, Arlis. She deserves someone who's going to love her. I fucking *refuse* to allow her to settle for some asshole who sees her as a price to pay to join a pack, just so you can worry about her less. You are *not* going to do that to her! Forget the half-breed bullshit. Don't even bring them here."

Arlis tilted his head slightly, staring at him for a long moment. "Shit! Is this more than you just scratching an itch while you're visiting? Have you *bitten* her?"

Trayis reached up and rubbed the back of his neck. "I have."

"Is she your mate?"

Trayis sighed. "I don't know."

Arlis frowned at that.

"Sometimes with VampLycans, it takes time to sink in if we find our mate. It's the fucking Vampire blood. The stronger it is, the more it can screw with the Lycan instincts."

"You just gave me a *direct order* over one of my pack. I take it you have feelings for Shay?"

"Yes," he admitted. "And you'd likely have a problem with some of them."

"Like?"

"Like I want to beat the hell out of some of your pack for the way she's been treated. I'd love five minutes alone with Tegan."

"That's why you were throwing vibes at my table this morning..."

"I'd have already tracked his ass down if he'd hurt her, Arlis. She doesn't have a bruise on her, I checked, and that's the only reason he's still breathing. Your sentry or not."

Arlis had the nerve to smile smugly.

"What's so amusing? I just threatened one of yours with death."

"It's just that Shay isn't the woman I imagined you'd go for."

"You and me both, brother. She's too damn soft and sweet. It makes me feel protective in ways I've never experienced before." He remembered what had been said at breakfast. "I don't see her as a pup, though. There's nothing childlike about her. She's sexy as hell."

"I'll take your word for it. And not that you need it, but you have my permission."

Trayis frowned. "For what?"

"To take her with you when you go home."

"Fuck!" He reached up and rubbed the back of his neck again. "I'm not ready for a mate!"

144

"Neither was I when Ginny came into my life, but I realized she was mine. That worked out great."

"Did Darlene tell you that Shay tried to get ahold of you earlier? Not to change the subject, but shit went down today."

Arlis frowned. "Besides Tegan?"

"Shay went to buy condoms off territory, since she thinks we should hide our relationship from everyone."

"Why would she hide it?"

"Because she believes your damn pack will think less of *me* for being with her," he snarled, angry all over again. "That's beside the damn point. She ran into a fifteen-year-old Lycan kid at the human store. It turns out he's her uncle."

Shocked, Arlis's mouth fell opened. "What?"

"Her grandparents weren't just hanging out at that cabin doing nothing when you sent them away to keep Shay safe. They had a son they didn't bother to inform you about. I remember you saying you didn't kick them out of the pack until Shay was in her teens, after they tried to get her banished. The boy was born in your territory, and he would have been one of your pack."

"Why would they hide him from me?"

"From what he told Shay, it seems his asshole parents told him you forced his big brother to mate a human, and they blame you for his death. Shay said the kid hates you for that, *and* her; he's been fed a lot of the lies. His parents have made you out to be worse than that bastard Frank."

"Fuck." Arlis growled. "*That's* the pack they went to. Frank's. I guess I'm not too surprised Mildred and Elvis hid the boy. I knew they hated me for protecting Shay, and they accused me of picking her over them. Every child should be celebrated. But why the hell didn't *Fred* tell me about the boy when he took them in? He should have. He was still alive when they joined that pack. Then again, he had a soft heart for strays with sob stories. I can imagine Elvis and Mildred lied their asses off to gain his sympathy. Goddamn it!"

"Shay's worried you might have to hurt her uncle. She fears he'll try to attack you because of the lies he's been told."

"I'd never hurt a youth."

"I know that. She knows it, too. But it upset her enough to cry when she found out about him and realized how badly he's been manipulated."

"Fuck. I'll go to her cabin now to get all the details and assure her."

Trayis moved to block him. "She's not at home."

"Where is she?"

"Waiting for me in the trailer. She's staying with me."

"Ah."

"I'll bring her by at breakfast in the morning. Or do you want us in your office when it opens?"

"Breakfast is fine. Eight."

"I remember."

Arlis stepped close and gripped his shoulders, holding his gaze. "I hope she's yours, brother. I want you to be as happy as I am. A mate is a wonderful thing."

"I'm afraid, with my personality…"

"I understand. There's one thing I can tell you about Shay, though. She's more human than Werewolf."

"I've figured that out."

"You won't accidently overpower her if you pull what you did at breakfast this morning. She'd have felt your vibes, but she wouldn't have buckled. Have her tell you about the assholes who've tried that shit with her."

His anger returned yet again. "I heard."

Arlis chuckled.

"There's not one thing funny about some of your pack trying to get her on her knees!"

"That's the thing, Trayis. Shay doesn't feel the vibes as strongly as a Were does. She gets mad and starts yelling when they try to use them to overpower her. As a Were, she's submissive…but as a human? She's got more backbone than any I've ever met. That human blood of hers protects her from being cowered. Some believe she's like her mother, but that's not true. Layla was frail on the inside, as well as on the outside. Shay looks like her physically, but inside, Shay's sturdy."

He let that information sink in. "I need to get back to her, now that everything here is settled."

"Thanks for coming."

"Always." He hugged his brother and left.

He nearly ran to the trailer, anxious to see Shay. He knocked, calling out to her. She must have been waiting near the door, maybe sitting in the chair beside it, since the locks slid back within seconds. He stepped inside, grabbed her around the waist as he entered, and slammed the door behind him. He slid the locks back into place to secure them.

"Is everything okay?"

He noticed the slight scent of fear and sweat on her, as if she'd been extremely nervous. "Frank is a prick, but he's a terrified one now, with a new understanding of how close Arlis and I are. The other alphas stood with my brother, too. They made it damn clear that to attack this pack would be seen as an act of war against them all."

Her relief was evident. "Thank goodness." She wrapped her arms around his neck.

He lifted her higher into his arms and walked toward the bedroom. "I'm sorry that took so long. I wanted to stay until all of them were gone. You should have tried to nap."

"As if I could sleep. I was worried about another sneak attack. I kept wishing I'd packed my shotgun."

He halted in the hallway, his eyes widening. "Shotgun?"

Her cheeks pinkened. "I can't shift. Sylvia and Dean, my foster parents, bought it for me as a housewarming gift. You know, since I was determined to live alone."

"I like them already." He continued into the small bedroom. "Can you shoot it?"

"Of course. Dean took me out to practice on targets until I could hit anything I was aiming for."

He eased her down on her feet and kissed her forehead. "I bet you look cute as shit with a shotgun in your hands."

She shook her head, giving him an exasperated look. That was adorable, too.

"I'm just being honest. Does it knock you on your ass when you fire it, doll?"

"I know how to brace my legs, Trayis," she said dryly.

He kicked off his shoes and removed his shirt. "I want to see that sometime."

"You're so weird."

"Why? Because it makes me a little hard imagining you firing a shotgun that's probably way too big for you to handle? Yet, you do." He opened his pants, shoving them down. "Strip. I want you—now."

She removed the shirt, wearing nothing beneath it. He grabbed her once he was naked, pulling her smaller body against his and lifted her again. He loved the way she wrapped her legs around his waist without thought and eagerly met his lips with her own, opening her mouth to his exploring tongue. Her passionate responses instantly made his blood boil with need. His fangs elongated as his dick became painfully engorged. He wanted to be inside her, wanted to bite...

He broke the kiss, turned, and just fell back on the bed, Shay bouncing slightly on top of him. A giggle came from her as he rolled, pinning her under him. He lowered his head, sucking one of her nipples into his mouth. She had to feel the tips of his fangs against her breast, but she didn't jerk away. Her fingers slid into his hair instead, holding him close as she moaned his name.

149

Don't bite, he kept repeating in his head. *Don't fucking bite her.*

The desire was too strong, though.

He pulled away, remembering the condoms. "Hang on."

He grabbed the box, ripped one open, and rolled it down his shaft. He hated the things, since it meant putting a thin layer of latex between their bodies.

An instant image of Shay with a rounded belly flashed through his mind, making him pause.

"Trayis? Are you okay?"

He realized he'd frozen, and blinked, struggling to push away the thought of Shay pregnant with his son or daughter. "I'm fine." He returned to the bed, flipped her over onto her hands and knees, and positioned himself behind her. "You are so damn beautiful, doll."

She moaned his name again as he gently eased his dick inside her tight, welcoming pussy. Shay felt perfect...better than perfect. His fangs ached and his gaze locked on her skin. He even gripped her blonde hair, loosely fisting it, to bare the top of her shoulder. He wanted to bite her so badly.

"Don't fucking do it," he whispered.

Shay tried to glance back at him. "Do what?"

"Nothing." He released her hair, gripped her hips, and began to fuck her. He closed his eyes, listening to her moans, and just allowed his body to drown in pleasure. "Hold still, doll. I'm going to do all the work. Just...enjoy...this."

Her moans filled the bedroom. Trayis felt her inner muscles tighten, and he fucked her harder, fighting the urge to come. Shay had the uncanny ability to make him lose control.

She cried out his name when she climaxed, and he damn near roared as he spilled into the condom. They both stilled, panting.

He hated to get up to remove the condom but he rushed into the bathroom to dispose of it and came back. Shay was curled on her side, smiling at him. She looked damn perfect in his bed. He climbed in and pulled her close, needing to hold her. She curled into him, pressing a light kiss on his chest, Trayis enjoying how good she felt in his arms.

* * * * *

Trayis rose from the bed an hour later, still wide awake. Shay slept on.

He felt unsettled that he'd gone to a place he'd never gone before in his mind. *Shay pregnant with my baby. Shit.*

He found his cell phone in the living area where he'd left it and saw a missed call from Wen. He hadn't even checked when he'd returned from the party, too fixated on taking Shay to bed. He sighed, walked to the far end of the trailer, and returned the call.

Wen answered on the second ring. "About time you called me back. I was beginning to worry. Is everything okay?"

"It's fine. I forgot my phone in the trailer. My brother threw a party and I attended."

Wen snorted. "Lucky you. I was ass deep in drama."

151

"Is everything okay?"

"Mya was sleeping with Roe *and* Brigs, telling both they were the only one for her. But she went to Roe after screwing Brigs—still wearing his scent. She was proud as shit that she'd pitted them against each other."

"Fuck." Mya was a younger clan member who was always causing trouble, screwing with different men, delighting when they fought over her. He'd spoken to her many times on the matter, forbidding her to incite jealousy for her own amusement. "How bad? Please tell me they didn't kill each other."

"We broke it up before too many bones were broken. Roe was winning, if you were curious."

"Not surprised. Did you punish Myra? I ordered her not to do that shit ever again."

"Of course. She's restricted to her cabin for a month. No visitors. No leaving. No more fucking two guys at once while lying to them about it. She threatened to leave our clan to go to another."

"Let her. Lorn already saw her in action when she went after his brother, Lavos. He'd turn her away. Velder's mate, Crayla, would probably beat her ass to a pulp the first time she caught Mya pulling her shit, then send her back to us still bleeding. As for Crocker, he'd give her a week to find a mate once he caught on to the little head games she plays, or kick her ass out. Anything else?"

"Not really. In retaliation for me restricting her to the cabin, Mya tried to imply to Gerri that we used to be a hot item. Trying to make her jealous. I assured her I've never touched Mya, or *any* of her friends who pull this shit. Nor have you."

Anger stirred in Trayis's gut. "Goddamn. Mya loves to cause shit. Did your mate believe you?"

"Of course. Gerri can't stand Mya and her little group of bed-hoppers. She's gotten very familiar with the troublemakers since I've taken over in your absence. They've been acting up more than usual with you gone. Speaking of, when are you coming back? Your job sucks."

A bit of guilt surfaced. The clan was his responsibility. It's why he rarely left Alaska. "A few more days."

"Good. How is it going with the virgin issue? Did you let her down easy?"

He stared toward the bedroom. He could see Shay sleeping from where he stood. "Not exactly. It's complicated."

"You just tell her you aren't looking for a mate and leave it at that."

He reached up to rub the back of his neck, a newly frequent habit. "I invited her to spend another night with me. She's in my bed right now."

Wen stayed silent for a few seconds, save for sucking in a deep breath. His voice came out low. "Another night? As in, you're actually *sleeping* in a bed with her after you fuck her? Like, all night until morning and waking up together?"

"Don't sound so shocked."

"I'm *beyond* shocked, man. Stunned. Amazed. Floored!" Wen cleared his throat. "What's going on in your head?"

"Fuck if I know. She's sweet, and I keep thinking how damn adorable and cute she is."

"That's, um… That's how I think about Gerri."

"Don't say that."

"I can't lie to you, man. I won't. Are you feeling any jealousy? Protectiveness? Want to keep her close? Hold her all the time? Can't keep junior in line?"

Trayis released his neck. "Junior in line?"

"You've never heard that saying before? You need to leave home more often and talk to younger people. Are you popping boners all the time when you look at her or pick up her scent? Like you have no control over that shit and just want to bend her over and go to town on her ass, even when you know you shouldn't?"

He closed his eyes. "I can't believe I left you in charge, Wen."

"Answer the question."

He sighed. "The attraction is…very strong."

"Do you want to sink your fangs and your dick into her at the same time?"

He clenched his teeth. "Yes."

Wen laughed. "It's official then. I'll have someone give your cabin a good cleaning and fill your fridge with food. I'm guessing you never eat there; I only ever see drinks in it. Your mate's actually going to want to eat in your home, instead of at the office."

"That's not funny. And I can't bring her to Alaska."

"Why the fuck not?" Wen's humor disappeared fast. "Who cares if you weren't expecting to find your mate while visiting your brother? You did. I was empty inside for the years Gerri and I were apart, Trayis, after her mom took her away. My life was shit until I went after her. Wasted fucking *years*, man. Don't make the same mistake I did. No holding off for the right time. Screw that. What's her name?"

He rubbed his neck again, feeling stressed. "Shay."

"Pack Shay up and bring her home. Don't overthink it. Listen to your instincts. Pay attention to how she makes you feel. Hold on to that—*and* her. Don't let her go, man."

Trayis knew it was sound advice, albeit too simple. Nothing in life ever was. "I need to go."

"Trayis?"

"Yes, Wen?"

"A mate is a precious thing. I made so many mistakes. If I could go back and tell my younger self one thing, it would be to not let my mate walk away. I still have nightmares about something happening to Gerri during the years she was away, without me protecting her. I got fucking lucky to have a second chance. Not everyone gets that. You found her. Bring her home. Got it?"

"It's not that simple, and we both know that."

"Do I need to interfere the way you did with Gerri and I? Because I will, man. I'll fly to Arlis's pack, pick up your woman, and bring her here the way you did with *my* mate. I'll always be grateful to you for doing that. I was such a dumbass, trying to keep the peace with my parents. You didn't let me get away with that shit, and I'm not letting *you* get away

155

with it now. You found your mate, Trayis. Don't make me get on a plane. You know I will."

A smile curved his lips. "Yes, I know you aren't bluffing. I'm going to bed now."

Trayis hung up and returned to the bedroom, got into bed, and pulled Shay into his arms. She did feel as if she belonged there. Maybe Wen was right.

The situation was completely different though. Wen had grown up with Gerri, had always had feelings for her. Trayis still had a lot to figure out. Things were just too new.

Chapter Nine

"Don't be nervous." Trayis kept a firm hold on Shay. She looked ready to flee as he led her to his brother's front door and opened it.

"I don't belong in the alpha's house for breakfast," she whispered.

He ignored that, almost dragging her through the front door, and firmly closed it behind them. The enforcers and his brother were already seated at the large table. Their mates were in the kitchen, bringing plates to them, the delicious smell of food filling the space. He was glad that two chairs were now empty where he usually sat, instead of one. He helped Shay sit before taking the seat beside her.

"Morning," Arlis stated, his gaze on Shay.

Trayis saw that her chin stayed down, gaze locked on the table. She did manage to mumble softly, "Morning, everyone."

"Shay? It's okay. Don't look so tense."

She glanced up at Arlis. "Thank you for inviting me."

Trayis felt his irritation growing already. She acted like his brother was doing her a big favor by having her in his home to share a meal. That needed to change—now.

He put his arm over the back of her chair, touching her shoulder just enough to let her know he was there, to comfort her.

"My brother told me about your run-in with the youth who claimed to be your uncle. Do you believe he's who he claims he is?" Arlis took a sip of coffee, waiting for her answer.

Shay stiffened a bit but gave a nod. "He looked familiar, and when he told me who his parents were, it clicked. He looks a lot like the pictures of my father. He's been lied to, Alpha."

"Trayis informed me. I'm going to reach out to Frank today and ask for a meeting with the youth."

Shay stiffened even more, her body becoming utterly rigid. Trayis watched her carefully. It looked as if she wanted to protest but she didn't say a word. His temper flared a bit more. She was a submissive, yes, but he couldn't stand seeing her so quiet. Her feelings and thoughts were important.

He lifted his arm from the back of the chair and stood. "Excuse us for a few minutes." He just bent, grabbed her chair, and pulled it back from the table. He lifted her, ignoring her gasp, and threw her over his shoulder, walking into the hallway that led to the downstairs spare bedrooms. Once there, he bent, gently setting her down on her feet. He met her gaze as he straightened and gently pinned her against the wall with his hands, crouched a little until they were almost eye level.

She stared at him with wide eyes. He sniffed, not picking up any fear. That was good. She should know he'd never hurt her.

"Doll, you need to speak up for yourself. You don't agree with Arlis, do you?"

"Are you *crazy*?" She clutched at his shirt, her gaze darting from his toward the room they'd just come from. "What are you doing?"

He focused his hearing, picking up zero conversation from the other room. They were all silent, probably trying to overhear what was being said between him and Shay. He was fine with that.

158

"Giving you a straight talk. You were invited here to discuss the situation with your uncle. He's your family. Forget that Arlis is your alpha. I won't sit there watching you *not* speak your mind. Do you understand? You're strong, Shay. Your opinions matter. You need to give them. Now go march your cute, sexy ass back to that table and tell him that you disagree, and why."

She gaped at him a little, her eyes even wider.

"You heard me. Otherwise, we'll stand here talking until you're convinced that I'm right."

"He is my *alpha*," she whispered. "It would be disrespectful to argue with him!"

"That's bullshit. You need to tell Arlis what you're thinking. Not just sit there in silence." He cupped her face. "Do you want him to reach out to the other pack to talk to your uncle?"

"I think it would possibly get him into trouble somehow. That's the last thing I want."

"Okay." He nodded. "Then what's the best way you think this should be dealt with?"

"I just wanted to warn Arlis to be aware in case the kid tries to attack him. And I don't want my uncle getting hurt because he's been lied to. I told him about Sylvia and Dean, offering him the chance to talk to them. I'm hoping he shows up here, wanting to get some answers. My grandparents might react badly if Arlis goes through official pack channels. They could see it as a confrontation or challenge."

"Then you need to say that to Arlis."

She bit her lip.

"This isn't a formal meeting, Shay. This is breakfast at his home. Arlis asked you a question, and you need to answer him honestly." He leaned in, holding her gaze. "I'm with you."

She nodded hesitantly.

He backed off and offered his hand. She took it.

"Chin up, doll. Speak your mind. Being honest isn't disrespectful when you've been asked questions."

She still looked timid as shit as he led her back to the table and helped her sit. He took his place next to her and gave his brother a silent nod. Arlis smiled, looking amused. So did everyone else in the room. He had no doubt they'd overheard every word he and Shay had exchanged. His brother confirmed it when he cleared his throat.

"You think we should wait to see if this kid comes to us?"

Shay lifted her chin and nodded, meeting her alpha's gaze. "I'm afraid it will make it worse for him if you go to Frank. He's a jerk who might piss off Mildred and Elvis, which might make my uncle a target of all three of them for speaking to me in the first place. My grandparents have lied to him his entire life, twisting things in their favor. He's got to be confused after speaking with me. The last thing he needs is more bullshit from them."

Arlis nodded and glanced at Martin. "Spread word to the sentries about the kid. Tell them to give him safe passage to Shay or to Sylvia and Dean if he requests it. Even me. I'll make the time if he wants to talk." He looked back at Shay. "Don't worry. Even if he challenges me because of

160

what he's been told, I don't harm youths. I'd just pin him down until he calms, and then set him straight about a few facts."

"Thank you." Shay sounded relieved.

Trayis felt better about the situation. Shay would have one less thing to worry about. He gently squeezed her hand encouragingly, before releasing it. She offered to help the other women serve breakfast but Ginny waved her off.

"We've got it, but thank you, Shay." Ginny brought her a plate and touched her shoulder, to show support and acceptance.

The enforcers brought up some business, casually discussing it with his brother over breakfast. Shay seemed to finally relax, and the rest of the meal went well.

Afterward, they said their goodbyes and he escorted her outside.

"That wasn't so bad, was it?"

"No. Thank you."

"You say that a lot, doll. What's on your agenda today?"

The look in her eyes tugged at his heart. "You want to spend more time with me?"

"I do."

She smiled. "I have a few hours of work to do, but then I'll be free."

"Dinner at my place tonight, then? There were a few more movies on that shelf I'd like to watch with you. Bring another overnight bag."

"I'd love that." Happiness lit up her beautiful eyes.

"It's a date." He pulled her closer, keeping hold of her hand. "Are you working at home or in the office today?"

"Home. One of the sentries brought my laptop to me from the office."

"I'll take you there."

"What are *you* going to do today?"

"Make some calls to my clan and washing a load of laundry."

"Exciting."

He chuckled at her teasing. "Very." He escorted her to her cabin, gave her a kiss, and left. It was getting harder to do. He enjoyed spending time with Shay, the idea of being parted from her less and less appealing.

* * * * *

Shay was working when she heard a slight beeping before her cabin door flew open. She wasn't concerned; only Marcia knew her code to the lock.

Her best friend stepped inside. "Are the gossips messing with me? You and Trayis actually slept together?"

She saved the document and stood. "Yes. And you and Kale? I heard you were with him in his cabin. Is that true?"

Marcia grinned and nodded. "It is! Now—tell me about Trayis. *Everything*. I heard he was carrying your scent at the party the alpha threw. Spill!"

"First, did Kale ask you to mate him?"

Marcia grinned, reached up, and yanked the neck of her shirt to the side. "Kale just went to formally tell our alpha, before someone gets too close to us and smells our mixed scents."

Shay's mouth fell open when she saw the already-healed claiming scar. Tears blinded her next. "Oh, Marcia. I'm so happy for you! I knew you were mates!"

"I'm happy too!"

"How did your parents take it?"

Marcia's expression grew somber. "I don't know. I left Kale's cabin and came straight here."

"Who told you about me and Trayis, then?"

"Are you *kidding*?" Marcia yanked her phone out of her back jeans pocket and tapped on the screen, showing her a bunch of text messages. "Literally everyone is talking about it. I turned on my phone this morning to check if I had any missed calls and saw this text explosion instead. How serious are you two? Is Trayis your mate?"

Shay felt a stab to her chest. "No. It's just sex."

Marcia inched closer. "I'm sorry. You look sad... But you had your V card punched at least. Was he gentle? Did you enjoy it?"

She nodded. "So much."

Marcia reached out and touched her arm. "I'm glad. That's a nice bright side. I'm sorry I disappeared for so long. Mating frenzy kind of took hold of Kale and I. We'd probably still be in bed but he had to report for duty."

"Don't apologize. I really *am* happy for you."

Marcia nodded. "I know. How badly do you think Mom is going to flip the hell out when I tell her?"

"She has to accept it. It's done. But you need to go tell her before she hears about it on her phone. The news is going to spread like wildfire. It always does when a couple mates. The pack will want to throw a party to celebrate."

"Will you come with me to break the news?"

"Uh...*no*."

Marcia winced. "It's going to be bad. Mom is convinced a submissive male would be a perfect match to balance out my natural aggression."

"Well, she's wrong."

"That's why I want you to come with me."

Shay sighed and finally nodded. "Okay."

"You're the best!"

Shay reached up and pushed her hair off her forehead. "Is the word 'sucker' stamped here?"

Marcia laughed and grabbed her hand. "Maybe. Come on." They left the cabin, Marcia practically skipping. "Spill every detail about you losing your virginity! Is Trayis freaky in bed? Did he bite?"

Shay felt her cheeks flush. "I'm not going to kiss and tell, but it was great. And I'm fine. Don't worry about me."

"He's a freakin' *VampLycan*, Shay. I'm so proud of you, though, for going for it."

"Did you hear about Tegan in any of those texts?"

Marcia stopped and released her hand. "No. What *about* Tegan?"

Shay sighed, telling her what had happened.

Marcia snarled. "I'm going to claw the shit out of him!"

164

"Arlis punished him. Let it go."

"As if! Not only did he attack you, but he was spying on Kale's cabin, listening to us having sex. How can I let that go? Kale is going to want to rip his head off."

"Tegan is in a world of shit already. I almost feel sorry for him."

"You're a sucker, Shay. A soft-hearted one."

"There's more to tell you but it can wait. Let's get this over with. Sylvia and Dean need to hear your news from *you*. Why isn't Kale with you to tell them?"

"I talked him out of it. He's telling Arlis, and then he really does have to work. And I love Mom, but I don't think she's going to take this well."

"She just wants you happy. That means Kale. She'll have to adjust her thinking."

"From your lips," Marcia muttered. "Let's go."

They resumed walking down the path to the area where most of the homes were located. They walked up the porch steps of Shay's foster parents' home, and Marcia knocked loudly, waiting for one of her parents to open it. She backed up to the very edge of the porch. Shay stayed at her side.

Dean answered the door wearing just jeans. The top snap wasn't done. Shay noticed scratch marks on his shoulders...fresh ones. It was a good thing they hadn't just walked in on their own. They'd have caught the couple having sex.

Marcia groaned. "Jeez. You'd think you two were newly mated. Is Mom dressed?"

"I'm putting something on," Sylvia yelled from inside their cabin.

"Get in here." Dean waved them inside, his gaze locked on Marcia. "Why are you hanging back there by the stairs? We've been worried. You haven't answered when your mother called you."

Sylvia came to the door, wearing a robe. "There you are! It's rude not to return my calls. I was beginning to think something had happened to you."

Marcia reached out, and Shay took her hand to give her support.

"Shit," Dean muttered. "What is it? The two of you standing over there, clutching hands, tells me it's trouble. What have you both done? Is the alpha going to come knocking next?"

"I mated," Marica blurted. "To Kale."

Sylvia gasped. Dean swayed on his feet. Shay glanced between them.

"They're perfect for each other," Shay added quickly. "She's been in love with him for years."

"What she said." Marcia squeezed her hand hard enough to hurt.

"Breakable bones," Shay reminded her.

Marcia eased her grip.

Sylvia recovered first, coming out the front door and approaching her daughter. She sniffed loudly, and then reached for Marcia's throat, tugging the neckline on one side, then the other, staring at the claiming mark.

"Please be happy for her," Shay whispered. "She was afraid to tell you. A submissive would have been a disaster waiting to happen. She needs someone stronger than her. Not weaker. Kale is a good Were who can handle anything she can toss his way. A submissive would have had issues with his pride and eventually grown resentful, but Kale won't. Remember that talk we had about my dad and *his* parents? Please don't be like them."

Sylvia flicked her gaze to Shay and gave a sharp nod. She released Marcia's shirt and pulled her into a hug. "We're glad you found your mate."

Dean stepped out of the house and hugged them both, then reached out pull Shay into their embrace as well. She felt squished but didn't complain. This was family and acceptance. Relief swept through her, too. It was going to be okay for Marcia and Kale.

"When is Kale coming by? We'd like to welcome him into our family."

Shay felt proud of Sylvia for asking, and even more relief.

"After his sentry shift ends. I wanted to tell you without him here, in case you flipped your lids. An argument isn't a good way to introduce him as my mate. He's letting our alpha know about our mating now."

Dean looked down at Shay. "And what about *you*? Is there something you'd like to tell us as well?"

Her mouth opened then closed.

He loudly sniffed, taking in her scent. Sylvia leaned in a bit, doing the same. Both of them frowned simultaneously.

She inwardly winced. "I'm not mated. No need to check me for claiming marks."

"But she's not a virgin anymore," Marcia chuckled. "She did Trayis! The gossips weren't lying for once. Who knew our shy little Shay would go after a *VampLycan*? I'm so proud of her!"

Dean snorted. "I knew you two were up to something."

Marica shrugged. "We thought Kale might be my mate. Shay wanted her V card punched." She glanced at Shay, winking at her. "We made a pact at the party to celebrate the alpha couple's newest son by going after the men we wanted. Mission accomplished."

"Come in." Sylvia grabbed them both by the arms. "We want details."

Shay had no choice but to enter the house, but she wouldn't be giving them sexual details. Those were private, between her and Trayis.

Sylvia led them into the kitchen and began to make lunch. They all sat at the island, listening to Marcia brag about what a loving, terrific mate Kale was.

Dean leaned close to Shay, drawing her attention. Her adopted father looked concerned. "You seem sad."

Marcia stopped talking and softly cursed. "I'm sorry. This must be hard on you."

"It's not that. I'm happy for you and Kale. Honestly."

"But you said Trayis isn't your mate. That's got to suck." Her best friend and adopted sister never held back her honest opinions. "You have the hugest crush on him, have for years. Part of you was hoping, wasn't it? I'm so sorry, Shay."

"There's more to tell." Shay took a deep breath and blew it out, sharing what happened when she'd gone to buy condoms. They listened, sympathy and shock showing on their faces.

"Those bastards," Dean snarled. He looked furious when Shay was done. "Mildred and Elvis have twisted the truth to avoid facing their own guilt for what happened to your parents. It was *their* fault your mother broke. Instead, they've lied to that poor kid."

Sylvia reached over and took her mate's hand. "Are you honestly surprised? I'm not. Elvis and Mildred were always willing to do anything to get their way. Remember when they decided I should mate Marcus?"

Shay's mouth fell open.

Dean snarled. "Who could forget?"

"I didn't know that," Shay admitted.

Sylvia shook her head. "It was stupid. Marcus was like a brother to me, and we felt zero attraction for each other. It was always Dean in my heart. I'd known since I was five that he was mine."

"I figured it out about three years later," Dean grinned, lifting his mate's hand to kiss it. "You were always smarter than me."

Sylvia chuckled. "True. You're stronger though. We make a hell of a team." Her gaze went to Shay. "When we were teens, your father's parents decided I should be his mate. They pushed hard for Marcus to pursue me. We tried to ignore them." Sylvia snorted. "When Dean claimed me instead, they tried to force Marcus to cut us off, to never speak to us again. They insisted we'd betrayed him. But Marcus was thrilled for us."

"He was." Dean chuckled. "He's the one who encouraged me to claim my mate when we hit the age of consent, instead of waiting like some couples do. He said Sylvia and I were made for each other, and it was stupid to put it off. He also joked that it would get his parents off his ass if she was claimed already." His humor faded. "I miss him."

"Me too," Sylvia whispered, tears filling her eyes. "He loved you and your mother so much, Shay. Never let those asshole grandparents of yours make you believe anything else."

Dean teared up too. "His grief when Layla died..." His voice broke. "We knew he wasn't going to survive. With his last words, he extracted our promise to raise you. He knew we'd love you for him."

Sylvia nodded, wiping away tears. "He didn't want his parents to get you. We were going to fight them if they tried to take you from us, but they didn't."

Shay nodded. She'd heard that part before. It still hurt that her grandparents had hated her, though. Everything they'd done had ensured she'd never be accepted by some of the pack. "I'm grateful to you both."

Sylvia smiled. "You're a joy, Shay. We might have lost our best friend and his mate, but we gained you. Always know that. You're in our hearts always, as if you're our biological daughter."

Dean nodded. "You're our baby, Shay, no matter how old you get."

"This is going to become a cry fest," Marcia sniffed. "Stop. I don't want Kale showing up unexpectedly to find all of us bawling. He'll think you don't accept our mating."

Shay laughed and wiped at her own tears. "And I have a date with Trayis tonight. He'll think I'm attacked daily if he sees me with swollen eyes one more time."

Marcia leaned closer, bumping her shoulder. "Is he protective?"

"Yes. It's very sweet."

"Oh, that's promising." Her adopted mother winked. "Maybe both of our daughters will get mated."

"Don't think that way. It's just sex." Shay didn't want them to get the wrong idea.

"Shay, Trayis hasn't hooked up with any women in this pack for as long as I can remember—and he's seeing you *again*? That's more than just sex."

She met Dean's gaze. "Some pack members sleep together regularly. It doesn't mean anything."

"They aren't you, Shay."

She frowned. "What does that mean?"

He winked. "You're special. And Trayis isn't an idiot. He's figuring that out."

"What Dad said," Marcia added. "I saw the worry in your eyes when I threatened to leave the pack, but it seems *you're* the one who might be doing that."

"What do you mean, you were going to leave the pack?" Sylvia released Dean's hand and got up, staring intently at her daughter.

"I would have left if Kale hadn't been mine," Marcia admitted. "I couldn't stand the idea of him mating someone else. It would have hurt me too much to see him with someone else."

"Good thing they mated, right?" Shay forced a smile. "Let's not discuss me and Trayis anymore. What kind of party do you think the pack will throw for Marcia and Kale's mating?"

That got the family talking about something else. Shay relaxed, watching them. An hour later, she excused herself, needing to finish her work before Trayis arrived to pick her up for their date.

Chapter Ten

Shay smoothed her hands down the dress, wishing she had a full-length mirror instead of just the small one over the sink in her bathroom. She only owned two dresses, and the black one was the nicest. She'd even dusted off her single pair of heels from when she'd decided to try to date humans a few years before.

The knock at the door had her rushing for it but she stopped, took a few deep breaths, and then unlocked it. She smiled as she opened the door, staring at Trayis. His gaze swept down her body and she liked the look on his face. It was even better when he softly growled.

"You look sexy."

"Too much?"

He gently reached out and wrapped his hand around her waist, pushing her back inside her cabin and shutting the door behind him. "No. You look good enough to eat, doll."

She grinned. "Really?"

"Yes." His gaze locked with hers. "What's the occasion?"

"None. I just wanted to look nice for you."

"I'm glad but there's one problem."

"What's that?" She felt nervous again. Had she messed up? Was she trying too hard?

"Our condoms are in the trailer."

That made her smile again. "Oh."

He released her and slowly circled her body, taking in every inch. Another low growl came from him. It turned her on, big time. No one had ever looked at her the way Trayis was right now, as if she were the sexiest woman alive.

Her cell phone rang, breaking the moment, and she startled. She rushed toward where she always left it charging on her counter and stared at the screen. Martin, the head enforcer, was calling her. That wasn't good.

"Shit." She unplugged it and answered. "This is Shay."

She sensed Trayis coming up behind her.

Martin cleared his throat. "I need you to go to Dean and Sylvia's."

Fear clutched at her. "Are they well? What's wrong?" She'd left them hours ago with Marcia, waiting for Kale to get off work to officially introduce him to her family. Had they not liked each other? Had words been said? "Was there a fight?"

"No. Ellis approached a sentry and asked to be taken to their home."

She frowned. "Who?"

Martin sighed. "The kid, Shay. Elvis and Mildred's pup."

She nearly dropped her cell, her hands trembling. Her uncle had come. "Is he alone?"

"Yes. He approached from Frank's border through the woods. He didn't ask for you specifically, but I thought you'd want to be there."

"Thank you." She ended the call and turned, staring up at Trayis.

"I heard." He took the phone from her. "Let's go."

"What if he doesn't want to see me?"

"What if he does?"

She hesitated. "He didn't ask for me, though."

"Let's go," Trayis repeated, wrapping an arm around her waist and tugging her toward the front door.

"Our date—"

"Can wait."

She allowed him to lead her out of the cabin. He closed the door and helped her down the steps in her high heels. Once they reached the dirt path, she regretted her poor choice in shoes. She stopped to take them off but Trayis scooped her into his arms instead.

She raised a brow. "What are you doing?"

He grinned. "I love the heels. Leave them on."

"It's a bit of a walk into the middle of the territory."

He snorted. "You don't weigh much, Shay." He strode toward the main living area. "I'm out of shape if I can't tote you around easily. And I'm not. Enjoy the ride."

She wrapped her arms around his neck and smiled. He might not be a full Werewolf but he seemed to have the arrogance of one. "I didn't imply otherwise."

"Didn't you?"

"No. But I haven't gone on many dates."

"Good."

She smiled wider. They passed a few sentries, who gawked at them a little, but otherwise stayed clear. She avoided looking at the males too closely, afraid to see censure in their expressions. Trayis swore he didn't

175

care if anyone thought he was slumming by being with her. She needed to have faith in his honesty.

"It's the one to the left," she pointed out. "With the bright green door."

Trayis carried her up the porch steps and put her back on her feet, releasing her. She paused before the door, staring at it. Her heart pounded.

What if her uncle didn't want to see her? What if he had planned to avoid her?

"Do we knock or just enter? What's pack etiquette with family homes?"

Trayis's voice startled her, and she twisted her head to peer up at him.

The door opened, drawing Shay's attention again. Marica met her gaze and opened the door wider, lifting her finger to her lips.

Shay nodded and entered silently.

Soft voices came from the family room. Shay walked quietly down the hallway and peered through the kitchen toward the lit fireplace in the family room. Sylvia and Dean sat in chairs and the boy she'd met in the parking lot was on the couch across from them. On the coffee table were familiar photo albums. One of them, the boy had open on his lap.

"They were extremely happy," Dean was saying. "Do you see the way Marcus gazes at Layla? How he's touching her in almost every picture? He worshipped his little human."

The photo album Ellis held was one that her parents had put together. Tears filled Shay's eyes, and a big warm body pressed up against her back. Trayis, offering her comfort. He wrapped his arm around her waist and lowered his chin to rest on the top of her head. She remained motionless, watching. She didn't want to interrupt or intrude. Marcia stood quietly next to her.

"That isn't what I was told." The boy's voice held obvious anger. "My parents said my brother was forced to mate her, that he hated every minute of it. They told me that he slept at their home a lot to avoid her."

"Lies," Sylvia murmured. "Marcus avoided his *parents* after he mated. They never accepted Layla, and they were very cruel to her. They told her she wasn't good enough for him, that he deserved a strong bitch as a mate. The breaking point came when they demanded that Marcus end her life. He was outraged. Layla was his heart, and so was the child she was pregnant with at the time. What kind of parents ask their son to murder his own mate and child? But that's what your parents did, Ellis.

"Keep turning the pages. You're almost to the photos where Shay was born. You'll see the love in his eyes for her. She was his little angel. I'm sorry they lied to you...but Mildred and Elvis were difficult at best. They could be flat-out vicious at worst."

He turned the pages, and Shay watched his face. Tears blinded her as he touched certain ones. She was too far away to know which pictures, but she was intimately familiar with that album. She had looked at it herself thousands of times. It was the only view into her parents' lives that she'd ever had.

Ellis finally closed the photo album and stared at Dean as he replaced it on the coffee table. "What *really* happened when my brother and his mate died?"

Dean cleared his throat. "Mildred had begun to send bitches to their house. Single ones, to try to take Marcus from his mate by any means necessary. Including trying to seduce him right in front of her. Not that it would have worked, because they were true mates, but it still devastated Layla to have those bitches go after Marcus so brazenly."

"Some would just walk in, strip naked, and tell Layla to get the fuck out. Remember, she hadn't known Weres existed before your brother. She'd never dealt with such brazenness or cruelty." Sylvia growled low. "It was insulting and humiliating. They frequently tried to provoke her into attacking, which would have been suicide. Layla was small even for a human. She had to call Marcus or myself to get them out of her home. At its worst, it happened a few times a week. Your mother figured Layla would eventually flee. Our alpha forbid the women of our pack to continue pulling that shit, but your mother just reached out to other packs. Told them her poor enforcer son was miserable and had been forced to mate a human. It was all lies."

"Marcus seethed with rage every time," Dean added. "Your parents were slowly driving his mate insane and causing her pain. They were determined to make her life hell."

"Then somehow...she got some pills." Sylvia's voice broke and she sniffed. "We don't know how. Layla *never* left her home. They were human pills, normally prescribed by human doctors. No packs had them in their infirmaries because we don't have issues sleeping. That's what never

178

made any sense; how she'd gotten them. Marcus swore they hadn't been in the house previously. She certainly didn't bring them with her."

"We had to assume someone gave them to her," Dean growled.

Sylvia nodded.

Shay let that sink in for the first time in years...and suspicion rose. Had her grandparents given her mother the pills somehow? It made her sick to think about the possibility.

Trayis tightened his hold and pulled her closer to his body.

Ellis stated her exact thoughts. "You think my parents did that, too?"

Sylvia nodded. "They came quickly, before word had even spread that Layla had died. It was too fast...as if they'd been waiting for the news. Elvis and Mildred barged in and said horrible things to Marcus, about how he was better off. Marcus attacked Elvis and accused them of giving her the pills. The enforcers had to break it up and force your parents out of their home.

"Marcus couldn't survive without Layla. His heart was broken beyond repair. He asked us to raise Shay, to protect her from your parents. It was a relief when they didn't demand that she be turned over to them—but then they asked our alpha to kill her. He refused to harm a pup, which infuriated them. They wanted Shay to die, too. She was barely two years old, and the sweetest little girl. Arlis had to ban them to the outer perimeter of our territory for her safety."

Ellis leaned forward and covered his face with both hands. Even with her limited abilities, Shay could feel his grief. "They've lied to me my entire life..."

Shay wanted to go to him and give him a hug. Trayis held her in place.

It was Sylvia who rose and took a seat next to Ellis on the couch. She wrapped an arm around him. "They let hatred of humans blind them. You're old enough to see how it is with some members of a pack. Old ways die hard. They won't be swayed from their hatred. It's not a reflection on *you*, Ellis. You came here to learn the truth. That proves how different you are. It's *their* shame. Not yours."

"That's right." Dean stood and went to the other side of the boy, taking a seat. "Marcus was a brother to me. We were best friends. I'd be honored to call you a brother—or a son." He patted the boy's back lightly. "You're always welcome here. If you want to visit...even if you need a place to live. Our home is yours. We accept you with open arms and hearts. Arlis is a compassionate and loving alpha. He'd accept you into our pack if you ever want to come back. You were born in our territory."

"Yes," Sylvia agreed. She turned her head then, meeting Shay's eyes. "Shay's here. Do you want to see her?"

He didn't answer and kept his face covered.

"We'll give you a few moments alone," Sylvia murmured. She released him and stood. Dean did the same. "Come into the living room when you're ready."

Sylvia approached their little trio, motioning for them to go back down the hallway.

Trayis led her to the living room down the short hall, Marcia proceeding them. Dean and Sylvia followed. They stopped near the front door and Shay wiped her tears.

"You were right. He came," Sylvia whispered. "We showed him the albums of us growing up with Marcus, and all the ones we took from your house after your parents died. Now he knows the truth. It's up to him what he does with it."

"Thank you." Shay gave her a sad, grateful smile.

"It's breaking my fucking heart," Marcia murmured. "Poor kid."

"He has us," Dean reminded them. Then he gazed at Trayis. "Speaking of all things family, what are your intentions with Shay?"

"Dad!" Marcia hissed.

Shay just gawked at her adoptive father.

Trayis smiled. "We're figuring that out."

Dean gave him a sharp nod. "I know you could flay me alive in a fight, but Shay is my daughter by heart. It's my responsibility to look out for her."

Sylvia snorted. "You're not much of a fighter to begin with." She winked at Trayis. "We're a family of taskers for the pack. Only our Marcia is aggressive."

"Taskers?" Trayis glanced at Shay.

"Performing tasks that help the pack. You know...like what I do for Arlis," Shay informed him. "Marcia trains young female pups how to fight. Her older sister Valley cooks for the elders, to keep them fed. Most of them don't want to learn how to use modern appliances. Sylvia helps with that as well, and teaches them how to use computers and whatnot. River, Rod, and Reed keep all the sensors and cameras up and working in our territory. They're also great with computers."

Trayis grinned. "River, Rod and Reed?"

"See?" Sylvia lightly punched her mate.

Dean chuckled. "I love to fish at the river. And I got to name the boys."

Sylvia rolled her eyes. "My mate does roof maintenance and he's a plumber. Anyone who has a water issue calls him. That is, when he's not catching fish. He gives a lot of them to the pack to make sure everyone has plenty to eat."

"Taskers are important to a pack." Marcia sighed. "At least that's what I was told when I got turned down to be an enforcer." She grabbed her breasts. "Having tits sucks. There are no female enforcers in our pack."

"I see." Trayis looked amused.

"Are there any female enforcers where you're from?" Marcia peered at Trayis with interest.

"I can honestly say none have asked to be one in my clan."

"Hmm."

"Drop it, Marcia," Dean ordered. "I wouldn't allow it anyway. I hate when you get into fights." He gave Shay a pointed look. "Usually over *you*." His tone softened though. "But I'm very proud of that. I know I've wanted to kick some ass a time or two for the same reason Marcia was always getting into fights."

"Me two," Sylvia said.

"Me three," Trayis growled.

All of them stared at him with surprise. He opened his mouth to continue but a slight noise down the hall had them all turning. Ellis approached them. His eyes were a little red and puffy, as if he'd shed some tears of his own. He kept his focus on Shay.

"May I speak with you?"

"Yes." She stepped closer to him.

"I'm sorry for how I treated you when we met. I thought...I thought you were lying to me."

"It's okay." She wanted to hug him but his body remained stiff, as if he wouldn't welcome touch from her. "It's not your fault. None of this is."

"I have a lot to think about. But I'm going to confront my parents when I go home."

Shay hesitated. "Maybe that's not the best idea. They could shun you."

Anger glinted in his eyes. "Maybe I'll shun *them*."

Dean changed the subject, fast. "Do you know what you need? A snack. Let's go have one. We always think better with food in our stomachs. Then we'll talk."

Ellis nodded and allowed Dean to lead him back toward the kitchen.

Shay went to follow but Sylvia blocked her way, shaking her head. "Let Dean calm him. He'll assure him again that he's got a home here if he's shunned. We won't allow him to become rogue."

"Maybe Kale and I could go over to their territory, track down Elvis and Mildred, and beat the fuck out of them," Marcia growled low.

Sylvia chuckled, shaking her head. "No. It's not our way."

183

"It's the way I *want* to be." Marcia sighed again. "But it wouldn't help in the long run. I know. I still want to kick their asses. I have for as long as I can remember." She jerked her head toward Shay. "For fucking with my sister."

"I'd like to meet them, too," Trayis said.

Shay glanced at him over her shoulder, liking the suddenly rough sound of his voice. "You're doing the black thing with your eyes again."

"That's cool but freaky." Marcia chuckled. "Kind of sexy, too."

"What is?"

The deep voice startled Shay, and she realized that Kale had opened the front door and entered without knocking. He must have just gotten off work.

Marcia rushed to her new mate. "He's here! Mom, you know Kale."

Shay clutched Trayis, holding her breath, waiting to see how Sylvia would react.

Her adopted mother simply smiled warmly and embraced the couple in a hug. "Welcome to our family."

Shay relaxed, breathing again.

"Let's get back to our date," Trayis said quietly. "Dinner should be waiting. I almost forget that I ordered something to be delivered." He pulled Shay closer and addressed her family. "Call us if we need to come back. We will."

"Shay never takes her cell anywhere." Marcia waved her hand over Shay's dress. "Unless she's got it stashed in her bra or undies."

Trayis gave her family his cell number then led her outside. Shay glanced back as the door closed.

Trayis immediately scooped her into his arms. "They're fine. The boy needs time. Dean seems like a good influence, he'll talk to him until he calms." He quieted briefly as he carried her down the porch steps. "I like your family, Shay."

"I think they like you, too. Maybe we should stay for a bit."

"The boy needs man time with Dean. I barely remember being that age, but I know it was difficult to control my emotions. It would be bad if he went home in a rage to deal with his asshole parents."

That reminded her of something. "How old are you, anyway?"

He chuckled, taking her into the woods toward the trailer. "It doesn't matter. Vampire blood seems to halt our aging process once we hit adulthood, and then it's very slow."

She cuddled into him, wrapping her arms around his neck. It was kind of nice being carried around by him. "So you're really old and don't want to tell me."

He chuckled. "Exactly."

"Keep your secrets, then."

"I do have some." His tone grew serious.

She considered that. "Will any of them hurt me?"

"I don't think so. That's the last thing I want, Shay."

She believed him. "Okay. Good enough."

"You still look incredibly sexy. I can't wait to get you alone."

She grinned. "Walk faster."

He laughed, picking up the pace.

Chapter Eleven

Trayis was glad he'd asked a favor from Ginny. His brother's mate had pulled through for him. The table had been set with nice dishes and covered food waited as they entered the trailer.

Shay grinned up at him. "That smells so good."

"It does. I had Ginny call the caterer she'd used for the party and order us something special." He opened the fridge, spotting the bottle of wine waiting. Two glasses were chilling on the shelf next to it. He pulled them out and turned.

Shay looked surprised.

"I might come from Alaska but I'm not a complete barbarian."

That drew another smile from her. "This is romantic."

"I wanted lit candles but that's a bad idea in a trailer." He put the bottle and glasses on the table with the food. "Burning it down probably wouldn't be cool. Then there's the whole smoke issue. This place is small and cramped."

"Don't forget the forest fire risk. Too many trees," she teased. "Embers and all that."

"I have three fireplaces in my home." He waved her to take a seat as he did the same, opening the wine and pouring it into their glasses.

"That sounds nice."

"One's in the open living room, and I wanted one in my bedroom. It gets extremely cold in Alaska during the winter. The third is in another bedroom. My cabin has three bedrooms total, and three and a half baths."

"Wow. Somehow, I imagined it would be tiny like mine."

He threw back his head and laughed, imagining a VampLycan in such a small cabin.

"What's funny?"

He lifted the covers off the food, presenting it to Shay. He'd requested a few filet mignons for each of them and stuffed clams with fresh vegetables. There was also mashed potatoes with cheese and herbs mixed in. "One of my kind would end up rolling over in bed and falling out of your loft space."

"I can see that." Her gaze darted over his chest and then she held his gaze. "I doubt you'd fit on a twin-sized bed, anyway."

"I have an extra-large king-size bed. We make them ourselves."

Her mouth opened but then she closed it.

He shrugged. "I'm tall. I hate having my head against the headboard and my feet hanging off the end on standard human mattresses. Some of the clan are excellent tradesmen. I asked one of them to make me a frame and headboard. Someone else creates larger-than-normal mattresses from human ones we buy. Then we have other members who make the bedding to fit."

"You have taskers, too."

"I guess so. It's just not what we call them. They're skilled tradesmen."

She peered at him as she unfolded the cloth napkins and silverware Ginny had laid out. He knew she'd been the one to personally deliver the meals and set the table. Her scent lingered.

"I like that."

He smiled. "We work together in my clan, and we all find something to do that we enjoy. Everyone is happier that way. It's also nice to be able to create or build something in the winter months when the snow comes."

"Tell me more about your clan."

He cut a piece of steak and took a bite, carefully considering what to share. He swallowed. "We're close, like a big family, with the exception of a few troublemakers."

She nodded. "Every pack has their fair share."

"Mine has fewer of them. It's a clan leader's duty to nip that shit in the bud fast."

"What if the troublemaker won't stop?"

"There're four clans. They can go live with another one if they wish, but none of the leaders will put up with trouble for long."

"Do VampLycans ever go rogue or get banished?"

"It's rare. One clan had quite a few VampLycans leave, but Decker was in charge of them at the time. He never banished anyone, though." Decker killed them. He wasn't about to mention that to Shay. He didn't want her to fear the clans. "Most fled to other clans to escape his rule. Decker was a bad leader. He's dead now. Lorn took over. I like him."

"Have you ever thought about joining another clan?"

189

"No." Guilt surfaced. He needed to tell Shay the truth. He still worried about how she'd react. He'd learned enough about her to figure there was a chance she'd run away from him, believing she was too far beneath his station. It had been bad enough when she'd suspected he might be an enforcer.

"This is so good." She moaned around a bite of tender meat.

"It is. The company is better."

She blushed, and damned if he didn't want to kiss her. He cut another piece of filet instead and stuffed it into his mouth. He couldn't wait to take her to bed and strip off that form-hugging dress she wore.

"Have you ever thought about joining another pack?"

She stilled, fork and knife held in midair. She gazed at him a moment, and then she ducked her chin, continuing to cut her food. "No. Never."

"Shay?" He tensed slightly. He'd upset her somehow.

She looked at him. "I'm grateful for the one that I have. No other pack would take me in."

"That's beside the point. Would you ever consider leaving if you found your mate?"

She dropped her gaze, her shoulders slumping. "That won't happen."

Anger on her behalf began to seep into him. "That's bullshit," he snarled.

Her head snapped up, eyes wide. No fear showed, though. Just surprise.

"I'm asking because I need to return to Alaska soon, Shay."

She continued to stare at him, looking confused.

190

It made him even angrier at his brother's pack that his hint wasn't enough. He spelled it out for her. "Would you come with me?"

Her mouth opened and closed a few times. It was so fucking cute. All his anger drained, replaced by amusement.

"I don't expect you to agree to become my mate without knowing what you're getting into beforehand...but I thought the first step would be you coming to Alaska with me. Seeing our home. Meeting my clan. I'm hoping you'll feel secure enough to become my mate once you do."

She dropped the silverware to the table. Trayis's body tensed, and he half expected her to bolt. He was prepared to catch her before she could get out of the trailer.

Instead she slid off the bench and stood, facing him. "You want *me*?"

"I do."

Tears filled her eyes. "Really?"

Hating the bench seating at that moment, he stood with her in the narrow walkway. They touched. "I do, doll. Will you come to Alaska with me? Give my home a shot and see if you could be happy there?"

"Do you think I'm your true mate, or do VampLycans not have those?"

He cocked his head. "We do have them, but sometimes the Vampire side of us confuses the Lycan instincts. I have strong feelings for you, Shay. So strong, I'm certain you're it for me. I wouldn't ask otherwise. I don't want to lose you. How do you feel about *me*?"

Tears spilled down her cheeks. "Have you thought about kids? They could turn out like me."

"You mean adorable? I'm definitely okay with that." He gripped her hips. "Answer my question. How do you feel about me?"

"I care. A lot. Scary deep. What if I have a baby that can't shift?"

"You're half Lycan and I'm all VampLycan. Our kids will shift. Even if I'm wrong, I don't care about that. I will love them all the same because they'll be ours." He smiled. "Scary deep, huh? That sounds serious."

She clutched his shirt. "What about your alpha? Won't he be upset if you bring someone like me home?"

It was tempting to blurt out the truth but he was still too worried she'd bolt. He'd have to ease her into that reality. "We aren't prejudiced in the clan. Wen, as an example, is mated to a full human. Remember? I told you I adopted Gerri."

She nodded.

"It would have been fine if Wen had fallen in love with a Vampire, too. In my clan, the most important thing is being happy and having a strong bond with a mate. Every mate found is precious. A leader would have to be a heartless dick to refuse them the right to be together."

She just stared at him, mute.

"Are you worried about not seeing your adoptive family? We can visit more often. Even if it's just for short visits. I did that not too long ago."

She looked confused again.

"That human I adopted? Her mate is cousins with Graves and Micah. Gerri was brought to your territory for her safety, until I could pick her up to take her back to the clan to be with Wen again. Most of your pack wasn't aware, since I only spent a few hours here and then flew back to

Alaska with Gerri. We can visit more often. I can't be gone from Alaska for long stints but short trips would be doable."

"Oh, Trayis," she sniffed. "I want to say yes…but I'm afraid you'll lose respect in your clan. You have no idea how badly I want to agree, but I never want you to face consequences because you're with me."

"That's ridiculous."

"It's *not*. I care too much about you to be the cause of any pain in your life. I'm not that selfish. Your happiness matters too much to me."

"Doll." He leaned down and kissed her. They were done talking. She would just keep saying silly things. He slid his arms around her waist and lifted, walking backward toward the bedroom.

Shay moaned against his mouth, meeting his passion. She had plenty of that. His body burned with need. He bumped into the bathroom wall but kept moving until the mattress stopped him. He gently put her on her feet and spun her around, reaching for the zipper on the back of her dress. He wanted to tear it off but then she'd never be able to wear it again. That would be a crime.

"I can't think when you're touching me," she panted.

"That's the point."

"This is serious, Trayis. I'm a half-breed."

"My entire *clan* is half-breeds, Shay."

She twisted her head, giving him a wry look.

He nodded, helping her remove the dress. "Full-bloods are the rarity in my clan."

The dress fell to the floor and he got a look at the delicate garments hidden underneath. They were white and lacy. Her taut nipples teased him—and his patience was gone. "I'll buy you new ones."

He eased her back on the bed, tearing at the flimsy straps of the bra, then her tiny panties. He needed to taste her—badly. His fangs slid down and the urge to bite hit hard. It was hell to resist, but he didn't break her skin as he sucked on her breast.

Shay was his. He no longer could deny that.

She'd admitted to not being able to think when he touched her. It sounded like a great plan to keep her off balance. One way or another, he would take her home with him when he returned to Alaska. When they got there, he'd prove that she could be happy with him and his clan. Arlis was about to lose one of his pack, but Trayis would gain a mate.

He paid attention to her other breast, growing more aroused by the sounds of her moans. Her fingers slid into his hair, and he loved the feel of her fingernails raking his scalp. He lowered down her body, placing wet kisses over her stomach. He couldn't get enough of her taste.

Shay tugged on his hair. "I need you inside me now!"

He chuckled. "But I want to play."

She yanked on his hair harder. "Please?"

He rose up her body and kissed her mouth. She wrapped her legs around his waist, rubbing her pussy against his stiff dick. He groaned, not wanting to reach for a condom, but getting her pregnant before she agreed to mating would be unforgivable.

He tore his mouth from hers, glanced around frantically for the box, and lunged to the side, where he'd placed them on the nightstand. Shay released his hair and splayed her hands on his chest, using her fingers to tease his nipples.

He managed to get the condom rolled over his stiff shaft, and then he slowly entered her tight body. Shay moaned his name and he pinned her tight under him. His woman felt like heaven.

The urge to bite struck again, but still he resisted. It was getting more and more difficult. Once they were sharing blood, he wouldn't have to worry about taking too much from her.

"Trayis. Yes!"

He fucked her hard and fast, making certain to rub against her clit with every thrust. Her moans urged him on.

She was his, and he wouldn't let her go. It was a done deal.

* * * * *

Shay woke alone but she heard Trayis softly speaking to someone. She sat up in bed, staring down the hallway. He'd left the bedroom door open. He paced at the far end of the trailer with his cell phone pressed to his ear.

He looked tense and angry, despite keeping his voice low. She slid out from under the sheets and stood, walking toward him. Had he informed his alpha of his choice to bring her home? She still worried that it would cause him problems.

"You need to be harsh with her punishment, Wen. She's testing your authority." He paused, closing his eyes. His other hand rose to rub the

195

bridge of his nose as he paused to listen. "I get that you can't fight her. If Mya were a male, you'd kick her ass for sneaking out and causing more trouble. Put her in a holding cell. That's what I'd do."

Shay paused in the hallway just outside the bathroom door.

"Take away everything but her clothes and treat her like a child, since she's acting like one. Put a female guard on her. I'd pick Vassa. She'll be furious with Mya for fucking her brother and causing him to fight his best friend. That should make things miserable for Mya. She needs to learn to follow your orders."

It became clear to Shay that Trayis was giving his alpha advice.

Her knees nearly buckled under her. That duty and privilege fell to a head enforcer.

Trayis was also using his alpha's first name instead of title. They had to be very close, like Arlis and Martin. Her alpha and his head enforcer were best friends.

Her stomach rolled. She'd suspected Trayis might be an enforcer, but he was second in charge of his clan.

"I understand, Wen. I'll head back tomorrow." He listened again before speaking. "Have Tymber send me the flight information he books for Shay and I. We can leave in the afternoon. Just tell him not to stick us with some crazy bush pilot like the last time. I don't want Shay to become afraid at any point on our trip." He paused again to hear whatever Wen said, and then he laughed. "Thanks. See you soon."

Trayis ended the call and closed his eyes, tilting his head back and taking some deep breaths.

"You were giving him advice."

His eyes flew open and he turned his head, meeting her gaze. "Shit. Did my phone call wake you?"

"You're head enforcer," she blurted. "We can't do this. I *won't* do this to you." She spun, rushing back into the bedroom to get dressed.

"Goddamn it," Trayis snarled.

She heard him coming as she bent to pick up her discarded dress. His arm snaked around her waist and he lifted her off her feet. Then he had her pinned under him on the bed. She stared into his eyes, panting.

"Shay, stop."

"You were giving your alpha advice!" Panic filled her. "I'm so far beneath you it's not funny!"

Trayis pinned her tighter, holding her wrists, and he arched one of his eyebrows. "You are beneath me only because I'm on top of you. Watch this." He rolled, taking her with him, until she lay sprawled over his body. "Now I'm beneath *you*." A sexy smile curved his lips and amusement sparked in his eyes.

Shay's frustration peaked. "You're making jokes? There's nothing funny about this!"

He released her wrists and cupped her ass, giving it a squeeze. "I already told you. VampLycans aren't like packs, Shay. You have to stop thinking the way you do. *No one* will challenge you over being with me. You're under no obligation to prove a damn thing. Besides, it wouldn't matter if you were the toughest Lycan bitch in this pack. It wouldn't make a difference to me."

197

She stopped struggling, waiting for him to explain.

"You've seen me shifted. Our women can do the same, of course. But my entire clan is aware a Lycan in a fight with a VampLycan wouldn't be fair. We've got too many advantages. Nor do women challenge each other over men in my clan, like in some Lycan packs. But even in *your* pack—correct me if I'm wrong—the male can halt it from happening. I know Arlis would forbid anyone from challenging Ginny. Am I wrong?"

"No."

He sighed. "That call? It was about a female troublemaker in our clan who likes to fuck different men just to get them fighting against each other. That's the only problem we currently face. A bored narcissist who loves to pit males against each other by using sex to pump up her ego. Her name is Mya, and she finds that bullshit entertaining. So do a few of her friends. They're like those rude bitches who approached us at the picnic. They have nothing better to do with their time than start shit. All we can do is hope they find mates to end their games or keep punishing them until they learn to stop."

She bit her lip, and then braced her hands on his chest, straddling his waist as she sat up. "Have you ever been with this Mya?"

He grimaced. "No. Before you ask, I haven't touched her friends, either. I made a mistake once by getting sexually involved with a woman from my clan. She wanted us to become mates but I didn't feel that way about her. It was just convenient sex for me. She took it too far when she began acting as if she had the right to issue orders to other clan members. I set her straight and ended it immediately." He stroked her skin. "I'm not

198

saying this to make you feel jealousy. Just a history lesson. She wasn't in love with me either. It was about my status."

Shay hated that he knew she'd feel the green-eyed monster, hearing about him with someone else. "You said VampLycans aren't like Werewolves, but you just admitted she wanted to be your mate without love. She was willing to settle. It was your position she was after and the respect that would go with it."

He smiled. "I think that's a woman thing, regardless of what species they are. Some women are more into power than love."

"So are men."

"True. Point being, it was a mistake I made and learned from. I stopped seeing her and she left to go live with another clan once she realized I wouldn't change my mind. You won't have to deal with any of my past lovers, Shay. If anyone says otherwise, know it's a lie. Mya tried to pull that shit with Wen and Gerri. She implied Wen used to be her lover. Not true. She just wanted to hurt his mate."

"Because Gerri's human?"

Trayis snorted. "No. It pissed Mya off when Wen wouldn't allow her into his bed. She said that shit to his mate to get back at him, probably hoping Gerri would leave him. Mya can be vindictive, and she holds a grudge. And we've got more available men than women in our clan. Mya fully takes advantage of that. It's why mates are so damn important, regardless of their race. Our men shouldn't have to deal with a few cruel women who're willing to use sex to play with their emotions in some fucked-up head game."

Shay thought about the Bitch Trio. They'd happily lie to cause mates to fight if they held a grudge against someone. It was something petty and cruel they'd do just out of spite. "How did your alpha react when you told him about me?" She carefully studied his eyes to gauge his sincerity. "Be honest—and tell me his exact words."

Trayis held her gaze, and then he rolled once again, pinning her back under him. He adjusted his body until he could use his elbows to keep his weight from crushing her, and he cupped her head in his large hands. He leaned in until only inches separated their faces.

"Remain calm. I'm *not* allowing you to run from me."

Dread pitted in her stomach. His alpha was upset. She knew it. She lifted her hands, placing them on his shoulders, just wanting to touch his warm skin. "He's disappointed?"

"No. Wen isn't the leader of my clan, doll." He took a deep breath, locking gazes with her. "I am."

Those two words...

They *devastated* her.

She kept repeating what them over and over in her mind. *I am.*

Trayis frowned, watching her closely with narrowed eyes. "Breathe, doll. In and out."

She realized she must have been holding her breath at that point and sucked air into her starving lungs. Then her heart began to pound—and pure panic set in.

"Don't," Trayis rasped. "I'm not letting you bolt. You're *mine*. My position doesn't matter. This is why I didn't want to tell you, Shay. I knew you'd overreact. There's no reason to. Clans aren't the same as Lycan packs."

Shay's mind worked past the shock and she began to think clearer. "This can't work, Trayis."

"Bullshit."

She gave him a look of pure disbelief.

"Don't look at me like that." He arched one eyebrow. "I mean it, Shay. This can and *will* work between us."

"You're the alpha of your clan and I'm the lowest member of my pack!"

"Get the hell over it." He looked angry for a split second but then his features calmed. "You're the *only* one who gives a damn about that. No one else will. My clan will be happy that I've found my mate. Hell, Wen is having someone clean my cabin and stock it with food just for you. I tended to almost live at the office, so I ate there all the time. Not anymore. We'll make our cabin a home together. You're going to be great for me, Shay. I can't wait to take you to Alaska. We'll be happy together."

She wasn't sure how to convince him how wrong he was.

Trayis gently eased his hold on her and adjusted his body but he kept her pinned beneath him. "It's going to work out fine, Shay. I'm taking you home. Once we get there, you'll understand better. My brother's pack has done a number on your head with that low-status bullshit. It infuriates me. They've put you down so much that you can't see your own worth. Well, *I* do, doll. You're incredible, compassionate, sweet as hell, and I refuse to let you go."

Tears welled in her eyes. She was falling in love with Trayis, probably was already there, and the last thing she wanted was to give him up. But it just couldn't work out for them in the long run. They were too different.

He stabbed his fingers into her hair, trapping her head between his hands, and leaned in closer. "It'll be fine, Shay. Can you trust me?"

"I want to." That was the truth.

"Then have some faith in me. All your worries are for nothing."

"What about the other clans? Even if your people are loyal enough to forgive you for choosing me, will it cause a territory war?"

He scowled. "You mean like that dickhead Frank thinking less of my brother for mating to Ginny and trying to start shit? No. Since Decker was killed, the clans have completely united. We're not into warring for land. I keep telling you, doll, we aren't like the packs. Hell, for the first time in what feels like forever, we're even completely at peace with the GarLycans."

"You were at war with them?" That news surprised her.

"Not at war. We just had some tensions, but those have all been put to rest. Lord Aveoth is the GarLycan leader. He's a good, honorable man. You'll get to meet him and his mate, Jillian. They visit sometimes. She's mostly human, with some VampLycan blood." He played with her hair. "She can't shift either, from what I've been told, and she grew up believing she was completely human. She had to go through the crash course of finding out humans weren't the only people on this planet. No one gives a damn, Shay." He suddenly grinned. "It's going to be fine. Will you trust me?"

She desperately wanted to. "I can try."

202

He brushed a kiss over her lips. "Don't run from me, doll. I won't let you. And we need to leave tomorrow. Wen is fed up with filling in for me, thanks to Mya. In the morning, I want you to pack your bags. You're going to love Alaska...and my clan is going to love *you*. Will you come with me?"

She stared into his eyes and found herself nodding. "I want to be with you."

He looked immensely happy. "Now, stop thinking for a while and allow me make love to you again." He took possession of her lips.

Chapter Twelve

Shay zipped up her last bag. She was really going to leave her home, go with Trayis to Alaska, and begin a new life with him.

Tears flooded her eyes. It was almost too good to be true that he wanted her as his mate. The only downside was leaving everything familiar to her.

"Don't you dare. You start bawling and I'll do it, too," Marcia warned. "I'm so fucking happy for you but at the same time, Alaska seems so far away."

"Trayis said you and Kale are welcome to visit anytime you want. I'll be coming back to see you and the family. And we'll talk on the phone."

"You mean when you're home and you actually hear your cell phone ring?" Marcia smirked. "Maybe your mate will force you to start carrying it on you at all the times. That would be something new."

"Shit." Shay rushed over to the counter and unplugged the charger from the wall and grabbed her cell. She unzipped the bag and shoved them both inside.

Marcia laughed. "Even with a mate, you haven't changed."

"We're not mated yet."

That had her friend's eyes narrowing. "Why is that?"

"Trayis wants me to be certain before we seal the bond. He said once we get to Alaska and I meet his clan, all my reservations should be gone. I'm still really worried his clan will reject me and maybe give him trouble for choosing me. He says they won't, though."

The suspicious look left Marcia's features and she smiled. "That's sweet. And I can't believe he's a clan leader!" She stood from the couch and grinned. "You have a few hours before Trayis picks you up. Do you know what we should do, now that you're packed?"

"Go spend more time with your parents and Rod?"

"We did that thing this morning, after you called to tell me Trayis is whisking you off to Alaska to be his mate." Marcia got a glint in her eye. "Let's go find the Bitch Trio and announce the news in person. Imagine their faces!" Pure glee sounded in her voice. "After all the years of shit they gave you, it's going to be epic! Trayis, the super-hot VampLycan—who it turns out is also a clan leader—picked *you* to become his mate. Those bitches will be green this time instead of blue. No dye in their hot tub required!"

Shay smiled but shook her head. "I'm not that petty."

"*I* am. You know I'm going to rub that shit in their overdone faces every chance I get. I'll take videos and stuff to send you." She paused before admitting, "They showed up at our cabin last night to talk to Kale."

Shay's mouth dropped open. "What? Why?"

Marcia's hands fisted. "To cause shit. He answered the door, since I was unpacking my stuff at the time, after he helped me move into his place. Barbie was going on about how she just knew he'd never mate someone as 'manly' as I am, and they'd come to see if he was okay, after hearing such vicious and cruel rumors about him. I tried to get around him to rip off her lips, but he held me back. Then Lucinda said something about him protecting them from me, and how that proved they meant

205

more to him than I did. *Then* the cunt totally went there and flat-out stated she'd bedded him before."

"They really are horrible."

"I know. Kale pretended like he couldn't remember ever doing her, and he told them he just didn't want to waste his night cleaning up their body parts or burning bloody trash. Then he snarled and told them to never insult his mate again, or he'd let me rip them to shreds. They fled pretty quickly after that. I love him so much."

Shay walked over to her and gave her a hug. "I'm happy for you."

Marcia squeezed her back. "I'm happy for *you*, too. Just sad that you're leaving. Who knew our little pact to go after the men we wanted at that party would end this way? We got *them*, but we're losing each other."

"We're not losing each other. You know how much I love you. Distance isn't going to change that."

They broke apart when Marcia's phone beeped. She checked her cell. "I have to go. My class isn't behaving for Valley. They want to use her as a punching bag. I totally understand that. She's annoying as shit at times, but big sis has honored the favor she owed me by babysitting my students. Stop by to say goodbye before you leave! We're practicing at the creek meadow today."

Shay nodded. "I will."

"So, want to take bets on who gets pregnant first?" She suddenly grinned. "Never mind. It's going to be you." Her gaze dropped to Shay's stomach. "Any chance of that already being a possibility?"

Shay shook her head. "We've been using condoms."

"You won't when Trayis officially claims you. I guess we'll find out if the assholes were right and you get knocked up right off the bat." Marcia grinned. "I better be the second person you tell right after your mate."

"You got it," Shay promised. Tears filled her eyes.

Marcia grabbed her and yanked her close again in a hug. "I'm going to miss you—but this is amazing. You worried you'd never find a mate or have kids. Trayis looks virile as hell. He'll probably give you a bunch of kids, since you can't control your ovaries. I'm thinking at least two dozen."

Shay laughed and lightly punched her as she broke away. "Not funny."

Marcia chuckled. "Very funny, actually. I've got to go. Valley is way better at handling cranky elders than troublesome little girls. They're all future hellions. I'm going to make sure this pack gets a female enforcer one day. It's my mission in life. Don't forget to stop by to say goodbye!"

"I won't."

Shay watched her best friend leave before she turned, climbing up into the loft to make sure she didn't forget anything. The good thing about having such a small home was not owning many possessions. She'd packed two duffle bags full of her things. Trayis had told her that would be fine.

She'd already visited her family earlier that morning to break the news that she was leaving with Trayis, and that he'd asked her to be his mate. Her foster parents had been overjoyed at the news but sad to see her go. Ellis, her uncle, had returned to his home, but Sylvia and Dean had promised to take him in if it didn't go well with his parents. Trayis had assured her that Arlis would accept him into the pack without a qualm.

Guilt hit her over leaving when Ellis's future was up in the air, but they could return if needed. Trayis had even offered to accept her uncle into his clan. Either way, the kid would be looked after.

Trayis continually amazed her with his generosity. It made her feel certain in her choice to leave with him.

She smiled, putting fresh sheets on the bed in case someone else wanted to move into her place once she was gone. The clock on the tiny nightstand read just after eleven o'clock. Trayis would return at noon to pick up her and her bags. They would visit his brother and then drive to the airport.

She felt nervous about flying on a plane for the first time, but Trayis would be with her every step of the way. He said they'd have to take a few flights to reach his home, and his clan had booked them first-class tickets on the trip to Anchorage. From there, it would be on a smaller plane to reach his territory. He really did live in a remote area.

She was halfway down the ladder when someone knocked on the door. She jumped the rest of the way and strode to it, yanking it open with a grin on her face, assuming Trayis must be early.

It wasn't him standing on her porch, though. It was Tegan.

The sight of him came as a shock. His hair wasn't brushed, his clothes were dirty, and his eyes were bloodshot. Part of his face was swollen and bruised. It was clear he'd taken a beating. One arm was bandaged in a few places, probably from broken bones. Both of his hands were wrapped, too, some of his fingers held immobile by the bandages.

He moved before she could react and struck her with his uninjured forearm.

Pain exploded in the side of her cheek. The force of the blow sent her flying backward, and she hit something—probably the coffee table—and landed on the hardwood floor.

He crouched next to her as she stared back, stunned. "Kale is getting the enforcer position. They sent me to the outer border patrol because of *you*!" He snarled the words. "Now it's my turn to get even."

Shay tried to roll way, her face throbbing and her head hurting.

He hit her again. The blow landed on the back of her head, making her forehead strike the hardwood floor, and she nearly passed out. Her limbs didn't want to work as she was lifted, thrown over his shoulder, and then they were moving. She heard him slam her front door then he leapt off her porch, her stomach painfully colliding with his shoulder.

She finally lost consciousness when he began to run.

* * * * *

Trayis knocked on the door again. "Shay?"

She wasn't answering. It worried him. Had she freaked out by changing her mind about leaving with him? He pulled out his cell phone and dialed her sister.

Marcia answered on the second ring, sounding out of breath. "Who is this?"

"It's Trayis. Is Shay with you?"

"No. She's at the cabin."

209

"She's not answering her door. I'm here now."

"Maybe she's taking a shower." Marcia lowered her voice. "I know the door code. Just punch in the numbers. You're her mate now, I'm sure she wouldn't mind." She told him the digits he needed.

He punched them in, the lock clicked, and he entered the cabin—then froze. "Shit!"

"What? Don't tell me she got that human cold feet thing? Just ignore her and tell her to shut it."

Trayis crouched, staring at the broken coffee table and a few drops of blood. He pressed his finger to one of them and lifted it to his nose. Then he tasted it. "The coffee table is broken and Shay's blood is on the floor. She's not here." He knew that without having to check the loft. He inhaled. "I smell a male. It's faint, but not a scent I know."

"I'm on my way!" Marcia disconnected.

He called Arlis.

"Hey, brother. Are you on your way to say goodbye? We're at the house."

"I need you and your enforcers at Shay's cabin *now*."

"What's wrong?" Arlis's voice deepened, going tense.

"She's gone. The coffee table is smashed like someone landed on it. Her blood is on the floor. There's an unknown male scent lingering and Shay is missing. I think someone took her." He rose quickly and closed the door, hoping to trap the male's scent inside before the fresh air could destroy it.

"We're on our way."

Trayis searched the cabin quickly. Her packed bags were near the door with her purse, but no Shay. Then he waited by the door, time seeming to pass very slowly.

Who would take Shay? It wasn't her family. He'd met Rod that morning, and had spent time with Dean and Sylvia. The remaining foster siblings had no reason to hurt her.

He heard voices and waited until he identified his brother's from the porch before opening the door. "Get inside and sniff. You know everyone in your pack. We need to find out if this was one of yours or if her grandparents sent an outsider after Shay."

Martin and Arlis entered. He caught a glimpse of Marcia running out of the woods but closed the door before she reached them. He held his breath, watching as his brother and his head enforcer took in the broken table, the blood drops, and both sniffed around.

Martin snarled and glared at Arlis. "Tegan. He smells of dirt, but under that, I know the bastard's smell."

Arlis grimly nodded. "Agreed."

"The one who attacked her before?" Rage filled Trayis. "Where is he?"

The door lock clicked and Marcia rushed inside. "What's going on?" She saw the damaged table and rushed forward, crouched and sniffed. "Shay's blood. Fuck—is that Tegan's scent?" She stood fast. "I'm going to fucking rip his balls off and make him choke on them! That bastard hurt her. Where is she?"

"Calm," Arlis ordered.

Trayis wanted to roar in fury. A pack male had hurt Shay, and now she was missing.

Arlis pulled out his cell and made a call. "Alert all sentries and every member of our pack to be on the lookout for Tegan. It seems he's taken Shay." He paused. "Yes, Darlene. I'm serious. Shay's missing, there's blood in her cabin, and Tegan's scent is here. Wide alert to every phone *right now* except his. I want him found!" He disconnected and faced Trayis. "I assigned him to outer patrol duty. He isn't supposed to be here. Hell, he should be too hurt still to do something like this."

"He'll know the schedules and patrol routes of the sentries." Martin looked equally pissed. "He would know how to sneak to the cabin and snatch Shay without being caught. Fuck! I knew we should have killed him."

"Why would he go after Shay?" Trayis would kill Tegan. It was a done deal. He just needed to find the bastard first. "Where would he take her?"

Arlis shook his head. "I don't know."

"He's an immature asshole who never could take responsibility for his own fuckups," Martin snarled. "He probably blames Shay for his punishment."

"Enough," Arlis growled. "We'll find them. He'll have known to avoid the sentries, since he's familiar with their routes, but a tasker might have seen him."

"What kind of tasker?"

"We have people who clean up trash, collect food, and check traps we've set up to catch game." Arlis paused. "He'll avoid the cameras, since he knows all their locations."

His brother's phone rang, and he answered it. "What?"

Trayis stepped closer, picking up a female's voice. She spoke too low for him to hear her words.

Arlis hung up. "Tegan was seen less than an hour ago near the river by our north border. A trash gatherer called when the alert came in. Brad said he saw him there yesterday, too." Arlis looked at Martin.

"That's up where he's assigned. It's remote, few of our pack venture there, and it would be a good place to hide a female."

Or to kill one—taking his time, without worry about interruption.

Trayis shoved that thought out of his head. He turned, yanked open the door, and saw that a dozen members of his brother's pack waited outside. A few of them were Arlis's enforcers.

Arlis stopped next to him and tore off his shirt, also kicking off his shoes. "It will be quicker to shift and run. I'm not as fast as you but I know the way. Let me lead. We'll find Shay, and then Tegan is all yours."

"I'm killing him for harming Shay." Trayis would go insane if anything happened to her. She was *his*.

He never should have left her alone to pack her bags. He knew some of her pack were assholes to her. He'd just never suspected one of them would physically harm her in any way.

Everyone stripped. They shifted and Arlis took the lead. It was tough on Trayis not to dart ahead. He could move faster than any Lycan, but his brother knew his territory better.

Chapter Thirteen

Shay woke in an unfamiliar room. It stank of mildew, dirt, and rotted wood. Her back was against a coarse wall, her hands painfully bound near her butt. She lifted her head and saw light filtering through some cracks in the wood planks. It took her a moment to realize she seemed to be in an old shack.

The floor under her had suffered water damage. It was a small space, maybe eight feet square from wall to wall. There was a half door, more like a wooden hatch, across from her. No furniture or anything else in the room. It was possible it was a storage shed instead of a shack.

Her head hurt, near her temple. She couldn't see or feel what was wrong but her memories returned fast. She'd been attacked. That's why her head hurt.

Tegan had done it.

But Tegan wasn't with her now. She lifted her chin and stared at the ceiling. There was more water damage in the wooden slats. In the corner, some of them had fallen in, revealing a hint of rusted metal above, which would be the roof.

"Shed," she whispered.

A sturdy breeze hit the wall she leaned against and her eyes grew wide when the entire shed moved in a subtle swaying motion. The wind died down and the shed stilled.

"What in the hell?"

She tried to wiggle away from the wall but the rope binding her hands grew taut. She twisted, adjusted her ass on the damaged floor, and was able to see behind her. There was a tiny hole in the wall. The rope attached to her ran out that hole. She gave it a hard tug but the rope held. It seemed she'd been tethered to something outside.

"Tegan?" She stared at the hatch. "Hello?"

He didn't respond.

The wind began to blow again, hitting the wall behind her, and the entire structure swayed once more. Shay closed her eyes, focusing on the movement. Had the bastard somehow hoisted the shed off the ground? It would account for how the wind could make it move so much, including the floor beneath her.

Shay opened her eyes, studying the ceiling again, then the walls. The entire place looked as if it was about to fall apart any second.

She used her fingers to brush against the wall behind her. "Ouch!" She rubbed her thumb over the slight injury and felt a splinter. "Shit..."

The other walls seemed to be literally falling apart. Water and time had done damage to the structure. She hoped the one behind her was just as weak. Shay adjusted her body to bend her legs up and to the side, to get her feet closer to the wall behind her. Fortunately, Tegan hadn't removed her shoes. After scooting around on her butt, she managed to bend and twist enough to get her shoes against the wall.

She pushed, but the wall only creaked. It was tough with her legs bent and twisted to the side the way they were, but she managed to kick the wall a few times. The brittle wood cracked. On the third kick, a chunk of the wall completely broke. She pulled her feet back and wiggled around again to peer out of that small hole where light poured in.

And saw the tops of trees.

Her mouth fell open, stunned. It had to be a mistake. She adjusted again, rolling onto her side as far as the rope would allow, and inched closer to see out of the hole she'd made. Fresh air blew in when the wind began to stir and the shed swayed again.

What she saw filled her with absolute terror. She was somehow suspended high up in the air, overlooking the woods below. It wasn't a trick of her imagination. The hole also revealed more than treetops as she twisted her head at an uncomfortable angle to get a better view.

The river was directly below, twisting for miles. And she hung hundreds of feet above it.

"*How*? Where in the hell am I? How did he get a shed up here?"

She faced forward, her neck beginning to ache from having it twisted to the side to see out, and rested her cheek on the rough wooden floor. The wind blew again, the small building swaying, and fresh terror filled her. She needed to think and figure out how to escape.

Little time passed before she heard an odd sound. She struggled to sit up, using the rope to help her since she couldn't use her hands to balance well, and the weird half door creaked open.

She stared at Tegan, taking in his bruised face. He didn't enter but instead just glared at her. She could only see his head, shoulders, and the arm he used to hold the door open.

"You're awake." His gaze shifted from her face to the small hole she'd made. "I wouldn't mess with those walls, you stupid bitch. I won't have to be the one to kill you if you do it yourself."

"Why did you attack me, Tegan? Where am I?"

Anger contorted his features. "I got *demoted* because of you."

She gawked at him but recovered quickly from the shock. "You got demoted because you took drugs."

"Because you, Marcia, and that fucking Kale were plotting against me until I needed something to calm me down! I should be an enforcer. Not *that* asshole. Then our cold-hearted fucking alpha sent me out here after doing *this*." He released the door and held up a bandaged hand. Some blood soaked it now. It hadn't been that way before. "Arlis broke my fingers because of *you*. They were healing until I had to tie you up. Now they're hurt all over again."

"Tegan...where am I?"

"Doesn't matter. There's nothing for miles. All the old lookouts for hunting parties are in this fucking condition. I have to shift and sleep in fur to stay warm, but I've got broken fucking bones. That means rewrapping my arms and hands to hold the bones in place *each time I shift*. Would you like to do that, Shay? Me either. How 'bout if the weather turns? Would *you* like to sleep in here? Knowing it could fall out of this tree at any time?"

She pulled together the information in her head. "This is an old pack treehouse?"

He snorted. "More like a deathtrap. This one just hasn't crumbled apart yet. Some of the others have."

She felt sick to her stomach. They were old lookout spots. The pack used to post sentries in locations where they could see for miles to give their people plenty of warning when large groups of human hunters went after wolves. It had been a huge problem about forty years before.

"Tegan, please just let me go. I wasn't plotting with Marcia and Kale against you. I didn't even know they were together until you told me. I swear."

"Bullshit!"

She tried to remain calm but he was quickly angering her with his stupid paranoia. "You give me a lot of credit, but the truth is, I'm the lowest member in our pack. No one gives a shit about what I think, and they sure wouldn't listen if I came up with some plan to hurt you. But I *didn't*. The fact that you stole drugs got you into this mess more than anything else. Then you attacked me in the office."

"I picked up wifi when I snuck into our territory to grab you, and got my text messages." He glared at her. "Do you want to know what people were telling me?"

She had a bad feeling she could guess. "What?"

"The alpha's freak of a half-brother is fucking you. I bet he'll be pissed if what our alpha did to me gets you killed."

He really was stupid. "You think Trayis will blame *Arlis* for you taking me because you were punished? Are you still on drugs? That doesn't even make sense, Tegan."

He snarled, looking enraged. "I deserved to become an enforcer!"

"Sure you do," she placated. "This isn't the way to get it, though. I'm sure another spot will open. Just let me go and I'll never tell anyone about this. It will stay between us. You don't want to ruin your chances."

He turned his head, staring off at something. Then he glared at her again. "Nineteen years."

Now he was making even less sense. "What does that mean?"

"That's the last time a spot opened. Nineteen fucking years ago. I'm not waiting two fucking decades for another chance to become an enforcer. A new alpha will mean new enforcers he trusts being assigned."

She couldn't wrap her head around his thinking. He had to be certifiably insane. "Trayis *isn't* going to kill Arlis over me."

"He will. Greif is a terrible thing. I've seen it. The freak will blame everyone he holds accountable when you die."

She was done trying to be reasonable. He was beyond that. She went for fear instead. "That would be *you*, Tegan. Trayis will kill *you*. You'll never become an enforcer. The only future you'll have will include your body being torched once he's done tearing you apart. Let me go if you want to live. I'll ask for your life to be spared. You need help. You're not well."

He snarled, rage twisting his features into a hideous mask, and fur sprouted over his cheeks.

"Trayis asked me to become his mate. Did the gossips tell you *that* in those texts? I'm supposed to leave with him today. He should have come to get me by now, and he'll realize I've been taken. He'll be looking for me. You have one pissed-off VampLycan hunting me right now, Tegan. Let me go, or you'll literally have no future. You kill me and you're dead."

"Lies!" he roared.

"I'm not lying."

He turned his head again. She had no idea what he kept looking at. Then he smiled, the insanity showing in his eyes as he met her gaze once more. "If that's true, I could make Trayis kill Arlis in exchange for your life."

He was totally insane if he thought that would happen. The only one Trayis would kill would be Tegan. She didn't point that out to him. It seemed anything she said, he twisted it into something crazy.

"I'm checking my texts again to see if you're telling the truth. If *you're* being mated, someone will have told me. I'll be back soon. And I'd advise you not to move around. This thing is barely holding together. You won't survive the fall if it goes—and I want it to be *my* choice if you live or die."

He slammed the small hatch closed and small wood chips flew inward from the force. She heard soft wood creaking and Tegan muttering words she couldn't understand, but all sound faded as he climbed lower on what must be a ladder somewhere outside.

Shay struggled with the rope but, unlike the structure around her, it wasn't weakened by age or water damage. Once again, not being able to shift had left her in a bad situation. Stupid thumbs prevented her from being able to wiggle out of the rope holding her wrists.

She stilled, thinking about that carefully.

Then she took some deep breaths, pulled her hand back as far as she could, and slammed it against the wall behind her.

It hurt, but the wood broke instead of her thumb. Pieces of the plank splintered and imbedded into her skin. "Shit! Ouch!"

She used her uninjured hand to feel around and found a large sliver of wood, and she tried to saw at the rope. The wood crumbled, too weakened from water damage, but that didn't mean she was giving up. Tears of frustration filled her eyes but she blinked them back.

Trayis would be looking for her but she was too high to find by smell. Even if she screamed, she doubted anyone would hear her this far out. It was up to Shay to save her own butt.

* * * * *

Trayis hated the slower pace of the pack as he followed Arlis and a few of his enforcers. Sentries had also joined them. Their numbers grew to over twenty. He kept sniffing, hoping to pick up any trace of Shay's scent on the wind. It hadn't happened so far.

They reached the river and everyone began to shift. Trayis did too, standing quickly. His gaze went to Arlis.

"This is where our territory ends. Tegan was assigned to guard this area." His brother looked at his pack. "Spread out and find him. Keep him alive. We need to make him tell us where he's taken Shay."

Frustration welled in Trayis. "What's around here? Any caves or somewhere he could stash her to hide her scent?"

Arlis walked toward him. "A few. The sentries know them and will search those first. We've all done patrol time here."

Trayis turned, staring at the river. "What if he killed her, Arlis?"

221

His brother put a hand on his shoulder. "He wouldn't dare."

"You didn't think he'd be stupid enough to grab her, either, did you?"

Arlis flinched and released him. "I should have locked him up instead of sending him out here. I'm sorry. I honestly didn't think he'd do something like this. He's always been a bit of a hothead but his temper cools fast. Maybe he'll bring her back."

Trayis turned to face him. "I'm going to kill him for hurting Shay. She was *bleeding*."

"We'll find her. Everyone is looking for them. He must be around here somewhere. It's the most remote area of our territory but more of the pack are arriving every second. We'll cover the area faster with such a large group. Shay *will* be found."

"What if he's seriously injured her?" It tore Trayis up inside, imagining Shay in pain, held captive by a crazy Lycan. There was so much the bastard could do to her. "If he raped her..." He snarled, killing mad.

"I can imagine what you're thinking. Tegan is rash but not flat-out stupid. He knows that's a death sentence."

"We need to find her fast. What else is out here? He'd know we'd try to track her, right?" He stared across the river. "Is there a way to the other side? A boat your pack keeps nearby? Maybe he'd take her into another territory."

"Doubtful. We don't keep boats this way. Damon's territory borders ours here. Tegan knows that's one alpha he doesn't want to fuck with. The last time one of ours ventured that way, Damon had a little fun with the youth who was stupid enough to trespass."

Trayis scowled.

"Damon didn't hurt him, but he returned him with an escort and...um, the kid was wearing a dress and makeup. That's Damon's idea of a joke. They don't hurt females, so rather than beat on the teenager as punishment for crossing his border without permission, they dressed him like a girl. An adult male would be another matter. Tegan knows that."

"What if Tegan sent *Shay* that way? What would Damon do to her?"

"Nothing bad. She's a woman. Hell, you know Damon. He already knows Shay can't shift. He'd hear her out then just call me to have her picked up. He'd offer up some of his trackers to help find Tegan if he knew about this. It would piss him off if anyone hurt a woman."

Trayis nodded, agreeing. He and the alpha weren't friends but the male had honor. "He hasn't called?"

"No. That's why I'm thinking Shay is still in our territory."

One of the sentries rushed out of the woods. "We got a scent lock on Tegan!"

Trayis shifted and ran toward the sentry, who turned, shifting as he ran. Arlis followed *him* that time, on all fours. More of the pack ran toward them and a howl filled the woods. The scent of male fear filled Trayis's nose. It was Tegan.

More howls rose, giving them a better location. The pack was hunting the male, and it didn't take long to figure out Tegan had become aware of it. But once Trayis had his scent, he increased his speed. He outran all the other Lycans, swiftly gaining on Tegan.

He spotted the male running toward a ridge and snarled, bursting into more speed. The male turned, spotted him in VampLycan form, and Trayis heard a whimper.

Then Tegan stopped abruptly, spun around, and pulled a gun.

Cold fury filled Trayis as he kept racing forward. Let the man put bullets in him. It would hurt but he'd still reach the bastard.

Instead, the crazy Lycan raised the muzzle of the gun to his own head, using a bandaged hand to grip the trigger. "I'll blow my brains out! Stop!"

Trayis came to a halt with just ten feet between them. He shifted, rising to his feet. "Where the hell is Shay?" he shouted.

"You'll never find her on your own! You need me."

Trayis glanced at the gun pointed at the male's head. "That won't kill you."

"It'll take days for me to heal, if I don't scramble my brains. Days Shay won't have. She'll die. You're *fucking* her, right, VampLycan?"

The other Lycans approached from the woods, and Trayis held out his hands, motioning for them to stop. They did, staying behind him. Only Arlis shifted and reached his side.

"What are you doing, Tegan? Where's Shay?" At his silence, Arlis growled, "Answer! That's a fucking order from your alpha." He threw vibes toward the male.

Tegan trembled but didn't lower the gun from his head. "*I* should have become your enforcer. Not Kale! He and that cunt Marcia plotted together so you'd pick him instead of me!"

Arlis stepped a foot closer, frowning, his tone quieter. "Tegan...are you still doing drugs?"

"What do *you* think? You broke my arm in two places, and my fucking fingers! It *hurts*. Especially since I have to keep using them."

Trayis wanted to lunge and grab the asshole, rip the gun from his fingers, and then torture the truth out of him. He couldn't risk the gun going off though. The bastard was right. A bullet to the brain would put him down for a few days and he'd be unable to answer questions until the injury healed. Even then, that kind of damage to his brain might make him forget shit. Like where he'd put Shay.

"Tegan," Arlis pushed more vibes at the male, "drop the gun and tell me what you did with Shay. You're pack. We don't harm females. Especially our weakest member. Enforcers would *protect* her. Not hurt her. You want to be an enforcer? Show me you have the instincts to be one."

Tegan shook his head and stared at Trayis. "Kill Arlis—and I'll give you Shay."

Trayis gawked at him, beyond stunned by the demand.

The crazy Lycan nodded. "She's still alive. You want her, right? Kill that unfit fucker who calls himself our alpha, and you can have Shay."

"You fucking moron," Martin muttered behind them.

"You always hated me!" Tegan screamed, lifting his other arm and motioning toward Martin. "Kill Arlis *and* all his enforcers! I'll make a better alpha." He glared at Trayis again. "You get the bitch. I get the pack. Sounds fair, right? Do it *now*. Kill them all! Show them just how brutal a VampLycan can be."

225

"Lock your knees," Trayis hissed to Arlis—then he unleashed every drop of his rage, sending vibes in every direction.

Out of the corner of his eye, he saw Arlis sway but manage to stay on his feet. The Lycans behind them hit the ground fast, going to their knees.

Trayis lunged as Tegan began to fall...

The gun went off before he reached him.

He caught the bastard and used his claws to rip the gun away. The weapon and part of the Lycan's hand flew out of sight, into the bushes.

Tegan didn't scream from the pain. He was already out cold, his body slumped. The bullet had hit its mark and blood poured out of a hole in his temple.

"FUCK!" Trayis roared.

Arlis struggled toward him, still swaying like a drunk. "Control it!"

Trayis leashed his emotions. It was hard to do at the moment.

His brother gripped his shoulder and crouched next to him, taking a few deep breaths. "*Shit.*" He felt Tegan's neck. "He's still breathing but he might bleed out. I see you took most of his hand... Who knows what the bullet did inside his skull? I don't see an exit wound."

Trayis carelessly dropped Tegan. The Lycan was out cold. "I thought I could get to him in time."

Arlis glanced over his shoulders at his pack. "You put every last one of them on their knees. Damn, I forgot how powerful that Master Vampire blood amps up your alpha side. I damn near went down, too." He stood, turning to the recovering Weres. "Get the healer, *fast*. Don't let Tegan die. I want him guarded at all times. The second he wakes, I want to know."

He crouched next to Trayis again. "We'll find Shay. I'm only picking up *his* blood. None of hers. That means she's probably alive. I can't see her not putting up a fight if he'd tried to kill her. And he needed her alive. You heard him. He wanted to use her as leverage to get you to kill us."

Trayis hung his head, closing his eyes. "*Fuck.*"

"We'll find her. Let's go. He's not going to be any help. Maybe we can backtrack his scent. He wasn't worried about hiding his trail once his scent was caught and the hunt began. He was running for his life."

Trayis opened his eyes and stood. "He's insane, Arlis."

"I know. He's on drugs again. I smell those, too."

Trayis had to pull himself together. Shay was out there somewhere. And he'd just lost his chance of making her kidnapper tell him where she was.

He turned, staring at the other Lycans. "I'm sorry about the vibes."

Martin spoke first, and he actually grinned. "Don't be. I've never been put on my ass like that before. It was an experience."

Some of the other enforcers chuckled, and Trayis relaxed. They didn't seem angry with him for pulling that stunt. He turned to hold his brother's gaze.

Arlis nodded. "You had to try. It was all you could do. Let's see if we can find Shay by backtracking him."

Chapter Fourteen

Shay lay on her side and twisted, the ropes tight on her wrists. She rolled her shoulders, curled her upper body into a tight ball, and wiggled her ass. It hurt but she was making progress. Her body didn't want to contort enough but she kept straining, inching her hands along her ass, trying to get them out from behind her back. If she could get the rope in front of her, it would be a game changer.

She was certain her wrists were bleeding, rubbed raw by the ropes and the pressure she was putting on them. Her shoulders were on fire. She was pretty sure they weren't supposed to move that way. Even her back ached.

She slowly continued, though, until she'd worked her hands under her ass to the backs of her thighs. Now she was stuck in a ball.

"Shit." She panted a bit, uncomfortable, but it was working.

She slowly turned onto her back, brought her legs up high so they were lying against her chest and she was folded in half, and inched her arms upward. Then she twisted each foot to free herself. She grinned, hurting but triumphant. Her arms were in front of her now.

Shay stared at her wrists. They were indeed bleeding, and her hands had begun to swell from the tight ropes.

She sat up and stared at the knots. They looked super complex. "Fucking Tegan. Asshole!"

She used her teeth to try to loosen them but it only hurt her mouth. She cursed some more and stared at the rough hole in the wall, where the rope ran outside of the treehouse. Maybe the other end was close and not knotted so tightly. If she could dismantle more of the wall, her hands would still be bound but she wouldn't be stuck inside the structure.

She wiggled around yet again, bent her legs, and leaned back. The rope kept her braced so she didn't fall backward. Shay kicked out hard at the hole.

The wood gave and a bigger hole opened, letting more breeze in. She lifted her legs again and kicked higher, to widen the hole even more. The rotten wood gave easily, breaking apart and falling away.

She kept kicking until the wall in front of her was mostly gone. It revealed an even better view of just how high she was in the trees. The river flowed noisily below. Thanks to her foster father, she quickly figured out where she was. At least, she was pretty sure. She was facing north, the river was the territory border, and that meant most of the scenery she could see across the water belonged to Alpha Damon. Behind the far mountain in the distance would be the largest human city in the area.

She rolled, got on her stomach, and carefully wiggled forward until her face was peering over the edge of the floor. The rope trailed under it, and she wiggled out more, careful to not lose her balance. With her head and shoulders out of the treehouse, she got a good look under the floor of the treehouse. The rope was attached to a thick branch a good ten feet below.

"Shit."

There was nothing to grab hold of to climb down. The treehouse floor jutted from the trunk it was built into, with no sturdy, usable branches nearby. She stared at the thick branch she was attached to and softly cursed.

There was only one thing to do. It was going to hurt. And if the rope broke, she'd fall to her death.

Shay closed her eyes, breathing in fresh air. The branches far below blocked any clear view of the ground on her side of the river. If any of her pack were down there, she couldn't see them. That meant they couldn't spot her, either.

'Think," she murmured. "Worse case, the rope breaks. I'll fall to my death. Second worst thing, I break my wrists. Then again, I might reach the branch safely, and then somehow manage to get free and climb down."

She wiggled back onto the platform until her head wasn't outside and sat up. She stared at the rope attached to her wrist then gripped it with both hands. It was rough and would probably mess up her skin when she fell. She needed to hold on as tightly as possible, though, to avoid breaking her wrists when she fell.

Tegan was crazy. She couldn't trust him not to kill her. It would take him time to get close enough to the territory to check his texts. Then he'd be back. She needed to be gone before he was. There was no choice. She needed to save her own ass.

"This is going to hurt. Please don't break, rope. I don't want to plunge to my death."

She scooted closer to the edge and closed her eyes. "Just fall. You can do this."

Fear kept her in place...but then she thought of Trayis. He would have the courage to do whatever it took to survive.

She opened her eyes and stared out at the view. "Trayis, I'm coming back to you. I'm not going to allow that moron to kill me."

Then she sucked in a sharp breath—and then took the plunge.

Her body tilted. She stared in terror at the branches below as she tumbled off the platform. Her body dropped, she clutched the rope tight...

Then agonizing pain ripped through her arms and shoulders as the rope halted her fall, her arms yanked above her head. Momentum swung her forward, and Shay's chest slammed into something painfully hard and solid. It knocked the air from her lungs. Her wrists and palms burned like fire.

She opened her eyes, realizing she'd crashed into another dense branch several feet below the one she'd been tied to. She sucked in air, forcing herself to breath. She was bruised for sure, maybe had some broken ribs, judging by the pain each breath caused, but she wasn't dead. It took her a few seconds to push beyond the pain and evaluate her new situation.

She lifted her leg. It took two tries but she managed to get her foot high enough to catch on the branch. She hoisted herself up, getting more of her body onto the branch, slowly and painfully, and then sat up to take some of the pressure off the rope.

Blood coated her wrists but the bones weren't broken. Her palms had gotten torn up, just like she'd suspected they would.

And she was able to see the ladder Tegan must have used to climb to the treehouse.

It was about ten feet away, and it wasn't a ladder, really. Just spaced-apart rungs hammered into the trunk.

She scooted along the branch until she was under the knot tying her to the branch above. "Damn it." There was no way she could reach it from where she'd landed. It was too far up. She'd been lucky to climb onto another branch after she'd fallen.

She straddled the limb and stared at the rope. She had a couple feet of slack. "Try again," she muttered, lifting her wrists to her mouth and began to bite into them, yanking with her teeth at the knots. One of them began to loosen.

She grinned. "Fuck you, Tegan." She also kept looking down the thick trunk, watching and waiting for Tegan to come back as she used her teeth again on the knots. The base of the tree was hidden by too many branches, but she could see the rungs for a good thirty feet.

She finally got her wrists free.

The damage to her skin looked bad. She removed her shirt, used her teeth again to rip off strips, and wrapped her wrists as best she could. Her blood damped the material quickly, so she applied gentle pressure, tossed the cloths, then tore more strips. She wore only a bra with her jeans now, but her hands were free and wrapped.

Shay touched the still-sore spot on her temple. She could feel dried blood on her skin and hair on the left side of her head. It's where Tegan had struck her before leaving the cabin, ultimately knocking her out. That was the least of her worries. No fresh blood, so she'd worry about that injury later.

Her gaze went back to the makeshift ladder. Tegan wasn't climbing the rungs, but that didn't mean he wasn't down on the ground. She scooted on the branch, moving closer to the trunk until she reached a rung. Shay held on to it as she stood, staring down.

All quiet. Still no sign of Tegan.

Now she had to make a choice: climb down the tree using the rungs, or use the branches to reach the next tree, and try to climb down that way. Nerves made her hesitate. "Shit."

She remembered Tegan's hands, how messed up they were. So was his face. And she'd be above him. With her shoes on, she could try to kick the shit out of him if they met up on the ladder. He'd have a hard time holding on to anything—her *or* the rungs—with those bandages.

She took several deep breaths, her throat dry, heart pounding—and began to climb down the crude treads. Her gaze stayed on the rungs below her. No way was she going to let the bastard surprise her again.

Shay had never liked heights. It was probably a good thing she couldn't see much through all the thick branches as she climbed lower and lower. Her hands burned, the damage to them making it painful for her to grip the rough rungs, but she kept going. Time wasn't on her side. Tegan would come back. She wanted to reach the ground and be gone before he returned.

She wasn't overly familiar with that part of her pack's territory, but she'd seen plenty of maps at Rod's house. It was his job to keep those cameras operational. Some of them were near the river. She just wished she could remember where each of them had been placed. That information had never seemed important before now.

She finally breached the dense branches and could see the ground. Exhaustion had her panting. The area around the base was thankfully clear of Tegan. She paused before traversing the lowest rungs, searching for any sign of movement. The only thing that stirred was the breeze. The river noise was much louder, now that she was only twenty feet in the air, free of the noise-reducing leaves and branches.

It was tempting for her to drop to her knees to kiss the ground when she climbed down the remainder of the trunk, but she resisted. She longingly stared at the water, incredibly thirsty, but instead she turned away from it, stumbling into the woods and toward pack territory. She was too afraid of running into Tegan to linger.

Shay kept moving, slowly but surely, her gaze darting around as she strained to hear any sound of Tegan. She also looked for hiding spots in case she needed to get out of sight.

A glint caught her eye, and she spotted one of the cameras. She quickly changed direction, stopped in front of it, and waved her arms. Hopefully, someone was watching the monitors.

"Please see me!"

Trayis had lost Tegan's trail. It had been easy to follow for a bit, his stench the strongest where the crazy Lycan had realized he'd been scented and ran in fear. Before that, he'd traveled over the rocky shore of the river. The trail was gone.

He snarled, enraged.

Arlis and half a dozen of his pack spread out, looking for any sign of Tegan's scent or footprints.

One of the sentries whistled. "Here."

Trayis rushed over to see what the sentry had found. A partial print in the dirt. They fanned out again, looking for another mistake Tegan had made.

Ten yards away, someone picked up his scent on a bush, where he'd obviously brushed against it. It seemed Tegan had changed direction.

"This is the third time," Martin snarled. "It's like he was staggering around like a fucking drunk, even though he remembered to hide his tracks."

"We aren't giving up." Trayis sniffed the air and kept his gaze locked on the ground. "Keep looking."

The satellite phone one of the men had given Arlis rang. Trayis looked over, watching his brother answer it. Arlis met his gaze—and his eyes widened as he listened to whoever spoke. "Where?"

Trayis rushed toward him, his heart pounding.

"Got it. Section nine-two-four. Where the fuck is that?" Arlis smiled briefly at Trayis. "Shay's alive! They have her on one of the cameras. She's waving in front of it to get our attention."

Relief hit Trayis so hard, he could barely breathe. "Where?"

"You said nine-two-four?" Martin pointed. "That way. Maybe a mile."

That was all Trayis needed. A direction. He shifted, running as fast as he could toward where Martin had pointed. He leapt over a fallen tree, skirted a boulder, and kept running. He didn't know if anyone followed, nor did he care. He had to get to Shay.

He frantically tried to pick up her scent—and finally caught it, slightly changing direction. He had to dodge more trees, rocks and bushes. Her scent grew stronger, and he locked on to it, picking up a sudden burst of speed.

He leapt over another bush and spotted her.

She spun, terror on her face, but then she cried out, "Trayis!"

Rage nearly blinded him when he saw her. She was injured. There was slight swelling and some blood on the side of her head, near her temple. She wore only jeans, bra and shoes, and he saw damaged skin on her exposed stomach and ribs. Her wrists were bandaged in rags—and he could smell her blood.

He catalogued all of that before he finally made it to her, skidded to a halt, and shifted back to skin. He rose up, swiftly pulling her into his arms, holding on tight. *She is alive.*

"Shay!"

She clung to him. "You found me!"

He let her go and dropped to his knees, staring at her stomach. There was bruising and scratches. He inhaled, picking up several scents. Some of them were Tegan but those were faint. He jerked his head up. "Did that bastard do this to you?"

"The head and wrists, yes. The rest, it's a long story. I might have some broken ribs."

He rose to his feet again. "I'm going to bite my wrist. You're going to drink my blood."

She looked stunned.

"It will heal you. Do you trust me?"

"Yes."

He lifted his wrist, let his fangs drop, and bit into his skin. He gently turned her until her back was to his chest, wrapped his arm around her, and then lifted his bleeding arm to her lips. "Drink, doll. *Now.*"

She opened her mouth and let him press his torn skin to her lips. He held her as tight as he dared, beyond relieved that she was in his arms. He heard his brother and the rest of the search party coming, but he concentrated on Shay.

She was drinking *his* blood. His dick stirred at the thought, at the pull of her mouth on his flesh, but he ignored his arousal. There wasn't a damn thing sexy about this moment. Shay was hurt, literally bleeding in his arms, and he wanted her healed.

She trembled slightly and stopped drinking. He pulled his arm back, seeing that he'd stopped bleeding. It was tempting to bite himself again to force her to drink more.

"How is she?" Arlis walked up to them, looking concerned. His brother glanced from his arm to the blood on Shay's lips. "Good idea. You can heal any injuries." He lifted his hand and motioned to the others. "Back off."

Shay lifted her head, holding his gaze, and Trayis saw her tears. It tore him up inside. "I'm here, doll. I'm so sorry that crazy fucking Lycan got you."

"I'm okay."

He adjusted his hold then lifted her, cradling her in his arms. His attention went to her head. The cut there had stopped bleeding long ago but he could see the skin knitting together where it had been split. His blood was working. Then he lowered his gaze to her stomach, watching as the scratches began to heal.

"Thank you for the blood. I was thirsty but that wasn't what I had in mind," she quipped.

"Get her some water," he ordered Arlis.

"On it." His brother walked off.

"Vampire blood heals faster than a Lycan's. What exactly did he do to you, Shay?" He didn't pick up any scent to indicate Tegan had sexually assaulted her. That was a huge relief.

"He hit me in the head hard enough to knock me out, and I woke up tied to a rope tethered to a rickety old treehouse." Her gaze lifted to the sky. "Way up."

Rage consumed him all over again. "You climbed down?" He thought about her falling from a long distance. She was so fragile, and some of the local trees were immense. Shay didn't heal as well as a Lycan. She could have died.

"I'll tell you about it later." Her gaze locked with his. "I'm really okay." She gave him a brave smile. "I'm so happy to see you. Did we miss our flight?"

He lowered his body and just sat on the ground, cuddling her in his arms. Trayis *needed* to hold her. "All that matters is that you're safe, and I have you."

238

He knew they were being watched, could sense the Lycans surrounding them. It didn't matter if they saw how much Shay meant to him. She was his mate…or would be soon. He rocked her gently. "How are your ribs feeling? You said they might be broken."

"I feel better. They hurt less. I'm just really thirsty."

Arlis came back and knelt in front of him. He opened a bottle of water and offered it to Shay.

"Drink slow," Trayis reminded her. "You could get sick otherwise."

She nodded, taking small sips. "Tegan is out there somewhere. He'll be coming back. He's crazy."

"No, he won't be."

Shay held his gaze.

"We caught his scent and chased him. The bastard pulled a gun and shot himself in the head to avoid being forced to tell us where you were."

He hated to see the horrified look on her face. "He had a gun? And he *killed* himself?"

"He's not dead." He would be soon enough. Tegan's time was up. He'd hurt Shay, kidnapped her, and Trayis wasn't going to allow him to live.

"He was on drugs again," Arlis added. "It can make our kind unstable. Especially the shit he stole from our healer, if he was mixing them together."

"He was *always* unstable." Martin walked into Trayis's view. "Tegan just hid it well. I saw plenty of crazy in that bastard when I had to try to make something out of him."

Arlis sighed. "You were right, Martin. I should have let you kill him. This could have been avoided."

"Don't bust your own balls, Alpha." Martin came even closer and lowered his voice. "You like to see the good in people and give them second chances. It makes you a great leader. I don't have your patience. That's why I'd be shitty at your job."

Trayis adjusted his hold on Shay. "Help me up."

Arlis and Martin gripped his arms, pulling him to his feet with Shay. He couldn't and wouldn't let her go. Not until he could assure himself she was really okay.

"Thanks. Shay needs a bath, and I need some time alone with her."

Arlis held his gaze. "I'll contact your clan to let them know you're going to be delayed."

"Just a day," Trayis decided. "Tell Wen or Tymber we'll leave first thing in the morning. No offense, but I want to get Shay to my clan."

Regret surfaced in Arlis's expression. "I'm so sorry this happened."

"I've dealt with some crazy in my clan, too. Remember my last visit in the middle of the night?"

Arlis nodded. "You came to pick up that human because of Wen's fucked-up parents. Who could forget? I'm glad that worked out."

"Me too."

Chapter Fifteen

"I'm fine, Trayis." Shay felt just a tinge of irritation at this point. He'd carried her the entire way from the woods to the guest trailer, refusing to let her walk. Then he'd cleaned her in the shower as if she were an infant. He'd washed her tenderly, slowly, checking over every inch of her skin— which was remarkably healed. Then he'd put her to bed and fed her, making her eat every bite.

"Humor me."

She sighed and nodded. If forced, she'd admit it felt nice to be taken care of. It was also comforting that he cared so much. If there was ever a doubt, it had been laid to rest. She was grateful there wasn't any bubble wrap in the trailer or Trayis might dress her in it head to toe.

Someone knocked on the door in the living area and Trayis snarled. "Your family is driving me crazy. What part of 'stay away' don't they understand?"

She opened her mouth but he got out of bed, stomping out of the room. She listened as he unlocked the door, snarling at whoever was there that she was fine and not accepting visitors. For some reason, Trayis didn't want anyone near her. She guessed it was an instinctual thing, after what had happened with Tegan.

He slammed the door and returned to the bedroom, sprawling out next to her.

"I'm all healed." She showed him her wrists. The skin wasn't cut or swollen anymore. In fact, his blood had totally removed every mark. "I feel great now."

"You could have *died*."

"I didn't. I'm so grateful that you were out there looking for me. And obviously it was traumatic for us both. Crazy people exist in the world, Trayis. I'm alright. Everything is okay now. You can relax."

"He could have killed you."

"You've said that many times. He didn't. Who was at the door *that* time?"

"It was my brother. We leave at six in the morning. Our flights have been changed."

"I'm sorry we couldn't go today."

"It's not your fault. I'm just glad you're here with me."

"Me too." She smiled and reached out, taking his hand. "Thank you for feeding me your blood. I didn't know that it could heal."

"My father was a Vampire. Their blood heals injuries, if given in small amounts. Too much can change a human and turn them."

"I figured, since I've heard how they make other Vampires."

"Lycan blood protects that from happening to them. They can't be turned by a Vamp. I didn't give you enough to risk it, though, since you're also human."

"I appreciate that. I like sunshine and real food."

He reached up and gently stroked her cheek. "It frightened me when I realized you were taken, Shay."

242

"I'm okay."

He nodded and let his hand drop. "You trust Martin, don't you?"

"Of course. Why?"

Trayis's eyes turned black. "I have something to do. Martin is going to stay outside to protect you while I'm gone. This won't take long."

"Where are you going?"

He hesitated. "Tegan is still alive. I won't allow that to stand, Shay. He took you, hurt you, and could have killed you."

She let that sink in. Packs had rules. Some of them were harsh but necessary. "I understand. He's crazy and dangerous. I guess they aren't going to get him help."

"You're thinking like a human again."

"I realize that. Though, we do have a pack therapist, who perhaps could have helped Tegan."

"He ordered me to murder Arlis and his enforcers. Tried to trade your life for theirs. My brother will kill him if I don't." He didn't look away from her. "I want to kill him for what he did to you. *No one* hurts you, Shay. You're mine to protect."

She knew it was necessary. Tegan had clearly had two mental breaks close together, and she'd witnessed both. First when he'd used stolen drugs and gone after her in the office. Then again when he'd attacked her and kidnapped her from the cabin. Being punished the first time hadn't worked. Tegan had become a threat not only to her, but to the entire pack with his insanity and stupidity. Humans would be at risk, too, if he were allowed to escape.

She nodded. "I understand."

"Do you?"

"I do. I deal with pack correspondences, remember? He's not the first Werewolf the packs have had to put down. And we have Graves. It's sometimes his job to take down dangerous Werewolves. Tegan had a chance to get himself straight, but instead he only made things worse. We've survived and remained hidden from humans by following strict laws. We police our own, and there's no long-term prison for Werewolves. They follow the rules or they're killed. There's no gray area. We can't allow there to be. Tegan earned his death."

The black bled out of Trayis's eyes. "I don't want you to feel responsible in any way. You're not. This is all on Tegan."

"I understand. I really do. God only knows what horrible thing he'd do next if he were allowed to live. He's crazy, stupid, and can't be reasoned with. I tried. And no one forced those drugs into him. He chose to take them. I'm fine with it, Trayis. I was raised in a pack. I get it."

"Good." He scooted closer and placed a kiss on her forehead. "Rest. Martin is right outside."

"I'm safe now that Tegan isn't running around."

"I don't care. I'm using a guard we both trust. I won't risk anything happening to you. Humor me, Shay. I had a bad scare."

She nodded. "Okay."

"Good. I won't be gone long."

"I'll be here."

She watched him climb off the bed and leave, listening to the door close at the other end of the trailer.

Trayis was going to kill Tegan. Part of her was glad she hadn't been invited to watch that go down. She might live with a pack, but she still didn't like violence.

A good five minutes went by before she heard the door open, and Shay sat up. It surprised her to see Marcia coming down the short hall toward her. She smiled when she saw her foster sister.

Tears filled Marcia eyes. "Martin let me sneak in while Trayis is away. He said to get my ass in, don't stay long, assure myself you're really fine, and then get the fuck out."

"I'm okay." She slid out of bed and stood.

Marica gently hugged her, let go, and then visually inspected her. "You don't appear any worse for the trauma you suffered."

"Trayis gave me his blood." She lifted her arms. "My wrists were fucked up from the rope and I had a head injury. I'm fine now." She didn't mention the damage she'd taken slamming into a branch after jumping from the treehouse.

Marcia looked surprised. "You drank his blood? And I worried *he'd* be the one biting *you*."

"He's part Vampire. His blood heals if it's taken in small amounts. My injures began to heal right away."

Marica smiled. "That's cool. Especially for you. That means he can heal you super-fast if you're ever hurt. I guess I can stop worrying about you leaving, at least a little." Then she tensed, growing somber. "Did Tegan do anything else to you? You should talk to another woman if he—"

"He didn't sexually assault me."

Relief had Marica sighing. "I'm glad. We were so worried."

"Tegan was just crazy and refused to listen to reason, still convinced you, Kale, and I had been plotting to screw him out of the enforcer position. Oh—and Kale got it? That's what Tegan said."

"Yes. He's taking over for Ted next week after he officially retires. I always wanted to be the first female enforcer for the pack, but I guess I'll have to settle for being mated to one."

"I'm sorry, Marcia. I know that's always been your goal."

"Kale thinks maybe I can help him do his job sometimes, to show Arlis and the others what I'm capable of."

"That's a good plan."

"He's a smart mate. Supportive." She winked. "I'd better go. I wasn't letting you leave without saying goodbye again, since you never got the chance to see me after I left your cabin earlier. I love you." Marica hugged her. "Be happy, call me often, and try to check your phone once in a while after you remember it's charging on the counter somewhere."

Shay laughed, hugging her back. "Promise. I'm going to miss you."

She watched her sister leave and then got back into bed.

Trayis approached the brick building the pack kept deep in the woods. Two enforcers were guarding it. Arlis was already waiting. His brother appeared grim as they faced off.

246

"I want to end him," Trayis demanded.

"He's yours. Unfortunately, he hasn't woken. He fucked himself up with that bullet. The healer said it could be a full day or two before he comes around."

"Fuck."

"I know you wanted to talk to him, let him know your feelings on what he did to Shay, and probably make him piss himself before putting him down. You won't get that satisfaction, brother."

That was disappointing.

"You could feed him some of your blood to heal him enough."

Trayis shook his head. "Bad idea. One, I already fed Shay some of my blood. I don't want to be weakened. And while she's recovering, I refuse to take blood from anyone else. It wouldn't sit right with me. Then there's the fact that if I had to give him enough blood to reverse damage to his brain, it would only make him tougher to kill. He'd heal a lot quicker from anything I did to him, at least at first. While that might be fun for me, since I'm furious, I'm not going to weaken myself. I'm taking Shay home in the morning. I want to be at my best while we're traveling."

Arlis stepped closer. "It's your right to kill Tegan...but allow me to do it for you when he's awake. Otherwise, you're going to have to take him out while he's unconscious. That's not our way."

"I know. It's only an honorable kill if he's fully aware he's been judged and sentenced to death for his crimes."

"I won't take him out fast. I promise. He'll suffer for what he did to Shay. My word." Arlis touched his chest, making the pledge. "I have my own issues with him. He tried to blackmail you into killing me *and* my enforcers. Shay is yours now, but she was one of mine. You know I care about her. I'd have adopted her if I hadn't been single when her parents died. But I still counted her as family before you claimed her."

Trayis was disappointed he wouldn't be the one to take out Tegan, but he nodded and touched his own chest. "I trust you to do it. He's yours. Make it painful."

They clasped hands. Arlis grinned. "Are you going to mate her tonight?"

"It's tempting, but I have my reasons for waiting until I'm back with my clan."

Arlis's eyebrows rose.

"She's half human. I'm going to tightly bond her to me, and there could be some side effects on the human part of her."

"She won't change, will she? As in, turn any part Vampire?"

Trayis shook his head. "Her Lycan blood will prevent that, but I saw what happened to Lorn's mate. She was a half VampLycan who was turned more Vampire than Lycan when she was attacked, and had to drink a lot of pure Vamp blood. It tipped the scales of her existing DNA. The human side of her allowed for that. Shay might become more Lycan than human. My blood could enhance her Lycan side."

Arlis released him with a stunned expression.

"It probably won't happen. But I don't want to risk it right before flying to Alaska. It would be a nightmare if she shifted for the first time on an airplane full of humans."

248

"*Fuck*. How did Shay react to that news?"

"I haven't told her yet. It's a small possibility. I didn't want to get her hopes up. She really feels less worthy for being so human." He glared at his brother. "Your pack has made her ashamed to be the way she is."

"We didn't mean to."

"I get that. Her grandparents didn't help. Speaking of two people I'd like to kill..."

"Get in line."

Trayis snorted. "You might get the chance if Ellis leaves his parents to live with Sylvia and Dean. They offered to take him in. And I can't see those bastards letting him return to this pack without raising hell."

"I hope Mildred and Elvis file a protest. I'll challenge them. They caused rifts in the pack plenty of times, and then had a son they didn't even inform me about. That was pure disrespect to me and the whole pack. Ellis already should have been one of mine. I'll fight to keep him if he chooses to live here."

"The kid might take it hard if you kill them."

"I'll keep that in mind."

Trayis backed off the subject. His brother didn't need more of his advice. He respected him as leader of his pack. "I'll say goodbye to you now. Shay and I are leaving early in the morning to head toward the airport."

"I remember. One of the enforcers will drive you both."

Trayis nodded. "Thanks."

"You're welcome. Come back more often. Stay longer."

Trayis chuckled. "Okay."

"Then again, you might be having a son or daughter soon." Amusement sparked in Arlis's eyes. "Shay's very human. At least for now. Let me know how that goes."

"I will."

They hugged and parted ways. Trayis returned to the trailer and thanked Martin.

"I let Marcia in for a few minutes. I felt sorry for her. She was all puppy eyes and pleading to see Shay for herself. Those two have always been closer than sisters."

"Thanks. I should have allowed it myself."

"You were in full-blown protective mode after what happened to Shay." Martin grinned. "It happens. Totally natural. For a VampLycan, you've got a lot of Were instincts inside you."

"Guilty."

"Have a good night. I'll be patrolling. Ted's taking over in a few hours. I don't think Tegan had any close friends who're willing to try to get a little payback. He was a dick to everyone. We're not taking any chances though. Rest easy tonight."

"I appreciate it."

Trayis entered the trailer and found Shay sleeping in bed. He stripped, set the alarm on his phone, and climbed into bed with her, holding her close. She murmured in her sleep but didn't wake. He'd never been so grateful to feel her safe in his arms.

Chapter Sixteen

Shay felt nervous, clutching Trayis's hand. The commercial flight they'd taken had been a pleasant experience. Being seated in first class had been nice. They'd served food, offered her a pillow and blanket, and she'd had a cocktail, since Trayis insisted that it would relax her.

Then they'd climbed into a small four-seater plane. That had been terrifying. Every breeze had bounced the little plane in the sky—and then she'd realized they would be landing on a road instead of at an airport. Trayis used his mind-control ability on the pilot to get him to agree to do it. They'd landed safely and Trayis had sent the plane off.

"Why do you have to control his mind?"

"We don't want any of the bush pilots to remember us using this road as an airstrip. Humans talk. What if someone overheard a pilot talking about it and it caused suspicion? They might think we're doing illegal human things, like drug running or something. It's best if we wipe their memories and let them think they dropped us off at an airport. Then there's nothing to investigate if the authorities get the urge."

That amused her. "Is there a huge drug problem out here in the middle of nowhere Alaska?" She peered around, seeing no sign of civilization except for the road. There were tons of trees and land, though.

He chuckled, raised her hand to his lips, and kissed the back. "No. The other reason is we like to keep our privacy. Humans got the bright idea to open a resort in this area a while back. A company invested in some stores and a gas station, too. They're the ones who paid for this road. But it's next to VampLycan territory, and the resort attracted human

251

hunters, and that pissed me off. Some of them invaded our territory with guns."

"I take it that it's no longer open?"

He shook his head. "We couldn't have a bunch of humans running around shooting at everything that moved, including my clan. It needed to be closed."

"How did you accomplish that?"

His eyes began to glow but it faded fast. "Their guests had a terrible time and never wanted to return. Let's just say no one recommended it to their friends. It closed after two years."

"The poor owners."

He shrugged. "They could afford the loss. We bought the resort, the tiny town they built, and the land it sits on. We just don't want humans coming out here. It might be tempting for some to break into the buildings and become squatters."

"No one lives there?"

"It's a huge lodge with dozens of guest cabins. We run patrols through that area every few weeks but we boarded up all the buildings after purchasing it, to prevent damage from storms and the harsh winters."

"So...it just sits there then?"

He nodded. "I'll take you on a tour one day if you want to see it. They sold it with the furnishings. It was more cost effective for them to abandon it all, rather than ship it a long way to a large city to auction everything for a fraction of the cost."

"I *would* like to see it." Shay glanced toward the road when she heard an engine.

"I'll take you soon. That will be Wen or Tymber picking us up."

"Wen is your head enforcer?"

"Wen and Tymber share that responsibility."

"But you left Wen in charge when you visited my pack?"

He nodded. "Tymber watched things for me the last time I left. Wen was on a mission. It only seemed fair to switch turns. It can be a pain in the ass to keep a clan in line. I consider them my friends." He grinned. "It's why I make sure they aren't overburdened by sticking them with my problems too often."

"Two head enforcers. That's different."

"We're VampLycans. I told you we're not exactly like a pack."

She turned her head and watched as a dark SUV made a turn in the road. The guy behind the wheel had dark hair, wore sunglasses, and he stopped about ten feet away. He left the engine running as he climbed out. He was super tall. A big grin split his face, revealing gorgeous, straight teeth any dentist would have been proud to work on.

"I'm so glad you're home." His face turned more toward Shay. "And you *are* fucking adorable. Look how short you are! Gerri's going to love you."

Trayis sighed. "Meet Wen, Shay. He might be large but he's like an overgrown teenager. Gerri is the human I adopted, and she's this lug's mate. It's amazing that she hasn't tried to strangle him."

253

Wen chuckled, going around them to their bags sitting on the ground and picking them up. "Who says she hasn't tried? I'm tough, though, and she's just not that strong."

Shay liked the enforcer immediately, and the way the two men joked with each other. Wen took their bags to the back of the SUV and opened the hatch, putting them inside. He walked to the front passenger side and opened the door. "My lady."

Trayis growled at him, released her hand, and shoved the slightly taller Wen aside. "I can get her door. I *do* remember my manners."

Wen shoved his sunglasses up, revealing blue eyes. He looked amused as he stared at Trayis. "Do you? Did they have vehicles the last time you went on a date? Have you ever actually *gone* on a date?" He winked at her. "Our esteemed leader isn't exactly a ladies' man, if you get my drift. We're so thrilled he found you. Welcome to the clan, Shay. Him having a mate is going to be awesome for the rest of us. His moods will improve." Then he lowered his voice. "He was kind of grumpy before."

"Fuck you," Trayis snapped, but then he laughed.

Shay grinned, climbing up into the passenger seat. Trayis leaned in and buckled her belt. "The roads here aren't so bad but they get worse closer to our territory."

"You don't do road repairs?"

Wen laughed, opening the back door and climbing in. "That would imply we wanted to make it easy for people to visit us. That's a big hell no. Especially from this side of our territory."

Trayis closed her door, rounded the SUV, and got into the driver's seat. "Ignore him. I try really hard to most of the time."

254

"Yeah, yeah," Wen muttered. "Clan leader abuse. See what I put up with?"

"You'll survive." Trayis turned the SUV around on the road and headed back the way Wen had come. They eventually left the road for a dirt trail. Trayis slowed to make the ride less bumpy. "This is a shortcut to my place."

"Which has been cleaned, stocked with food, and dinner should be waiting when you arrive. Tymber is grilling you some steaks. Just for the two of you," Wen added. "We don't want you overwhelmed, Shay. Tomorrow is soon enough to let the clan rush in to meet you. We kept your arrival on the down low to avoid a crowd waiting at the cabin."

She turned her head, staring at him. "Would there be one?"

"Once word spreads that Trayis has found his mate, everyone is going to want to meet you. The curiosity alone will drive them to rush to his place." Wen chuckled, his gaze going to the back of Trayis's head. "We never thought he'd take a mate. It's a huge deal. The other clan leaders might drop in, too."

Her nerves came back full force. "Great."

Trayis shot her a concerned glance. "It's fine, Shay. Damn it, Wen! You're upsetting her. Shut up."

"It's cool." Wen leaned forward and gently touched her shoulder for a split second to get her attention. "I mated to a full human. Trayis was so great about it that he adopted Gerri. Velder, another clan leader, has two sons mated to half humans, half VampLycans. The women didn't even know they were more than human until they got to Alaska. So basically, they'd inherited the human side more so than the VampLycan.

255

"Crocker doesn't have a mate. He's another clan leader. But he won't care that you're a half-breed. He'll just be jealous that Trayis found you. As for Lorn, the last clan leader, his mate is also half human and half VampLycan. She turned more Vampire for a while, but drinking Lorn's blood has her walking in the sun without burning, and we hear she can eat food again. No one is going to have a problem with you. Hell, even the GarLycan clan leader, Aveoth, took a mate with some Vampire bloodlines. That was a huge no-no, since Gargoyles are dicks about not breeding with us VampLycans. He said 'fuck you' to his clan and did it anyway."

Trayis shot her another concerned look. "Shay thinks some of the clan might have a problem because she can't shift."

Wen snorted. "Not a problem. Everyone has been great to Gerri except for my parents. And they left the clan. That's a long story, but they went crazy after my older brother died. I'll tell you about them sometime. You're going to fit in just fine. If anyone gives you any shit, it would be Mya and her few friends. Emphasis on the 'few.' She's kind of a bitch."

"Trayis told me about her," she admitted.

"Ignore Mya if she ever says she fucked Trayis. Not true. Neither of us are that stupid." Wen made a funny face. "Not even drunk, desperate, or in heat. Big hell no."

"Is she still locked up?"

Wen nodded at Trayis's question. "She sure is—and whining about it loudly. It's been amusing as shit. No one deserves it more. It was brilliant when you suggested that Vassa be her guard. She's protective as shit of her big brother Brigs, *and* she has a crush on Roe. Vassa has been verbally tearing her a new ass."

256

"Shit, I didn't know Vassa was attracted to Roe," Trayis admitted. "Maybe it wasn't such a good idea, since Mya screwed him."

"Nope. It's perfect. Trust me. I've been watching them closely. So has Tymber. It's been amusing as hell. Vassa won't physically attack her, since she takes her duty seriously, but women are *vicious* with words. She made Mya cry a few times. I didn't even think she was capable."

Trayis scowled.

Shay reached over and rubbed his arm. "That's a good thing. I grew up with the Bitch Trio, remember? I'd consider it progress if one of them were capable of crying. Usually they were the ones causing *me* to. Maybe this Mya will learn what it's like to be on the receiving end of being treated bad enough to get upset over it."

"Bitch Trio? Tell me more."

She turned her head to peer at Wen. "They really aren't worth talking about."

"Like Mya and her friends," Trayis offered. "Only the Lycan versions."

"Got it. Bitch Trio. Appropriate. We have the Blood Bitch Foursome, then." Wen chuckled. "I like that. I'm so calling them that from now on."

Trayis shook his head and sighed loudly. "See? He's like a big fucking teenager."

"You love me, man."

Trayis glanced at Shay and rolled his eyes.

She laughed. Her gaze went to the windows. The VampLycan territory was beautiful. She still didn't see any signs of civilization but eventually she spotted a few cabins. They were nicer than she'd expected.

Part of her had wondered if they'd be really old. Trayis had mentioned on the plane that they'd updated things over the years. She knew to expect electricity and cell service close to where most of the homes were located.

He finally pulled in front of a two-story cabin. It was a beautiful A-frame that had to be a good four thousand square feet, if she were to guess. The covered porch was massive, too. Trayis parked the SUV and turned it off. He reached over and took her hand. Their gazes met.

"Welcome home, doll. I hope you like it."

She smiled. "I love it. It's, um...big."

He chuckled. "Our *sheds* are larger than where you lived."

"No shit? Seriously?" Wen sounded stunned.

Trayis released her hand. "Stay there, Shay." He glanced into the backseat. "No shit. Wen, thanks for coming to get us. You're still in charge until tomorrow. Shay and I are going to enjoy our evening without interruptions. Make sure that happens."

"Fine. Tymber is in the back, though, grilling your dinner. The steaks should be about done. He knew when I left, so he guesstimated when we'd return."

Shay stayed still as Trayis got out and came around the front of the SUV. He opened her door and helped her down from the tall vehicle. Then he tucked her to his side, leading her up the porch steps to the front door. He opened it and used his foot to shove the door wide.

Then he surprised her by scooping her into his arms and carrying her inside.

She stared in amazement at the interior. It had beautiful log beams, a high ceiling in the living area, and a rock fireplace that dominated one wall. The kitchen area was under a loft. There were hardwood floors with a few rugs thrown in the living space near the couch and loveseat. The furniture was basic but looked comfortable.

He kicked the door closed behind them. "What do you think?"

She grinned. "It's stunning."

Footsteps sounded from a hallway on the other side of the kitchen, and then another big man walked forward, holding a platter. He grinned at them, entering the kitchen. He was tall, maybe six-five, with a muscled body covered in a tight T-shirt, faded jeans, and black boots. His black hair was long, pulled into a ponytail that had fallen over his shoulder. It nearly reached his waist. Light blue eyes were a stark contrast against his tan skin and hair color.

"Welcome home! Four steaks, medium rare. Baked potatoes and all the trimmings are on the counter. I even remembered to put out plates." The guy winked. "Now I'll get the hell out."

"Thanks, Tymber. This is Shay."

She waved to him. "Hi. It's nice to meet you—and thank you for dinner."

"I was glad to do it. I can't wait to get to know you, Shay. You must be someone very special to have caught Trayis." He grinned wide, his gaze locking on his clan leader. "You did good, man. See you in the morning. Wen and I told everyone there would be a meeting outside your office at ten. That way you can announce your mate." He inhaled, his nostrils flaring. "She's carrying your scent, but not strong enough yet."

"We haven't officially mated," Shay admitted.

Surprise widened Tymber's eyes.

"Yet. I wanted to wait until we got here," Trayis added. "Thanks for dinner and for helping to get this place ready for Shay."

"Anytime." Tymber passed by them, leaving out the front door.

Trayis gently deposited her on her feet. "Take a look around real quick if you want. I'm going to get our bags. I'll be right back, and then we'll eat. I'm starving."

"Me too." It had been a while since their in-flight meal.

He left but Shay didn't move. She just looked around, taking in every detail. The living room was large but cozy at the same time. The kitchen was updated, at least six times larger than what she was used to, and it had nice appliances. Even a dishwasher. It shocked her to find a home this nice in such a remote area.

Trayis returned with their bags and walked to the other side of the room to the curved staircase. "I'm going to drop these in the master. Want a quick tour?"

She nodded, hurrying after him. They'd used logs for the banister, too. She ran her hands over the smooth, polished rails. "This is amazing."

"We have a lot of time up here to learn skills. And tons of trees. It also saves money when we can build our own stuff from natural resources. Not that we're broke. The gold rush times were damn good to us."

Shay laughed. "Really? You mined gold?"

He chuckled when he reached the top of the stairs. "We did. VampLycans don't fear hard work, long hours, or physical labor. We excelled at it."

There were some bookshelves, most of them empty, and a leather couch in the loft. He entered a hallway and she followed. It led to three open doors. The first one was a bathroom. The second a compact guestroom. The third door opened into a bedroom larger than she'd expected. It had another fireplace along the back wall, and an open door to the left revealed another bathroom. Next to it were two slider closets. "Wow."

He dropped their bags near the bed and turned. "Under this, behind the kitchen area, is another master bedroom with a bath, a half bath, and some storage space, which could be turned into another large bedroom down the road, or even split into two smaller ones." He paused. "If we ever need more."

She felt her cheeks heat. "Do you want that many kids? I mean, you have two spare bedrooms already. You're implying we could convert two more. That would be at least four kids."

He nodded.

"That's probably good since, you know, I can't control my ovaries."

He grinned. "You say that like it's a bad thing. We can even expand the cabin to six or more bedrooms by adding onto the sides or the back."

"Whoa!" She was stunned. "That many, huh?"

"We live a long damn time, Shay. You'll be drinking my blood on a regular basis once we're mated. Even if your aging wasn't going to slow from your Lycan father, my blood will do that for you. You're thinking in human terms again."

"I tend to do that."

He approached her. "Let's eat, and think about making babies afterward."

"Good plan."

"Do you like the bedroom? We can move downstairs if you like the other master more. I just prefer being on the second story because of our winters."

She glanced at the fireplace. "I bet that's nice to have on chilly nights."

"The other master has a fireplace, too. I just like the views better from up here. In the winter, the snow can pile high enough to block some of the windows on the lower level."

"I'm great with this as our bedroom." She glanced at the huge bed. "That looks comfortable."

He chuckled. "It is. You'll find out yourself soon—I'm going to mate you in it."

She was looking forward to that.

Trayis took her hand and led her downstairs. They plated the food, fixed their baked potatoes with butter, cheese, and chives. "This was really nice of Tymber."

"He and Wen have a motive for being so welcoming. They say I work too much, which makes me moody." He winked. "Now that I have you, I'll cut back my hours. That means I won't be such an asshole."

She laughed. "At least you have a sense of humor about it."

"I told you the clan leader doesn't take himself too seriously."

"You did. I just didn't realize you were speaking about yourself at the time."

"I didn't want you to run away from me."

She couldn't blame him for that.

Chapter Seventeen

Shay showered, wanting to feel refreshed after all their travel time. Trayis waited in their bedroom. She wrapped a towel around her body then exited the bathroom. Trayis had lit the fireplace, and he sat on the edge of the bed. He'd removed his shoes, socks, and shirt. Even the button of his jeans were undone. His sex appeal left her almost gawking at him in appreciation.

He rose to his feet, his beautiful eyes showing golden streaks. He smiled. "You ready, doll?"

She nodded and loosened the towel, allowing it to drop. His gaze lowered down her body and a low rumble came from his throat.

"I'm a little nervous, though."

He stalked closer, until he stopped less than a foot away. "There's no need to be."

She reached up and placed her hands on his chest, peering at him. "Are you sure about this, Trayis?"

"Absolutely. You're *mine*, Shay. My heart is yours. My body. All of me. Forever."

"I feel the same way."

He gently gripped her hips. "You're thinking too hard again. I have a cure for that."

She grinned. "I know you do."

He lifted her off her feet and she clutched at his shoulders. He turned, walked them to the bed, and then gently placed her on it. "Stay there."

She watched as he quickly shed his jeans and crawled onto the bed next to her. She rolled toward him, touching his chest again. He had such a great body that she couldn't help but want to put her hands on him.

"We won't use a condom this time." His voice came out deeper. "I'm excited about taking you bare. Nothing between us."

She worried her lip. "Maybe you should, um...investigate me down there first, before we mate."

A grin split his face. "That's an adorable way to tell me you want me to go down on you, doll." He ran his tongue over his lips and the gold streaks in his eyes brightened. "And I'd be happy to."

She blushed. "Not that. To see if I'm ovulating. If I am, we could wait to seal our bond until I'm not. You know, to avoid me getting pregnant."

His humor faded in a blink. "I'd love to have a baby with you—and it *will* be able to shift, Shay. I almost lost you. The only reason I didn't mate you last night was because I didn't want us traveling right afterward. But I refuse to put it off any longer."

"But we should wait a bit before we risk becoming parents. I mean, this happened so fast."

He adjusted his body, stretched an arm up and resting his head on his hand. "You grew up with Lycans, Shay. Not humans. You know we don't date for years. Hell, we don't date, period. We follow our instincts and trust them. I'm ashamed it took me this long to figure out what you are to me."

265

She frowned. "We haven't known each other long. I mean, we *have*, since you've always visited Arlis and the pack, but you know what I mean."

"I do. We're together now. I should have realized the first time I took you to my bed that you were my mate, when I felt things I normally don't. The Vampire side can screw with the Lycan, just like you've got your human half screwing with your instincts. It didn't help that my brother's pack made you feel less amazing than you are. But I'm one hundred percent certain I want you for the rest of my life. No qualms. No hesitation. I'm all in, Shay. What is your gut telling *you*? Be honest."

"That I love you. You're all I want. And that's never going to change."

He smiled at that. "Now...don't think. Just say the first thing that pops into your head. Ready?"

She nodded.

"Do you want to have kids with me? Yes or no?"

"Yes."

His grin returned. "I'm going to mate you now, Shay. Link us together forever. It's not like we'll become instant parents tomorrow. But I've already imagined you heavy with my child." He scooted closer. "I want to make that a reality."

Her eyes widened when his very stiff cock pressed into her stomach.

"That's my reaction to thinking about you pregnant. Does that feel as if I'm worried or not ready to try? We're both half Lycan, doll. There's no such thing as too fast or a timeframe of when we should start a family together. Let me mate you. Say yes, Shay."

266

She didn't have to think about it. "Yes, Trayis."

He kissed her. She stopped worrying about everything, getting lost in him. His kisses had a habit of doing that to her. Passion flared hot between them. She rubbed against his firm body, moaning around his tongue.

Trayis pushed her onto her back, coming down over her. She adjusted, allowing him to climb between her thighs. She bent her knees, trying to wrap her legs around his waist, but Trayis wiggled his ass, inching down her body as he broke the kiss. His mouth went to her neck next.

She twisted her head to give him access, moaning when he lightly nipped. She could feel his fangs slide out and figured he'd bite her. He didn't, though. Instead using the sharp tips just to tease the sensitive skin and torture her with open-mouthed kisses.

"You make me burn up, doll," he rasped. "I want inside you so bad."

"Yes." It didn't take much for Trayis to turn her on. Just his kisses and having his body pressed against hers made her wet. He slid one of his hands between their bodies, playing with her clit. She bucked her hips against his fingers.

"Now," she moaned.

"Not yet."

He planned to torment her. She clawed at his shoulders, not worried about her nails doing much damage. They were human nails. He'd heal fast from any scratches. He lowered farther down her body, his mouth trailing to her breasts. All the while he rubbed her clit. She almost came when he sucked on her taut nipple.

"Trayis!"

He growled. It was the sexiest sound.

Then he rose up and pushed his thick cock into her.

The feel of him taking her so deep, so *bare*, had her crying out. Her nails bit into his skin when he began to furiously thrust his hips, riding her fast and hard.

That's what she'd wanted. Trayis all the way inside her.

"Neck," he snarled.

She tilted her head to give him access. His lips and fangs brushed across her skin, his body pinning her tighter to the bed, and she felt her climax building. He suddenly lifted his head and stilled. She opened her eyes and stared into his. They were mostly golden now, glowing fiercely.

He lifted his arm, biting into his wrist. She watched, knowing they'd have to exchange blood. As a half-breed who couldn't shift, she couldn't just bite into him the way Werewolves did during a mating. He'd have to bleed for her. And he did. He pressed his wrist to her mouth and she latched on.

His blood coated her tongue. She didn't have time to gag on the coppery taste or think about what she was doing, since Trayis began to move again, taking her even faster, harder. He adjusted his hips, rubbing his body against her clit.

Then his mouth was back on her throat—and he bit.

The sudden pain, along with the intense pleasure, sent Shay over the edge.

Ecstasy washed through her. She swallowed more blood, knowing how important it was to bond to her mate. Trayis groaned against her neck, his body quaking as he emptied himself deep inside her body. He kept moving, drinking her blood, and she took more of his.

He finally withdrew his fangs and licked her skin. Both of them were out of breath, and she felt a bit dazed. Not just from the great sex, but also what his blood was doing to her. She felt tired but exhilarated at the same time.

Trayis lifted his head and brushed his lips over hers, blood mingling from their mouths.

"Open to me," he demanded.

She parted her lips and he deepened the kiss. She ran her hands from his back up to his hair, sinking her fingers into the thick strands.

An odd sensation began in her belly, and heat spread throughout her entire body. She gasped, pulling away from his mouth. She felt feverish. She stared up at Trayis in confusion.

He grinned. "We're not done, doll. We're just getting started. When I give you my blood while making love to you, it's going to turn you on even more."

"I feel so hot..."

He began to slowly move inside her again. Shay moaned. He'd just come but he was hard again. "Yes, you do. So hot, so tight, and so *mine*."

His glowing gaze was locked with hers, and she didn't ever want to look away. His eyes were stunning. "You're mine, too."

"I am. Always yours, Shay. My mate. Say it."

"My mate."

He kissed her again, taking the second round slow, as he stroked her to another climax.

* * * * *

Trayis watched Shay sleep. He'd taken her twice but she needed rest.

His fangs remained out. The Vampire side of him wouldn't back down and had demanded to be present while he'd claimed his mate. He checked her pulse, finding her heartbeat strong and steady. She was small and frail, yet he'd taken a lot of blood from her twice.

He glanced at the wrist he'd bitten to give her *his* blood. Blood that would heal her. Make her stronger. Maybe even give her the ability to shift.

That had him smiling. He'd bet she'd be a dainty Lycan, cute as shit, just like her human self.

Hours passed but he didn't move from her side. Just watching her breathe fascinated him. He had a *mate*. It was something he'd doubted he'd ever find. Occasionally, during the long winter months, he'd considered finding a woman compatible to his personality and settling. Then summer would come, he'd get busy with his clan, and he'd realize all over again that he never wanted just any woman. He wanted his other half.

Now she lay in his bed, her hair spread across his pillow, and nothing had ever felt righter. Just looking at her made him feel happy and complete.

He ran his hand down to her stomach, cupping it. One day they might have children. He had always loved them. It was a celebration whenever a couple mated and had young. A part of him had felt envy each time.

Now one day he could have that with Shay. The next baby he held in his arms might be his own, instead of a new member he was welcoming to his clan, giving its parents his official blessing. Not that it was needed. He didn't believe in that bullshit. But the first generation of VampLycans had been raised by their Lycan mothers, while the packs were still present. They knew pack traditions and demanded certain things from Trayis.

He stroked her belly and Shay stirred, opening her eyes, and an instant smile curved her lips.

"You're so beautiful," he whispered.

Her smile widened. "You're so hot."

He chuckled. "I'm going to make you something to eat. Then I plan to make love to you again."

She rolled toward him, placing her hands against his chest, stroking him. One of her thumbs teased his nipple. "How about we make love and *then* eat?"

He kissed her. They could do that.

Chapter Eighteen

Trayis had just finished taking her to his office to give her a tour. It was the most solidly built barnlike structure she'd ever seen. They'd used logs to build it. The interior was open, with stairs leading to a loft area. A few desks were up there. The front area had some couches and tables. It delighted her to see the huge fireplace in the center, open on both sides, used to help keep the building warm in the winter.

There was a long table with chairs, as well, for conferences, and a small kitchen was behind that. Part of the back of the building had been blocked off to give Trayis a private office. It wasn't too large, but it boasted a fire-burning stove in the corner, near his desk.

"Why two fridges in the kitchen?"

He waved to the living room area as they returned to the main part of the building. "My enforcers hang out here often. One wasn't cutting it for storing drinks and snacks for all of us. We can go through a lot of sodas, waters, or beers in a day. That's one fridge alone. There's also a storage room we use as a pantry that I didn't show you, along the back. It has three chest freezers for meat."

"Ah. That makes sense."

He faced her. "Why do you look so nervous?"

She bit her lip and then released it. "It's almost ten o'clock."

"The clan is going to love you."

"That's what you keep telling me."

He grinned, taking her hand. "They will. Stop worrying. These people aren't like your pack."

"You keep telling me *that*, too. I just don't see how they can accept me and not feel as though you could have done better at finding a mate."

He released her hand, grabbed her around her waist, and yanked her up against his body. "Do you remember what we did most of the night when we weren't sleeping?"

She blushed. "Yes."

"You're fucking perfect, Shay. No one is better for me than you are."

She wrapped her arms around his neck and kissed him. He deepened the kiss. Her body reacted and she moaned, wanting him instantly. He groaned back, breaking the kiss. His eyes were streaked with gold when their gazes met, proving how turned on he'd become. The stiff feel of his cock trapped between their bodies was also an indication.

"You're fucking perfect. I'll keep saying that until you believe it."

The front door to the office opened and Tymber entered. He grinned upon seeing them. "Good morning." He closed the door and came closer. His nostrils flared. "*Now* she smells like your mate. Congratulations to the both of you, and to our clan!"

Trayis gently eased her down his body and put her feet on the floor. Then he adjusted his cock.

Tymber laughed, not even bothering to pretend he didn't notice. "Sorry to interrupt but everyone is waiting. Wen and I have kept them outside." He lifted his hand and waved at Trayis's hips. "You can finish what you two were starting after you announce Shay as your mate. For

273

now, think of something that pisses you off. No offense, but you shouldn't address them with a boner."

Trayis sighed. "As clan leader, I officially decree that I'm banning everyone from saying 'boner' from this day forward."

Tymber chuckled. "Blame Wen."

"Oh, I am."

"The word has caught on, so good luck with that decree." Tymber spun around and made his way to the door. "I'll tell them you'll be out in a minute." He paused before opening it, though, and then looked back, amusement on his features. "I'm glad no one says groovy anymore. I hated that one. I *would* say they'll get tired of using their boners but um..." He laughed. "That isn't going to happen. Pun intended."

He opened the door and stepped out, closing it behind them.

Shay was smiling when Trayis met her gaze.

He rolled his eyes. "See what I put up with? I sometimes already feel as if I'm a parent. They're just large children."

"I love your clan so far, Trayis. Everyone is really relaxed, and I can see how comfortable they are with you. You're a great leader."

"I try. I'm one of the first generation, and for whatever reason, I'm also one of the few the others listened to. When we broke into clans, the ones who moved here put me in charge."

She studied him closely. "First generation?" She let that sink in. "You're like two hundred years old or more, aren't you? I've heard that's about how long VampLycans have been around."

His expression grew somber. "Does that bother you?"

"No. Not at all. You look great for your age."

He chuckled. "We're still not sure how long our natural lifespans will be. It's kind of crazy to think about. At least as long as a Lycan but with the Vampire blood, who knows? It could be thousands of years. More. I've heard there's a Vampire in Russia who claims to be over three thousand years old who hasn't gone crazy and faced the sun."

Shay had a grim thought.

He seemed to guess what she was thinking. "You'll be drinking my blood, Shay. Often. It will affect your human half." He paused. "There's something we should talk about, but not right now."

She cocked her head, staring up at him. "What?"

He hesitated. "The clan is waiting."

"Please? Now I'm worried."

He reached up and caressed her cheek. "It's just that...drinking my blood might..." He paused.

"Might what? Spit it out."

He searched her eyes with his gaze before saying, "Activate more of your Lycan side."

The news stunned her.

"I know I should have told you before we mated. Lorn's mate was attacked by a Vampire, and she basically turned into one. It shouldn't have happened, since she's part Lycan. It did though. Lorn mated her, and drinking from him gave Kira the ability to not burn in the sun, and we've been assured she's eating food again instead of just a blood diet. It makes

275

me think that maybe my blood will give you abilities that have been dormant until now, from your Lycan half."

Excitement filled her. "You think one day I might be able to shift?"

"Possibly. I don't want to get your hopes up since I know that's something you really wanted, but I don't want it blindsiding you, either."

She grinned. "That would be amazing!"

"It doesn't matter to me, Shay. You're prefect just the way you are."

She loved him for that. "I know you mean it."

"I do. Now, are you ready to meet the clan? Don't be nervous. They're going to love you as much as I do."

"Except for your Blood Bitch Foursome," she teased.

He grimaced. "They don't love anyone but themselves. I hope you remember what Wen told you. It's the truth. I've never touched one of them. Mya especially tried to lure me into bed, but I was never that stupid. She's always wanted to mate to someone with a high ranking."

"Don't worry. If one of them says anything, I won't fall for their bullshit."

He grinned. "Good." Then he offered his arm. "Let's do this."

She felt a little sick to her stomach but pushed it back. Wen and Tymber had been really nice, and they were Trayis's two head enforcers. The three of them would handle any turmoil her being the clan leader's mate might cause. She had to have faith in that.

He led her to the door and she tightened her grip on his arm. The second he opened the door, she saw a ton of people milling around in front of the building. They had been softly speaking, but now all of them became quiet, turning their way.

Trayis led her a few feet outside the door and smiled. Wen and Tymber were waiting to stand on each side of them.

Trayis cleared his throat and spoke loudly. "Thanks for coming. My vacation was great—but the best part of visiting my brother's pack was finding my mate. Everyone...meet Shay. She's half Lycan and half human. If anyone has a problem with my choice, speak up and I'll deal with your bullshit now."

A woman with light brown hair, who looked about twenty, gasped. "No fucking way."

"Shut it, Yanca," Tymber growled. His big body tensed at Shay's side.

Another pretty woman grinned. "Yeah, shut it, Yanca. Jealousy's an ugly thing." She winked at Shay, holding her gaze. Then she bowed. "Welcome to our clan, Shay. I'm Stellia, the clan healer. We're thrilled to meet you." Her gaze slid to Trayis. "Congratulations. She's way better than any souvenir you've ever brought back on the rare trips you take."

The assembled clan chuckled, some of them nodding in agreement. Then almost as one, the group did a shallow bowing move, lowering their heads for a few seconds. Shay glanced up at Trayis. He winked at her but said nothing. She wondered if she should bow back, but Trayis didn't. She held still, taking her cues from him.

Then they came forward a few members at a time, clapping Trayis on the shoulder and saying hello to her. They were nice and, from what she could tell, seemed to openly accept her. No one touched her, but neither did they give her disapproving looks.

Some of the tension left Shay. She did notice that Trayis kept hold of her, with Wen and Tymber staying at their sides.

Yanca was the only one who didn't come closer, instead storming off into the woods. Shay noticed.

So did Trayis. "Yanca is one of the four."

"Don't mind what she said," a tall VampLycan male advised. "Troublemaker." He rolled his eyes. "No one pays them any mind. We're very glad you're here, Shay." Then he clasped Trayis's shoulder. "I'm so happy for you."

"Thank you, Maverick." He turned to introduce Shay. "This is one of our enforcers who took over travel duties for Wen, after he mated. It's *his* job now when one of us needs to go kick ass somewhere far from our territory."

Maverick nodded. "I'm hoping I find a mate one day in my travels, since I sure haven't found one here."

"But Yanca has offered. Mya, too," Wen teased, his tone giving it away.

"Not even in jest, man. Never," the tall VampLycan growled, but amusement sparked in his eyes. "I'd rather find myself a cute little Vampire mate over one of those four. She'd be way more loving and only suck the blood out of me, rather than my will to live. A guy would have to have a death wish to lock themselves to one of those four. Talk about misery."

Shay glanced at the VampLycans around her, gauging their reactions to his words. Trayis had told her no one would care if someone brought

278

home a Vampire, which was tough to believe. But no one had a negative reaction.

Trayis nodded. "A Vampire would cause me far fewer headaches than those four have. You find one you want to mate, bring her home."

Maverick winked at Shay. "You picked a good one with this guy."

"Shay was worried her being half human would be a problem," Trayis admitted. "I told her it wouldn't be."

Maverick held her gaze, his expression growing serious. "It's certainly not. We're a mostly smart clan. And it's Trayis who keeps it that way. He points out stupidity and doesn't suffer fools. He also chose enforcers with his same core beliefs. We had a lot of interaction with Decker's clan when he was in charge, because we border that territory. He used to be one of the leaders. Talk about someone who hated humans."

Maverick shook his head, looking disgusted. "Decker even hated *VampLycans* who were more blooded on the Vampire side. He killed children if they grew an aversion to the sun. We took in the few who managed to flee his clan and kept them hidden from the bastard. Our best day in decades was the day we heard he'd been killed. Point is, we got a front-row seat to that kind of hate over bloodlines, and it turned our stomachs. *Everyone* is welcome here. Bloodlines don't matter. Mates are a priority. No one gives a shit what blood runs in your veins, Shay." He jerked his head toward Trayis. "You're his mate, and that's everything. We're damn glad you're here."

She blinked back tears. "Thank you. That means a lot to me."

Trayis snorted. "*He* says it and you finally believe?"

She grinned up at him. "You're my mate, though. You'd totally lie if you thought it would help avoid hurting my feelings."

He smiled back at her. "I wasn't though. Is this issue put to rest forever?"

She nodded.

"Good."

"Now we get to plan a party." Wen sounded excited. "All the other clan leaders are going to want to come."

"And the friends we've made," Tymber added.

"Including the GarLycans," Maverick reminded. "I'm really liking the ones who've been visiting us and hanging out more often."

Trayis pulled Shay against his side and stared down at her. "They'll love you, too."

"I hope so."

"They will." That was Gerri, Wen's human mate, who introduced herself. "I'm not a huge fan of packs, but that's another story I'll share with you later. Clans are way better. We're going to become the best of friends, Shay! I hope I can call you that...?"

"Of course." Shay felt hope at seeing the genuine friendliness on the woman's face. It would be great to make friends. She looked forward to it. The more the merrier.

She let her worries go. The clan was accepting her without issue. No one seemed upset that she was half human.

And the news that she might one day shift was still circling her thoughts. Becoming Trayis's mate wasn't scary after all. It was turning out to be the best decision she'd ever made—right after the pact she'd made with Marcia to go after the men they wanted.

Trayis kissed the top of her head and hugged her tight. "Let's mingle, and then we'll sneak off and enjoy any time we have." Passion flared in his beautiful eyes. "We're newly mated, which means we shouldn't stay out of bed for long. Though as clan leader, I have responsibilities to tend to."

"I'll take over while you and Shay bond," Tymber offered. "I don't have a mate who needs my time." He glanced at them both. "Don't worry about a thing. I've got your backs. Take all the time you need."

Shay was touched. Trayis nodded at his enforcer in gratitude. It seemed they'd have a honeymoon after all.

Epilogue

Ten days later

"So that's how I returned to the clan and Wen." Gerri finished her story.

Stellia chuckled. "It was about damn time, too. As kids, anyone with eyes could tell those two belonged together."

"It's so romantic." Shay sat on the couch in the cabin. She loved her new home, being mated to Trayis, and enjoyed spending time with her two new friends. Both women had shown up the first day Trayis had returned to the office, to get to know her better.

But she and her mate had five wonderful days of alone time in the cabin first.

"Your story with Trayis is romantic, too," Gerri reminded her. "That took so much courage for you to go after him."

Stellia nodded. "Trayis can be intimidating to most people. I'm not surprised he didn't tell you right away that he's our leader. That's so him." Her gaze softened as she peered at Shay. "I've never seen him this happy. Thank you for that."

Gerri nodded. "He deserves someone as wonderful and special as you are. You do make him happy."

Shay blushed a little in embarrassment. "My life is a thousand times better with him in it. He's my entire world now." She stood. "Does anyone want something to drink?"

She made it just a few feet before a dizzy spell hit and she stumbled.

Stellia was there in a flash. The VampLycan could *move*. She put her arm around Shay's waist and turned her around, led her back to the couch, and helped her sit. Then she crouched in front of her.

Concern showed on her features as she kept hold of her wrist, seeming to take her pulse. "What was *that*?"

"I probably just stood too fast after sitting down for so long."

Unconvinced, Stellia jerked her head toward Gerri. "Get Trayis, please."

"No!" Shay shook her head. "He's at work. I'm sure it's nothing. I just got up too fast."

Stellia released her wrist. "Probably...but it could also be a sign that your mate's blood is doing something to your Lycan half. Trayis and I discussed this after he mated you. Do you feel any different inside? Does your skin tingle? Are you having any weird urges?"

"No. Nothing like that. I'm sure I just moved too quickly. That's all. It's happened a couple times now."

Stellia motioned for Gerri. "Get Trayis—now."

"There's no need," Shay protested. "I'm *fine*. Trayis is busy."

Stellia wouldn't have any of it. "Get him, Gerri. He'll have my ass if he's not notified right way." She gave Shay a stern look. "He's worried about you." She leaned in close, studying her eyes. "Try to think of something that makes you really angry."

"Why?"

"To see if anything happens with your eye color."

Easy enough—Shay hated that Gerri had fled to get Trayis. It was ridiculous. She was fine. Then again...her new friends were probably terrified of something happening to Shay while they were with her.

She closed her eyes, thinking about the Bitch Trio. That *always* pissed her off. A particular memory of them tormenting her about her mother and father surfaced. She opened her eyes and held Stellia's gaze.

"Well?"

A few seconds passed. Stellia shook her head. "Just a pretty soft brown. Sorry. Not a hint of black."

Shay shrugged but she felt a little disappointment. It would be incredible to finally be able to shift. Trayis had warned her that it could take months. Even years. Part of her wished it would happen right away. She'd tried to keep that hope buried since Trayis had brought it up, but it flickered to life sometimes when he went running on all fours. She wanted to join him so badly. And not by riding on his back, which she'd done a few times when he'd given her tours of the territory. Alaska was beautiful.

Stellia drew her attention by allowing her claws to slide out. "Do you trust me?"

Shay nodded. "Sure. What do you want to do?"

Stellia used the tip of one claw to make a shallow scratch on Shay's arm. She flinched at the sting of pain but it was over fast. It surprised her when the woman brought her claw to her mouth and licked at the minute bit of blood there.

A grin split Stellia's face almost instantly.

Then she surprised Shay again by leaning forward, licking the scratch.

Shay was both confused and a bit alarmed. "Um..."

Stellia winked. "Clan healer. Sorry about bleeding you, but I healed it with my saliva."

Shay glanced down at her arm to find it had indeed healed, as if her friend hadn't scratched her at all. "Why'd you do that? What did you find?"

"My taste buds have become an instant pregnancy test after all the years of taking care of the clan, if my nose can't pick up the scent yet. Congratulations!"

Shay gaped at her. "I'm *pregnant*? You're sure?"

Stellia nodded as she rose to her feet. "You're going to have a baby! I'll let you be the one to tell your mate. Trayis is going to be so thrilled!"

Shay watched as the woman moved fast toward the back of the house. "Where are you going?"

"Out the back door to avoid your mate. This is your news to share privately," Stellia called out, before fleeing from sight completely.

The front door was yanked open a few seconds later, and Shay twisted on the couch.

Trayis rushed in, out of breath. "Are you okay?" He slammed the door and jumped over the couch, bumped into the coffee table, and shoved it aside to kneel before her. He took both of her hands gently in his. "Are you shifting? I'll talk you through it, doll. Just don't panic. I'm right here with you. It'll be fine."

"I'm not shifting. At least, not yet. I just had a dizzy spell, so Stellia thought I might be."

A flash of disappointment creased his handsome face but it was gone as soon as it appeared. "Oh. I'm sorry. I know you want to really bad. It might take months though, if at all."

She squeezed his hands and smiled. Tears filled her eyes. "I love you."

"I love you, too." He glanced around. "Where's Stellia?"

"She rushed out the back door to avoid you."

He chuckled, holding her gaze. "I'm not mad that she was wrong. I was just worried you'd have your first shift when I wasn't here, and I wanted to be. Every important moment is ours to share."

"This *is* an important moment." She blinked back more tears.

He leaned in closer. "What's wrong?"

"Everything's *right*." She grinned. "At least, I hope so. Did you know that your healer can perform a pregnancy test with nothing more than her tongue and a bit of blood?"

Trayis blinked once. Twice. Then it seemed to sink in. His eyes widened and he glanced at her stomach, before peering deeply into her eyes.

"Hey, I warned you that I couldn't control my ovaries. Say something."

Tears filled *his* eyes this time. "I'm going to be a father?"

"Yes."

He suddenly pulled her off the couch, gently, sitting on the floor with Shay on his lap as he held her tight. "I fucking love you." He kissed the top of her head. "We're having a baby!" He chuckled. "It's going to be the cutest kid."

She curled into his chest. "It will be. Especially if we have a boy who looks like you."

"Or a girl who's a tiny version of *you*." He held her tighter. "We need to remodel the room next to ours. Have a crib made. Buy baby clothes. Toys." He continued to list what they'd need.

Shay laughed and lifted her head, reaching up to put her hand over his mouth. He stopped talking as she grinned at him. "We've got some time, and we aren't even sure what sex our baby will be yet." She lowered her hand.

"I'm just so excited."

"Me too."

He leaned in and softly brushed his lips against hers and then pulled back. "We'll plan for both regardless. I see lots of little ones in our future, anyway."

There was a fast knock, and then the front door opened. Wen peeked his head in. Then someone shoved him from behind, making him stumble into the living room. The door opened wider and Tymber stepped inside. They both stared at them on the floor in front of the couch.

"She's not shifting," Trayis announced. He looked at Shay. "They were in the office when Gerri rushed in. I just beat them here."

"Our leader can move when he's motivated. He left us behind, eating his dust." Wen shot a dirty look at Tymber. "This one tripped me a few times."

Tymber snorted. "You tripped me, too." He brushed at his clothes. "And I'd be more worried about your mate. You at least could have grabbed Gerri and carried her here with those damn long legs of yours. She's going to be pissed at you. Humans get tired faster, and she's had to run there and back. Because *your* dumb ass left her behind. I would've scooped her up myself, but that wouldn't have been appropriate."

"Shit!" Wen glanced at the open door. "My mate's gonna kick my ass...and I'm going to have to let her."

Trayis sighed loudly. "See what I mean, doll? They *are* like overgrown teenagers. I'm reminding myself right now that dealing with them has been good practice for becoming a parent." He kissed her cheek. "Say congrats, you two. Shay and I are having a baby. She's pregnant!"

Both of them stilled before wide grins spread across their faces.

Gerri came running inside then, bending forward to grab her legs, panting hard. "Did I miss it? Did Shay shift?" Her head lifted and her gaze locked on Shay and Trayis. "No? Oh." She panted some more. "Well, next time..." She gave Shay an encouraging smile. "It will happen. I have faith."

Wen dropped to his knees and gently rubbed her back. "I'm sorry, baby. I should have tossed you over my shoulder."

Gerri kept panting. "Shoulda. Coulda. Didn't. It's fine." She straightened, staring at her mate. "I'll remember that, though. Not only that you took off without me, but you would have carried me like laundry if you hadn't."

Wen groaned. "Shit."

Trayis's body shook as he laughed. "These are the future role models to our children. I don't know if I should apologize or not."

Shay tried to hide her laughter but failed. "I think they're great." She turned in his lap, wrapped her arms around his neck, and kissed him.

Trayis deepened the kiss. He could make her forget about anything. His hands roamed her body, making her moan against his tongue. He broke the kiss and glanced away.

Her gaze followed. Their three visitors were gone, the front door firmly closed.

"And that's how we get rid of them. Good to know. That's the fastest I've ever gotten them to leave." He adjusted her in his arms and stood, carrying her toward the stairs.

"What about work? You said it would be a busy day. You've had a lot to catch up on after spending so much time with me."

"That's why I have two head enforcers. They can handle whatever needs seen to. I get to handle you."

Shay cuddled against his chest. "You're going to spoil me."

"Every day, Shay. Every damn day. I'm so lucky to have found you."

"I'm the lucky one, Trayis."

He gently deposited her on the bed and crouched in front of her. "Let's agree that we're both blessed."

"Okay."

He lowered his hands, gently cupping her stomach and waist. "You're making all my dreams come true, Shay."

"You do the same for me."

Their gazes locked. Shay remembered she needed to call Marcia to let her know—but that would come later. After she made love to her mate. She leaned forward and kissed him. Trayis had become her entire world...and soon, they'd have a family.

About the Author

NY Times and USA Today Bestselling Author

I'm a full-time wife, mother, and author. I've been lucky enough to have spent over two decades with the love of my life and look forward to many, many more years with Mr. Laurann. I'm addicted to iced coffee, the occasional candy bar (or two), and trying to get at least five hours of sleep at night.

I love to write all kinds of stories. I think the best part about writing is the fact that real life is always uncertain, always tossing things at us that we have no control over, but when writing you can make sure there's always a happy ending. I love that about being an author. My favorite part is when I sit down at my computer desk, put on my headphones to listen to loud music to block out everything around me, so I can create worlds in front of me.

For the most up to date information, please visit my website. www.LaurannDohner.com